Queenie Malone's
Paradise Hotel

Also by Ruth Hogan

The Keeper of Lost Things
The Wisdom of Sally Red Shoes

Queenie Malone's Paradise Hotel

Ruth Hogan

wm

WILLIAM MORROW
An Imprint of HarperCollins*Publishers*

P.S.™ is a trademark of HarperCollins Publishers.

QUEENIE MALONE'S PARADISE HOTEL. Copyright © 2019 by Ruth Hogan. All rights reserved. Printed in the United States of America. No part of this book may be used or reproduced in any manner whatsoever without written permission except in the case of brief quotations embodied in critical articles and reviews. For information, address HarperCollins Publishers, 195 Broadway, New York, NY 10007.

HarperCollins books may be purchased for educational, business, or sales promotional use. For information, please email the Special Markets Department at SPsales@harpercollins.com.

Originally published in the United Kingdom in 2019 by Two Roads.

FIRST U.S. EDITION

Library of Congress Cataloging-in-Publication Data has been applied for.

ISBN 978-0-06-293571-7 (paperback)
ISBN 978-0-06-297964-3 (hardcover library edition)

20 21 22 23 24 LSC 10 9 8 7 6 5 4 3 2 1

To Bokey (aka Bokapup)—son of Eli

Her eyes they shone like the diamonds,
You'd think she was queen of the land,
And her hair hung over her shoulders
Tied up with a black velvet band.

—Traditional Irish folk song

Part 1

The zebra, the horse, and the kraken

1

Tilda

My mother killed my father when I was seven years old. Now, thirty-nine years later, she is dead too, and I am an orphan.

I haven't been back to her flat since the funeral on that hot and humid day in late August, and now the glowing colors and rich, earthy smells of autumn have been swept away by the cinereos hues and raw, salty winds of a seaside winter. As the taxi crawls along Brighton seafront in the thick, teatime traffic, I can just make out the gunmetal-gray waves smashing onto the pebbles. The lights on the Palace Pier are twinkling seductively in the late-afternoon gloom and, even after all these years, they still spark a flicker of child-like excitement inside me. We pass the street where Queenie used to live. Losing that life still smarts as sharply as a paper cut. The taxi turns left, away from the sea, and stops outside a tall, Victorian house. From the outside, my mother's flat is dark and still. As I turn the key in the lock and open the door, the silence and the musty air creep out to greet me, and the secrets of my mother's life—and mine—stir softly in their hiding places, waiting to unravel the familiar pattern of my past.

I sleep soundly, and wake feeling shamefully refreshed. I say "shamefully," because it doesn't seem quite decent that I should be feeling so chipper given the circumstances. It's like wearing a red dress to a funeral. I am here to pick over the bones of my mother's life like some sort of domestic vulture; deciding which linen, china, and furniture are worth keeping, and which should be consigned to the charity shops in town or left to the mercy of the bin men. The silence has been banished by the measured intonations of a Radio 4 presenter. The musty air has been sucked out into the bright, new morning through the open windows, and replaced by the altogether more appetizing smell of toast and freshly brewed coffee. I pour myself another cup and carefully butter a slice of toast, making sure that every square inch is thinly but evenly covered, and then repeat the process with thick-cut, bitter orange marmalade. I cut it precisely into four triangles and place the knife, perfectly straight, to the left of the plate, blade side inward. These are the rituals that keep me safe.

Outside, the sun is shining hard and bright, making the slab of crinkling waves flash and sparkle like cut glass. I'm tempted to open the French windows and stand on the balcony for a few minutes to feel the fierce wind buffet my body and lash through my hair, as if to underline the fact that I am still alive. But I resist. I'm not sure I know where the key is in any case. I'm simply trying to delay the start of a task that I feel sure is going to be both complicated and time-consuming. Deciding what to do with the furniture is not straightforward. I have already resolved to keep the flat, but whether as a permanent home or as a holiday flat and source of income I have not yet decided. Either way, it will need furniture. The kitchen table is staying; Victorian stripped pine, well used and well loved. During the last few years of my mother's life, she developed a passion for crossword puzzles, particularly those in the broadsheets. She said they kept her brain alive. She would spend several hours each morning sitting at the kitchen table with the newspapers spread in front of her, a dictionary and thesaurus close at hand—bad form to the purists, I know, but she rarely used them. When I visited her, she would sometimes ask for my help, as I sat drinking coffee and gazing out at the ever-changing sea. It was the closest we came to "companionable" during my adult life, a poor relation to the emotional intimacy more usually found between a mother and daughter, but the best that we could do. Her actions had placed a distance between us that remained until her death, and I long ago gave up trying or perhaps even wanting to build a bridge across it. We skirted around each other with the cool politeness of strangers, remote even when we were in the same room. Still, the table is staying. I am also keeping the ornate overmantel mirror, whose beauty is temporarily disguised under a generous layer of dust. I remember my mother checking her hair and patting her face with powder in the mirror before going out, taking care not to singe her tights by getting too close to the flames of the gas fire that burned beneath.

"Old age is not an excuse to let oneself go," she used to say.

Sadly, her eyesight was not as good as it could have been if she had deigned to wear her spectacles, and her generous application of face powder often made her look a little dusty, rather like the mirror. But this was offset by the "fresh from the salon' neatness of her hair, her smartly tailored coat, and the immaculately stylish silk scarf tied around her neck. This "going-out' ensemble was always completed with a brooch pinned either to the lapel of her coat or at her neck, in the center of the silk scarf. I once bought her a small, silver brooch with the word "Mother' engraved on it. I never saw her wear it.

The two wing-backed easy chairs in the sitting room are the epitome of abominable ghastliness and are going. Definitely. Aside from the fact that they are of a shape and design that can only be described as "Old People's Home' chic, they are covered in an eye-popping chintz that looks as though it has been created by Cath Kidston on LSD. The green velvet-covered sofa is inoffensive to look at, and reasonably comfortable to sit on, and is therefore staying for the time being.

After a purposeful start, my mind is beginning to wander and so am I. I drift from room to room, touching things, picking them up and putting them down again aimlessly. In the bathroom, my mother's toothbrush is still in a glass on the sink, alongside her neatly folded washcloth and a half-used bar of soap. Here my rationale deserts me; what exactly is the protocol for dealing with dead people's toiletries? These things are of no use to anyone, and should surely go in the bin?

But these are the last remaining relics of the flesh and blood that was my mother. They still have her on them. These humble objects retain a physical intimacy with her that would have discomforted me while she was alive, but which I am not yet ready to relinquish now she is dead. I put them into the toiletry bag covered in sprigs of tiny pink flowers, which she used on the rare occasions when she visited me. I don't know what else to do with them.

I go into her bedroom and sit down on the end of the bed. The bed in which she died. It will have to go. Her dressing table is positioned at the end of it. I sit gazing into one of the triptych mirrors, studying my face for any echoes of hers. Our bone structure is similar, high cheekbones, a strong, straight nose, and my dark hair and fair skin are like hers—were. But her eyes were cool and green and somehow glassy. I remember as a little girl, I used to think that they were the color of marbles. But I could never tell what she was thinking. I have my dad's eyes; dark and mercurial; one minute watchful, the next lively, and equal mirrors of fury and mirth. The small, deep scar above my left eyebrow is mine alone.

On the dressing table is a large wooden jewelry box, a brush, comb and mirror set, a large silver crucifix, and a bottle of my mother's favorite perfume, Chanel No. 5. I have never liked it. I have always found it too over-powering, but often bought it for her at Christmas and birthdays because she adored it. The brush still has a few strands of her hair woven in among its stiff bristles. There is also a small photograph in a plain silver frame. It is an old and faded black-and-white snapshot of a young woman wearing a pale summer dress and a single string of pearls. She is holding the hand of a small girl aged about five or six in shiny new sandals and very white socks, one of which is flying at half-mast. It is my mother and me.

2

Tilly

Tilly sat on the back doorstep in her new red sandals and carefully inspected the scab on her knee. She had fallen off her bike the previous Wednesday, when she had been momentarily distracted by the sight of Mrs. O'Flaherty's enormous bum waddling down the street wrapped in a bright orange Crimplene dress. Like two pumpkins fighting in a sack, as her daddy would say, and then her mother would press her lips together and pretend to look cross, like she always did when he said something funny but slightly rude. Tilly wasn't allowed to say "bum," but surely it was all right if you just thought it in your head? The orange pumpkins had captured her attention just long enough for her to miss the discarded roller skate that the front wheel of her bicycle had hit with enough force to catapult her from the saddle and send her crashing onto the pavement in a muddle of flailing limbs. She lay in the muddle for a moment, listening to the wheels ticking round until they stopped, and watching the tassels on the handlebar nearest to her face gently fluttering in the breeze. Her knee hurt and her elbow was sore, but her arms and legs seemed to be working normally. Luckily, Mrs.

O'Flaherty had not heard the crash she had unwittingly been responsible for, and had carried on to the end of the street and turned the corner with her pumpkins swaying jauntily behind her. Mrs. O'Flaherty was a kind woman, who had an easy way with children, which was just as well as she had seven of her own (she was, according to Tilly's mother, an "enthusiastic Catholic'). Had she seen Tilly's fall, she would undoubtedly have hoisted Tilly from her pavement muddle and insisted on returning her safely to her mother for the adminis-tration of a swab of stinging antiseptic, a bandage, and a comforting hug. But these would be the attentions of a normal, happy mummy, who baked cakes, wore an apron, and, more often than not, a smile; who smelled of Avon perfume and called her husband "darling." A woman like Mrs. O'Flaherty or the mummy from the soap powder advert on the telly. Not Tilly's mother. She would be cross about the fuss, the interference of Mrs. O'Flaherty, the clumsiness of Tilly, and the hole in the elbow of a perfectly good cardigan. There would be no hug, and the stinging would come from her mother's harsh words. Tilly picked herself and her bicycle up, cleaned her wounds as best she could with spit and a rather grubby hanky, and spent the rest of the day with the sleeves of her cardigan pushed up far enough so that the hole didn't show.

The scab was almost black now, with the white edges ripe for picking. It itched, and the skin around it was puckered and tight. Tilly lifted one edge experimentally with her fingernail, and immediately a trickle of blood ran down her leg and soaked into her very white sock. "I knocked it on the chair': the excuse immediately sprang to mind in readiness for her mother's inevitable rebuke. She often wished that her mother was more like the soap-powder mummy. Tilly thought she must be using the wrong sort. She pressed the scab back down with her finger and carefully rumpled her sock to hide the scarlet stain.

The borders in the back garden were full of flowers, and the lawn was neatly cut and edged. It looked like a picture-book illustration. The fragrant sweet peas were carefully coaxed and twirled around wigwams of cane sticks, and their fluttery flowers in every shade of purple, pink, red, mauve, and white were a testament to her daddy's loving care and attention. He had shown her how to nip out the side shoots that looked like tiny coiled springs. He said it made the stems grow longer and straighter and produce more flowers. She checked them every day, and nipped out each stray green tendril between the nails of her thumb and forefinger exactly as he had taught her. The borders were full of marigolds, snapdragons, and Livingstone daisies, their colors brash and bright like a 1950s picture postcard. Tilly loved the brazen daisies in their dancing-girl rows, not for their dazzling colors or shiny petals, but for the way they opened themselves up to bask in the sunshine, and then shut up tight once the clouds rolled in or the sun went down, like back-to-front umbrellas. It was magic.

Beyond the lawn was a small vegetable patch with a couple of rows of peas, some lines of crisp lettuce, four tomato plants in pots, and her daddy's precious raspberry canes. Tilly used to steal the pods of peas and eat them when they were still tiny and juicy sweet. Her daddy used to pretend to be cross, and then laugh and say it would be a miracle if any of them were allowed to grow big enough to end up on a dinner plate. Tilly liked it when he laughed, because he laughed with his whole face and not just his mouth. His cheeks would go red, and the skin around his eyes would wrinkle like an over-ripe apple; and his eyes, as dark as treacle, would shine with what he called "happy tears." Tilly's mother always said that the raspberry canes were a waste of time because the birds would eat them, but each year the canes were laden with the velvet-soft, deep pink berries, luscious with nearly sweet juice that trickled down her chin as she crammed the fruit into her mouth while hiding in the garden shed with her daddy. The fruit tasted all the more delicious because it was eaten like this—greedily, messily, and in secret. For Tilly, the smell of creosote would always be inextricably linked with raspberries, and years later, as an adult, the slightest whiff of it would make her mouth water. Her daddy would eat his share of the fruit, and then later, when he brought a meager half-bowlful into the kitchen, he would wink theatrically at Tilly as he handed the bowl to her mother, who would be wearing her best "I told you so' face. The raspberries were just one of the many little secrets and jokes Tilly shared with her daddy that brightened the rather dark and troubled palette that colored their daily lives.

Tilly stood up and tested her knee with a few tentative steps to see if the bleeding had stopped. The daisies were fully opened in the glare of the midday sun, and their technicolor petals shimmered in the heat. Tilly bent down and picked a snapdragon head. Just as she was squeezing its "cheeks" to make it bite her finger, her mother came to the doorstep. She was wearing a light blue cotton dress and a single strand of pearls. As she was standing there, she pushed a powder compact and a clean hanky into her handbag and snapped it shut with a loud click. She should have looked pretty, but her face was tense, and her expression strained.

"Come on, Tilly, we'll miss the bus. And pull that sock up."

She turned and went back into the house. Tilly dropped her snapdragon onto the path and tugged ineffectually at her sock. As she dawdled back past the flowers to follow her mother, she wondered who would look after them now that her daddy had gone.

3

Tilly

Tilly sat next to her mother, wriggling uncomfortably as the stiff, velvet pile of the bus seat prickled against the back of her bare legs. It was hot and stuffy on the bus, despite the breeze from the open door.

"Tilly, do sit still," her mother muttered as she rummaged in her handbag to find her purse.

"She's got ants in her pants, that one."

The lady bus conductor grinned broadly at Tilly while waiting patiently for her mother to fish the coins out of her purse to pay for their tickets. Tilly giggled. She longed to be a bus conductor with a shiny leather money pouch and a magical, whirring ticket machine, and to be able to say "pants' on a bus full of people without getting into trouble. Tilly's mother handed over the money for their fares and the bus conductor turned the handle on the side of her box of tricks and pulled out two orange printed tickets from the slot on the front.

"Here you are, love. Do you want to hold them?"

She passed them to Tilly with a wink, and made her way down the aisle, swaying gently with the jolting movement of the bus. Tilly definitely wanted to be a bus conductor. Not only was there a nice blue uniform, a pouch full of money, and the marvelous ticket machine, but you also got to be in charge of the whole bus. Tilly and her mother were sitting on one of the two long seats, just inside the door, that faced each other across the aisle of the bus. Opposite them sat an old couple and a young woman with a baby. The young woman was very pretty, with yellow hair pulled into a high ponytail and shiny pink lipstick. She was wearing a pale pink skirt with white flowers that was tight at the waist and then stuck out like a lampshade, and a close-fitting, short-sleeved sweater that was knitted in a white, fluffy wool that Tilly thought would be nice to stroke. The old woman had a rather cross face, and very stiff gray hair arranged in fat curls that were puffed up on top of her head like a pile of sausage rolls. Her dress was navy blue with tiny white spots, and stretched over the huge shelf of her bosom before disappearing into the deep crease between the shelf and her large tummy. Her feet were squashed into shiny navy shoes from which her podgy ankles spilled out like overstuffed haggises. She looked hot, cross, and uncomfortable. Tilly wondered if she was having a baby too. Her tummy certainly looked big enough to be holding one, and it would also explain why her dress was too small for her. Tilly was just about to ask her when the woman shot her such a stern look that she thought better of it. As Tilly looked at the young woman and the old woman sitting next to each other, she wondered when it was that bosoms changed from being two separate things into one big one. The young woman definitely had two, and you could see the shape of them very clearly under her sweater, but the old woman just had one big, rather solid-looking bosom shelf. Tilly puzzled over it for a bit, and decided that she didn't particularly want either.

She turned her attention to the old man, who Tilly thought must be about a hundred. He had tanned skin as wrinkled as a pickled walnut, great tufts of white hair sprouting out of his ears, and blue eyes that twinkled with mischief. He was wearing a tweed cap and a blue-checked shirt, and Tilly was sure that he would smell like a granddad. His gnarled, bony hands gripped the handle of a walking stick that he had planted firmly in front of him between his widely spread legs. He looked as though he had anchored himself ready for the jolting stops and starts and gentle swaying of the voyage ahead on the number 37. Tilly looked at him with unconcealed curiosity, and he stuck his tongue out at her. It was done in a second, like a toad catching a fly. Tilly wasn't altogether sure that she hadn't imagined it. She looked at her mother to see if she had noticed anything. Her mother was in a world of her own, staring out of the window. Tilly looked at him again. He stuck his tongue out—again. But this time Tilly understood. She quickly glanced at her mother again before pressing the end of her nose up with her finger and sticking out her tongue. A flicker of a smile crossed the old man's face before he pulled both ears forward, pressed the end of his nose up with the tip of his little finger, and once again poked out his tongue in reply. Tilly thought for a moment and was just about to respond in kind, when the bus conductor sashayed back down the aisle. She looked at them both like a teacher who knows that her pupils are misbehaving behind her back, but hasn't yet managed to catch them in the act.

"I've got my eye on you," she said in a stern voice to the old man, and then squeezed his knee as she passed him and climbed the stairs to the top deck. The old man's wife didn't look very pleased as she folded her arms firmly under her large bosom and jolted it crossly as if to wake it up. Tilly hesitated and the old man raised his eyebrows slightly as if to encourage her. Tilly readied herself; this was her best face and it took some concentration. She pulled her ears forward with her forefingers, hooked her little fingers into the corners of her mouth and dragged her lips into a wide grimace, rolled back her eyes so that only the whites were visible, and poked out her tongue as far as it would go. Beat that! The old man looked suitably impressed, and Tilly settled smugly back into her seat. But her claim to victory was premature. With breathtaking nonchalance and a flick of his tongue, the old man dislodged and partially ejected both his upper and lower dentures before sucking them back into place, keeping his eyes firmly crossed throughout the maneuver. Game, set and match. Tilly was completed captivated, and more than a little envious of his false teeth—they clearly gave him an unfair advantage. She was also then suddenly consumed with the giggles. She could feel them fizzing up inside her like the Alka-Seltzer tablets her mother gave her when she had a sicky tummy. She struggled to keep them inside her, but she was already shaking with both the effort and the failure to do so. Her eyes were brimming with happy tears and her face was as pink as a raspberry. The final straw came when she looked across at the old man and saw tears of laughter streaming down his face, his whole body rattling with mirth. Tilly was worried that his teeth might be shaken out of his mouth completely this time and skitter across the floor and bite her mother on the ankle. The thought of it finished her off. She exploded like a shaken bottle of pop. Her laughter bubbled through the bus, rising and falling like jam boiling in a saucepan as she tried to pull herself together. But it was hopeless. The more her mother told her to stop being silly and sit quietly like a good girl, the worse it got. She knew she was, in her mother's words, "making a show of herself," but the show had to go on because she couldn't stop it. And the old man wasn't helping. He was thumping his walking stick on the floor of the bus as though he were drumming the beat of the rising crescendo of hilarity that had gripped them both so firmly. Eventually the laughter subsided long enough for Tilly to batten down the hatches and display a reasonably sensible face. But her composure was precarious, too recent to be relied upon in the face of even the slightest provocation. As the old man's wife turned herself and her bosom away from him in disapproval, the bus jolted sharply and the baby sitting next to her was sick all over her bosom and her handbag. Tilly was lost again.

The next stop was theirs, and Tilly was glad to get off the bus. The smell of baby sick wasn't very nice, and the more the old woman tried to clean it up, the farther she seemed to spread it. She even managed to flick some of it onto the bus conductor, who had hurried downstairs to see what all the commotion was about.

The old man was laughing so hard by this point that his anchor had come adrift and he almost fell off his seat. Tilly reckoned that he'd definitely be going straight to bed with no supper that night. As for Tilly, her sides ached from laughing so much, but she wasn't so sure that she wanted to be a bus conductor anymore.

She didn't want to be a doctor's receptionist either. Ten minutes after they stepped off the bus, they were sitting on hard, wooden chairs in the cool and gloomy waiting room of their family doctor, Dr. Bentley, and Tilly was having a staring contest with his receptionist, who was seated behind a desk at one end of the room. She was a thin woman, with dark hair so tightly scraped back into a bun that it made the skin on her face seem a size too small. She had a long, pointy nose which she had looked down at them, over the top of her glasses, when they had walked in. She behaved as though her job was to protect the doctor from patients, who were usually just making a fuss about nothing. Tilly didn't like the way she seemed to think that her mother wasn't good enough. Good enough for what, she was too young to fully understand, but she felt it nonetheless, and she knew it wasn't nice. Tilly also thought that her face looked as though she had been sucking lemons. She smiled to herself as she thought about sharing the joke with her daddy, but the smile quickly melted like an ice cream dropped on the pavement as she remembered that he had gone away, and with the memory came the feeling that her tummy was full of mud. The receptionist was watching Tilly intently as though she might, at any moment, run amok and mess up the perfect piles of glossy magazines on the shiny table, or dishevel the box of leaflets proclaiming the benefits of Sanatogen and cod liver oil and malt. Tilly's mother made her eat a generous spoonful of the evil-smelling, brown, sticky gloop every day, because it was "good for her." Tilly didn't see how it could be. The very sight of the fat brown jar made her gag, and its contents coated the inside of her mouth for at least half an hour after she had been "dosed." It tasted like fish-flavored toffee, and made her burps smell like the bin round the back of the chip shop. The phone on the receptionist's desk rang, and she lifted the receiver to her ear without taking her eyes off Tilly.

"Doctor will see you now," she said to Tilly's mother in a clipped voice.

Her mother stood up a little too quickly, clutching her handbag, and said to Tilly, "Now wait here, and be a good girl."

She was almost at the door when she turned and added, "Don't touch anything."

Tilly scowled. "Be a good girl' was open to interpret-ation. It had possibilities. She could have looked through the magazines, or just moved them around, disturbing their perfect arrangement. She could have pushed her fingertips, one by one, onto the polished surface of the table, leaving a trail of smudge marks. She could have waved her hands through the heavy folds of the velvet curtains that hung at the window. All of this could be excused as the behavior of an essen-tially good but bored child trying to entertain herself while waiting for her mother. Tilly's instincts told her, however, that they would be guaranteed to annoy the receptionist more than spiders in her knickers. But she was scuppered by her mother's final words: "Don't touch anything." Tilly sat very still and thought very hard. After a moment, she jumped up from her seat. The receptionist was immediately on red alert. Tilly first went to the magazines. She placed both hands over the piles and moved them back and forth, leaving only the smallest space between her skin and the glossy magazine covers. Then, with one finger, she drew patterns in the air, sometimes only a hair's breadth above the polished surface of the table. Her finger moved steadily at first, tracing dramatic swirls and flourishes, but then suddenly swooped and dipped seemingly even closer to the table, like a swallow sipping water from the surface of a lake. The receptionist was getting crosser and crosser, in the way that grown-ups do when they are so thoroughly outwitted by a child. Tilly moved on toward the curtains, trailing the back of her hand perilously close to the rather miserable-looking rubber plant that squatted sullenly in a dull brown pot against one wall.

"Little girl," the receptionist finally snapped, "what exactly do you think you're doing?"

Tilly turned very deliberately to face her and smiled sweetly.

"I'm being a good girl and not touching anything," she replied.

Tilly spent the next couple of minutes pretending to stroke the curtains while the receptionist looked on in infuriated frustration. Tilly wouldn't have been in the least bit surprised if steam had started blowing out of her ears. Eventually, there was the sound of footsteps outside the door, and Tilly returned unhurriedly to her seat and sat down. She even remembered to cross her ankles and dropped her hands neatly into her lap to complete the perfect picture of innocence. The first thing her mother said as she came into the room was, "I hope you've been a good girl, Tilly?"

A question neatly fielded by Tilly's reply of "I didn't touch anything."

Outside, blinking in the bright sunshine after the gloom of the doctor's office, her mother took her hand. She seemed pleased with Tilly for once and even bought her an ice cream from the shop next to the bus stop. She immediately wished she hadn't, however, when the bus came sooner than they had expected, and Tilly had to negotiate getting on and finding a seat with one hand clutching her ice-cream cone, both eyes fixed on the pink ice cream that crowned it, and her tongue in constant motion attempting to finish her treat before it melted in the heat. As Tilly licked the last drips of ice cream off her fingers, she wondered vaguely what the medicine was that her mother had swapped her prescription for at the chemist. The only medicine she had ever had after a visit to the doctor, on account of a nasty cough, had been the same color as her ice cream and was called penny ceiling. On their way back to the bus stop, they had also stopped at the flower shop. Her mother had bought a lovely big bunch of roses, carnations, and some other flowers that Tilly didn't recognize but thought looked and smelled very pretty. They were for Auntie Wendy because it was her birthday. Auntie Wendy was her mother's best friend, which Tilly thought was quite strange because they weren't alike at all. Auntie Wendy was a noisy, friendly sort of lady, who said "hello' on the street to people she didn't even know, and thought nothing of answering the door in her dressing gown and curlers. She had two children and one husband. The husband was called Uncle Bill, and the children were called Karen and Kevin. Kevin was a boy and twelve years old, so Tilly didn't have much to do with him. But Karen was only two years older than Tilly, and friendly and lively like Auntie Wendy, so Tilly liked playing "shopping' and "hairdressers' with her. Auntie Wendy lived just two streets away from them and always had red fizzy pop, which was another reason why Tilly liked going to see her. They got off the bus at their usual stop, and Tilly noticed that she had two small splodges of pink ice cream on the front of her dress. She tried to lick them off, but her mother stopped her.

"Leave it, Tilly. You'll only make it worse."

Tilly wasn't really worried about the state of her dress; she just didn't want to waste any ice cream. The houses in Auntie Wendy's street all had boxy front gardens bordered by redbrick walls. Most of them had a square of lawn in the middle, edged on all four sides by a thin strip of earth planted with brightly colored flowers. Tilly thought that the houses and gardens looked like they were made of Legos. Except for Auntie Wendy's. Auntie Wendy's front garden was covered with crazy paving with the occasional hole for a plant or shrub, and was home to about twenty assorted garden gnomes. There was also a large plastic windmill, a small wooden wheelbarrow full of begonias, a stone statue of a naked lady, and a wishing well. One of the gnomes sat on the edge of the well dangling a fishing rod into it. He was Tilly's favorite.

"Oooh, look!" shouted Tilly excitedly as they reached Auntie Wendy's gate. "Auntie Wendy's got a new bird. Isn't he lovely?"

In pride of place, standing on an oval-shaped piece of mirrored glass that was held in place by a border of assorted stones, was a magnificent pink, plastic flamingo. Tilly loved Auntie Wendy's front garden. It reminded her of one of those places at the seaside where you could play golf (except, perhaps, for the naked lady). Tilly's mother didn't seem quite so keen.

"He's certainly rather colorful."

Auntie Wendy appeared from the side of the house before they were even halfway down the front path. She greeted them with a broad smile, open arms, and asked, "What do you think of my Englebert?" nodding toward the flamingo. "The kids got him for my birthday."

"I think he's lovely," said Tilly firmly.

Her mother smiled and handed Auntie Wendy the flowers.

"Happy birthday, Wendy."

Auntie Wendy took the flowers, clearly delighted, and then looked at Tilly's mother's worried face, pale despite the warm sunshine.

"What you need is a nice cup of tea and a piece of my birthday cake. But first, you have to let me try out my present from Bill."

She ushered them into the back garden and made them stand together under the apple tree. She disappeared into the house and reappeared almost immediately holding a small, black rectangular object in her hand. She held it up to one eye, and pointed it toward them.

"Say 'cheese!' "

Click.

4

Tilda

The black dog is behind me as I struggle to make progress along the promenade. Eli is my wingman. The freezing wind has already lashed my face into a numb mask and slapped my cheeks cherry red. If I were to unbutton my coat and hold it wide open, I should be whisked up immediately into the pale blue skies like a human kite, and with nobody to hold my string I might be lost forever. But Eli is always there to hold my string. For a moment, I'm almost tempted, but instead, I turn up the collar of my coat and burrow myself deeper inside it. A sudden gust steals my hat and whips it into the air like an escaped balloon. It swoops and rolls into the path of a man walking a safe distance in front of me. He tries to recapture the fugitive hat with flailing grabs and snatches, and it teases him for a moment before flying skyward and then pitching defiantly into the sea. The man turns to face me, raising his shoulders in an exaggerated gesture of regret like a mime artist. I am too far away from him to see his face clearly, but I have a feeling that it would be a kind one. I could have taken a more sheltered route through the town, but I needed the sea. Watching it through a window is never enough. I had to smell its raw saltiness and hear it bang onto the beach and roar across the pebbles. I have left the flat to buy food. I brought enough with me to make a decent breakfast, but I'm planning to stay for a few days at least, and will therefore need more than toast and marmalade. Without my hat, my ears are beginning to ring and the wind is whipping icy tears down my cheeks. I turn away from the sea and head up toward the town while the muscles in my face can still move. Eli follows at a distance; watchful, respectful, guarding. I know that no one else can see him. For as long as I can remember, I have been able to see things that most other people can't. It used to make life hard for me. It tainted me somehow, made me an oddity. But over the years I have learned that it is better to be the real me in secret, so I pretend to be like everyone else. It's not how I want to live, but it makes for a life less complicated. And it's made me stronger, tougher. I don't *need* anyone's company. I'm enough on my own.

I am in no hurry, and wander through the streets peering into shop windows that frame their goods like some wildly eclectic art gallery. My taste buds are being tempted by the warm scent of freshly baked bread and the sight of patisserie tarts and pastries, sitting in rows like little jeweled cushions. Finally, I begin the shopping that has been delayed long enough by my meanderings.

When I have bought enough food to sustain my body and enough wine to fortify my spirit, I head back toward the seafront. Despite the loss of my hat, the sea pulls me back like the seductive endearments of a cruel lover. The little shops along the promenade are opening up now, but there are few customers. This was once my playground for a short but blissful time; my childhood kingdom where I was happy, free and safe. I knew all the shopkeepers and stallholders by name. The fish man was called Walter, and every now and then he used to give me a free punnet of cockles, soused in pungent brown vinegar, and a little wooden fork with which to eat them. Madame Petulengro would let me gaze into her crystal ball and play Snap with her tarot cards, and Ralph and Ena, who sold postcards and rock and all sorts of seaside souvenirs, used to sing songs with rude words in like "bum" and "bugger." Well, Ralph did, and Ena used to tell me not to sing them when I got home. Conrad, who was foreign (probably Polish, I think now, but as a child, "foreign' was as much as I could tell), would sit on an upturned rowing boat on the beach outside Walter's shack mending fishing nets. He always had a cigarette between his lips that remained in place even when he was eating, drinking, or speaking. I was fascinated by his extraordinary proficiency in smoking, but his impenetrable accent coupled with his permanent cigarette meant that I never understood a word he said to me. But I remember that he had a kind smile. It didn't last, though, that golden syrup, "sun has got his hat on' happiness. It was so long ago, but even now with the memory of it comes the feeling that my stomach is full of clay. Queenie's was the only place where I have ever felt that I truly belonged, and it was the only time in my life when I felt completely safe. My mother must have known this. She must have realized that Queenie's was the happiest home I ever had, where I was surrounded by people I loved, people who loved me back. But still my mother sent me away. That it happened so soon after I came out of the hospital and that she offered no satisfactory explanation for my exile made it worse. I remember sitting on my bed next to the suitcase she had packed for me, begging her to let me stay. But she ignored my tears and led me downstairs to where the taxi was waiting. All she would say was that it was for my own good. It was a callous and undeserved punishment that I never understood, and she never attempted to justify any further. I don't recall anything about my accident, but I do remember with agonizing clarity that my mother snatched from me my childhood paradise of seaside, pier, and ballroom, and condemned me to a prison of polished corridors, drafty classrooms, and stuffy dormitories. The tang of the sea, vinegar on hot chips and fresh doughnuts was driven away by the stench of boiled cabbage and damp gym clothing. I was a fish out of water until I left, ten years later, with an excellent education and an irreparable sense of grievance. I came back for the school holidays, but it was never the same. I hardly saw my mother, and life at my beloved Queenie's and on the pier moved on without me. The subtle shifts and changes of everyday life were lost to me, and I became little more than a tourist. Even at Queenie's I was a guest in the place that used to be my home. The one consolation was that *she* always loved me just the same. Queenie was a second mother to me then, and there have been many times in my life when I have wished that she was my first.

I walk briskly, heavily shrouded in my thick coat, my shoulders hunched against the wind. I know without looking that Eli will have broken into a leisurely trot to keep up with my stride, and that his tail will be gently wagging. As I climb the steps to the front door of the flat, someone calls my name.

"Tilda, how are you my, dear? Sorting through your mother's things, I expect."

It is Miss Dane. Penelope Dane; my mother's neighbor from the ground-floor flat. She is at least as old as Winnie the Pooh, and stands as upright as a Girl Guide at a church parade. She is a lifelong exponent of the A-line tweed skirt, twinset, and silk scarf brigade, and doesn't hold with teabags, daytime television, or whinging of any sort. Or euphemisms.

"I'm really awfully sorry she's dead. I used to enjoy our little chats over a cup of tea. She was an extraordinary woman, your mother. Still, perhaps you'd like to join me for tea one day while you're here? Tomorrow. Around four?"

No, I wouldn't really.

"Yes, of course."

I had no idea that my mother and Penelope Dane used to have tea together. I had always assumed that they were simply neighbors on little more than nodding acquaintance.

I set down my shopping bags and reach into the depths of my pocket for the key. I look down at the street below. Eli is gone. He will be inside the flat already, waiting patiently for me.

It is almost lunchtime, and the wind and walking have made me hungry. I hang my coat on the coat stand in the hallway and take my bags through to the kitchen. The flat is warm, and light floods in through the large sash windows and French doors. The warmth is supplied by the excellent central heating system that was barely troubled during Mother's residence. She had it installed several years ago and then treated it like a front parlor; she only used it for best. It wasn't as though she couldn't afford the bills—it was simply that she regarded it as unnecessary for everyday use. I always packed extra sweaters when I came to stay with her, and woolly socks to wear in bed. When I arrived last night, I cranked up the thermostat, fully expecting a subsequent plumbing catastrophe. But the machine clicked obligingly, and somewhere, in the heart of the boiler, a flame had gently blown into life. It felt like a small act of rebellion against my mother to be so profligate with the pilot light.

In the kitchen, I begin preparing my lunch. Eli is lying under the table, keeping me locked in his steady gaze. I break some of the fresh, crusty bread onto a plate, and press some creamy butter onto its soft and still slightly warm insides. I add a couple of thin slices of cheese to the plate, a dollop of pickle, and a small bunch of grapes. I'm also going to have a glass of wine, or two. I feel half as though I'm on holiday. I fetch a glass from the cabinet in the sitting room and rinse it under the tap. It is etched glass with a large, delicate bowl and a tall, slender stem twisted like barley sugar. It is clearly also "for best," a precious confection spun out of fragile, glistening glass. But what good is its beauty if it is never seen and never used? It might just as well be a plastic tumbler. What was my mother saving it for? She could hardly have been expecting a chance call from a local dignitary, or a random visit from a passing celebrity or minor member of the royal family. My mother seems to have lived her whole life buttoned up in a stiff, starchy suit of "what ifs," "keep for bests" and "what will people thinks." A bright summer dress of "chase the stars," "seize the days" and "hang the consequences" might have fit her so much better if only she had dared to try it on. I think that may have been who she was inside, but I never got to see her. Her caution was stultifying, and she passed her days permanently under its sedation. And now I am beginning to be just a little afraid that I might be a bit like her. I am certainly hiding who I really am. It's not a legacy I welcome. I don't want to be that woman who wastes her whole life wearing the wrong dress. I fetch another glass from the cabinet and fill it with sparkling mineral water; and then another one, just for the hell of it.

After a leisurely lunch, which has dirtied three of the best wineglasses (I put the grape pips in the third), I am ready to resume the task of sorting through my mother's things. After the wine, I don't want to do anything sensible like tackling the post that is mounting in an unsteady pile on the bamboo table in the hallway. I wander through to her bedroom with the intention of emptying the drawers of her dressing table. I sit down heavily on the bed and, as I do so, my boot catches something heavy and solid underneath it. My mother was not a woman who shoved things under the bed as a matter of course. She was a woman who dusted under the bed as a matter of decency. It's a box, a polished, walnut box with an intricate brass lock. Its mottled lid glows and gleams with the rich colors of caramel, honey, and lemon curd. And it's locked. There are only two things that I can think of that someone would keep locked in a box under a bed: treasures and secrets. Either way, I need to find the key. I pick up the framed photograph from the dressing table and stare at the child I used to be next to the woman who so spectacularly failed to be the mother I wanted. What were her secrets and where was the key?

5

Tilly

The key was kept on the top shelf of the kitchen dresser, in a blue-and-white-striped china pot with a lid. Tilly had to climb up onto a chair so that she could reach it, and even then, her fingertips could only just clutch at the bottom of the pot, making it judder perilously close to the edge of the shelf. Tilly's heart thudded inside her ribs and she held her breath as the pot teetered between the clammy, fumbling grasp of her six-year-old hands, and a straight, hard smash onto the kitchen floor.

"Dear God, Jesus, Noah, and Moses, please don't let it fall," she prayed.

Tilly didn't know any proper prayers except "Our Father," which didn't seem appropriate in this case, and was too long anyway. The fate of the pot would have been decided before she got past "Hello be thy name." Tilly had been to Sunday school, but most of the time had been spent sitting cross-legged on a cold floor listening to stories about Noah's ark, Moses in the bulldozer, and the adventures of Jesus and his tricycles. Tilly hadn't paid that much attention. Whether it was God, Jesus, Noah, Moses, or simply the laws of physics,

Tilly would never know or care, but the pot toppled into her nervously waiting hands. She cradled it closely to her chest and climbed down from the chair. She took the long, slightly rusty key from its hiding place and slipped it into her pocket. She was going to leave the pot behind the bread bin, almost out of sight, until she got back, to save on the amount of climbing up and down, and the chances of dropping it. But then the thought struck her that maybe she could keep the key and hide it somewhere else. Her mother was unlikely to miss it, and then Tilly could use it whenever she wanted without first having to go through such heart-stopping furniture mountaineering and crockery juggling. This meant replacing the pot on the high shelf immediately. Tilly clambered back on the chair and repeated her prayer, this time including "Mary, Mother of God," for good measure. It worked. The pot was returned safely to its place on the dresser, and Tilly smiled to herself as her fingers traced the outline of the key in her pocket. They had stayed at Auntie Wendy's long enough for a piece of birthday cake and a cup of tea for her mother and a glass of pop for Tilly. Tilly had taken her cake and pop outside into the garden to play with Karen, while her mother stayed inside talking to Auntie Wendy. Tilly knew that they were talking about grown-up things because she had stood behind the door for a minute and listened after she had closed it. She couldn't hear exactly what they were saying, but it was clear from their quiet, serious voices that their conversation was not about Englebert the flamingo, or whether "hands that do dishes can feel soft as your face with mild green Fairy Liquid." She heard her mother say her daddy's name, and then she thought she heard her crying. Tilly was good at listening, and she did it a lot to try and get some clues on how the world worked. She knew from experience that grown-ups were very good at not telling children things, particularly things that they needed to know. For example, where was her daddy? Gone away to work, her mother had told her, but where? And more important, why? And when was he coming back? Her mother's answers were always vague, but Tilly really needed to know the facts, and so she would keep listening and hoping for clues.

Tilly and Karen were just in the middle of a game of hairdressers when her mother came into the garden to fetch Tilly and take her home. Her mother looked tired and her eyes were red, but Tilly was reluctant to leave their game just when she was hearing about Karen's "lazy, good-for-nothing husband making a pass at that bottle-blond trollop of a barmaid down the pub, while her hair was being given a pretend shampoo and set. She had no idea why Karen's pretend husband was playing football with a barmaid, and why it made her a trollop. She had no idea what a trollop was. But she might have found out had her mother not come and fetched her at that very moment. She was particularly cross because her mother's expression of disapproval when she heard what Karen was saying meant that it must have been something that Tilly would have very much liked to have understood, and that this would definitely be one of the things that her mother would not be telling her.

When they got home, Tilly's mother had gone for "a little lie-down." She had one of her mysterious headaches, which Tilly knew meant that she could be in bed for hours. She had told Tilly to be a good girl and play quietly, but that was it, no specific details. That left plenty of options open, and Tilly knew exactly what she was going to do.

Once the key was in her pocket, and the pot back on the shelf, Tilly opened the back door and went out into the garden. It seemed hotter than ever, and the heat shimmered in a haze above the concrete path. The tomato plants were wilting in their pots, like frail little old ladies in need of lemonade. Tilly would water them later, but first she was going to the shed. She took the key in both hands and wiggled it into the keyhole. It was a loose fit and rattled around making it difficult for her to unlock, but Tilly jiggled the key patiently as she had watched her daddy do many times, and her persistence eventually paid off. She stepped into the cool, quiet darkness and took a deep breath, filling her nostrils with the smell of old burlap sacks, potting compost, and, of course, creosote. It was familiar and comforting, like an old favorite blanket. But the gardening tools hung idle and somehow forlorn in their tidy rows along the wall. Tilly had wanted to be inside the shed to feel close to her daddy, but now she was here, and surrounded by his things, she missed him even more. Her eyes brimmed with hot tears that trickled down her cheeks in salty rivulets. She sniffed loudly and wiped her nose and face across the arm of her cardigan. Tilly didn't know exactly how long her daddy had been gone. It had only been a few days, but already it felt like a very long time. She reached up and took down the hand fork from its hook on the wall. She stroked the smooth, wooden handle, putting her hands where her daddy's had been last, as though she might be able to catch the faintest touch of him and hold it with her until he came back. Tilly reluctantly hung the fork back in its place and turned her attention to the wooden chest where her daddy kept packets of seeds, string, plant tags, and old newspaper cuttings about gardening. She poked around in the drawers, admiring the pretty pictures of flowers on the front of some of the seed packets and fiddling with the big ball of hairy, brown string that was beginning to unravel. Underneath the newspaper cuttings she found some things that she hadn't known were there: a spare pouch of tobacco, a packet of rolling papers, and a box of matches. Tilly was not allowed to play with matches. This was one of the definite rules, right up there with no swearing, no lying, and no giving Chinese burns, even as a joke. Tilly really liked matches. They were like little sticks of magic. She took the box and slid the cover off. She emptied the matches onto the top of the chest of drawers, and began replacing them in the box, one by one. This was not playing with matches; it was counting them. There were twenty-three. But what were the chances that anyone else in the world knew that? And what would it matter, if someone else did count them, and there were only twenty-two? Tilly carefully chose one match and closed the box. She gripped the match firmly between her finger and thumb, and holding the box still with her other hand, she struck it along the rough strip of sandpaper. The smell was lovely, and the flash and flame punched a small hole in the gloom just for a second, before Tilly blew it out like a birthday candle.

She was thrilled by her own daring and untroubled by her conscience. She hadn't played with the matches. She had counted them, and lit one. Where was the harm in that? Even so, she didn't plan on mentioning it to her mother. Tilly put the matches back in the chest and closed the drawer. She dropped the spent match into an empty flower pot, and took one last deep breath of shed smell, which now included an acrid tang of smoke. She would go and water the drooping plants and check the sweet peas, and then see if her mother was awake. She stepped outside into the sun-baked garden and closed the door softly behind her. She locked it and slipped the long, heavy key back inside her pocket. It would be her secret.

6

Tilda

The woman in the mirror looks ridiculous. She looks ridiculous and uncomfortable, like someone dressing up in her mother's clothes. And she is. The woman in the mirror is me. I have absolutely no idea why I'm so bothered about what I'm going to wear to Miss Dane's for tea. I don't even want to go. I hardly know the woman. My impression of her is part battle-ax, part busybody, part Women's Institute, and part my old Latin teacher, the sum total of which for me equals "just plain scary." I have only brought jeans with me, and for some reason, I'm afraid that these will be regarded as too scruffy by a woman with such fond attachment to her A-line skirts and pearl-button blouses, which is why I'm standing in front of a mirror looking utterly ridiculous in one of my mother's skirts. I have asked Queenie to come with me, but she refuses, saying that she hasn't been included in the invitation.

"It's just tea," she says, clearly amused by my outfit indecision, "not the Royal Variety Performance. You'll look lovely whatever you wear."

The clock in the sitting room chimes four. I am now faced with the choice of being punctual and looking utterly ridiculous, or late but feeling comfortable. I have wasted half the day looking for the key to the walnut box and I still haven't found it, and so I gave no thought to Miss Dane's invitation to tea until the last minute. In keeping with my recent catalog of small but significant acts of rebellion, I decide on jeans. After all, she can hardly put me in detention.

Miss Dane, of course, makes no mention of my lateness as she opens the door to me minutes later. She greets me warmly, but seems to be expecting someone else as well, as she checks the hallway outside before closing her front door. She shows me through to her sitting room and then goes into the kitchen to fetch the tea. The tea service is Clarice Cliff, the tea is lapsang souchong, and the biscuits are Fortnum & Mason. Miss Dane is clearly not a woman who keeps things for best, and at her age, who can blame her? Although on closer inspection of her sitting room, perhaps she simply doesn't differentiate between Sunday best and workday wear. The exquisite teapot is wearing a brown, knitted tea cozy that has Women's Institute bazaar running through every stitch. The Hummel figurines on the mantelpiece stand shoulder to shoulder with cheap Wade bunny rabbits and puppies that I can remember squandering my pocket money on as a child. The ramshackle pile of shiny coal is heaped into an expensive-looking Majolica punch bowl, and a majestic, cast-bronze statue of a stallion is being used as a doorstop.

"Now, are you warm enough, my dear? Come over here and sit by the fire. Perhaps you'd be kind enough to pour the tea? You're less likely to rattle the china than I am."

I wouldn't bet on that. Although I have to admit that Miss Dane's face looks slightly more benevolent in the soft light of the fire, one sudden move from her and I'll be straight into a perfect Latin declension of the noun "table' or reporting in somewhat stilted conversational Latin that the soldiers have laid waste to the citadel. I feel as though she is testing me, assessing my social skills to see if I pass muster. After all, she carried the whole tray of tea things from the kitchen without spilling a drop. Old age has apparently done little to weaken her body, and I suspect it may have even sharpened her mind. I manage to pour the tea without breaking anything, but I'm definitely not having a biscuit. I don't want to push my luck and drop crumbs everywhere, or forget myself and dunk. Now I need to think of something sensible and polite to say. Perhaps I could comment on the weather or inquire after her health. I have no idea why her opinion of me matters in the slightest, but for some reason as unfathomable to me as the shipping forecast, it does. I simply don't want her to think badly of me, and at the same time I'm annoyed with myself for caring. I needn't have worried. It seems that Miss Dane's purpose is interrogation rather than conversation.

"How are you coping? She was an extraordinary woman, your mother. You must miss her dreadfully?"

Am I obliged to answer this, or do I get a phone call and a solicitor first? Miss Dane has honed a natural talent for plain speaking into a martial art. Her question has caught me off balance. What I want to say is "mind your own business"—not to be rude, but because I don't want to talk about it, and in any case, it's not that simple. The truth is, I don't know, but my answer is, "Oh, I'm fine really. Thank you. Actually, we weren't that close."

Miss Dane recognizes a fob-off when she sees one. She must have been a schoolmistress. Why else would I feel like a fifth former who's just given a particularly weak excuse for not producing her homework?

"But, my dear, she was your mother, and you were her only child."

The cheeky little girl who still lurks somewhere deep inside me longs to reply, "Yes, thank you Miss Dane, I'm well aware of that," but the silence of a guilt-ridden fifth former prevails. Miss Dane watches me closely as I line up my teacup with the teapot on the tray, so that both handles are facing in the same direction.

"Do I make you uncomfortable?" she asks, almost gently.

"Most people make me uncomfortable, eventually."

This is torture by afternoon tea. I tell myself not to be so pathetic, and take a sip of the hot, black, smoky contents of my cup.

"Your mother was very proud of you, you know. She always looked forward to your visits."

She clearly wasn't going to drop the subject. Well, fine; let's debate the matter, shall we? "This house believes that Tilda's mother was a loving and devoted parent," with Miss Dane proposing the motion.

"She didn't like me," I counter.

"Of course she did!" An empty assertion.

"She sent me away to boarding school. I hated it." Good point.

"She must have had an excellent reason." Pathetic general rebuttal unsubstantiated by any facts.

"She drove my father away. He never came back." Answer that one.

"Well, that's how you saw it then, my dear, but you were only a child. There may have been mitigating circumstances of which you were unaware." I don't want to hear this.

"Yes, I was only a child. But I was there, and you weren't." Subject closed.

I am hot, and I can feel my face burning. It has nothing to do with sitting next to the fire, and everything to do with sitting opposite Miss Dane. How dare she tell me my life! She knows nothing about it. I take another sip of my tea. It tastes bitter in my mouth. I've had enough of the tea, and the company, but I remind myself that Miss Dane is an old woman who has also lost someone with the death of my mother. She probably has precious little company, and my mother was someone she counted as a friend.

"She loved you very much, my dear."

Her voice is softer now, but more intense. She leans toward me and fixes me with her calm, gray eyes.

"She was always talking about you, and that is why you must forgive me if I speak out of turn. I have heard so much about you that I feel as though I know you. She told me about your every achievement, professional or private, great or small, with such obvious love and pride. You were the most important thing in her life." She shakes her head sadly and adds, almost inaudibly but not quite, "Too important, perhaps."

I take a larger gulp of tea than I had intended. The

black liquid is still very hot and burns my mouth and throat, but the pain is a welcome distraction. I feel as though I have turned over two pages of a book at once and lost the plot. My reality is slipping out of focus like a view through a rain-streaked window. I do not recognize at all the woman she is describing as my mother. She is describing the mother I longed for, dreamed about, prayed for. The soap powder paragon. The mother who never came.

"Do you like cauliflower?"

Miss Dane's peculiar question is an even better distraction than the scalding tea. It catches me before I fall too far.

"My niece insists on doing my shopping for me, although I'm quite capable of doing it for myself. The wretched woman is always bringing me things I can't stomach. This week it was cauliflower. I can't stand the nasty knobbly things."

This is how I come to leave Miss Dane's with a burned mouth, a spinning head, and a cauliflower. As I reach the front door, she lays her hand on my arm.

"I am sorry if I have upset you, my dear, but the things I have told you are things that I believe you need to know."

She smiles at me for the first time I can remember. Yet I might still have dismissed her as a batty, slightly scary old busybody, had it not been for her parting words:

"Next time you come, why don't you bring your dog?"

Back in my mother's flat, sitting rigid with fury at the kitchen table, a hundred questions roar and scream inside my head like wailing banshees. Why did my mother never tell me she was proud of me? Why did she send me away? Where did my daddy go? Why didn't I know she loved me? Who the hell was she when she wasn't with me? My hands are shaking as I take a match from the box in front of me and strike it. As soon as it burns out, I strike another and another. I am only allowed ten matches a day, and after all ten, Eli crawls out from under the table and sits at my feet. But I am no calmer. I try to cool my scalded throat and boiling anger with glass after glass of chilled white wine from one of my mother's wineglasses. It's like throwing water onto a blazing chip pan. My rage explodes into molten wreckage and I hurl the precious wine glass into the butler's sink. The vicious shards of glinting glass fly and spin and ricochet before settling into a jagged mosaic that is a mirror of my own destruction. It's strange how the sound of smashing and shattering is soothing to the unquiet mind. Too much wine, too quickly, on an empty stomach has made me unsteady, and I lean back against the pine dresser, which is more rickety than I thought. The top section wobbles threateningly and the next smash I hear is not soothing at all. A small striped pot, one I remember fondly from the kitchen of my childhood, lies in sad pieces on the floor. Nestled among the blue and white fragments is something gold and shiny. It is a small brass key.

7

Tilly

It was too hot. Not the happy sunshine hot of flowery cotton dresses and stripy, swingy deck chairs, but the sulky, sticky hot of clingy nylon shirts and sweaty plastic stacking chairs. Lunch was horrid and Tilly would be glad when it was over. Not the food; the food was all right. Fish fingers, instant mashed potatos, and canned baked beans. The potatoes in the garden were running to seed, and the peas were being eaten by the birds. Tilly's mother was smoking a cigarette for her lunch. She wasn't very good at it, but Tilly thought that it must be because she was still a beginner. She'd only started about a week ago, and didn't seem to have gotten the hang of it yet. She smoked as though she was daring someone to tell her not to. She didn't look like she was enjoying it very much. Tilly thought she was probably just doing it to be awkward, the way Tilly sometimes put her shoes on the wrong feet and her cardigan on back to front when she was having a sulk about something and no one was paying any attention. But this was more than just a sulk, and that's why lunch was so horrid. Her mother's mood was like a boil waiting to burst. Tilly had learned to be careful when her mother was like this. She had often played a game with her daddy called "The Kraken Wakes." Her daddy would pretend to be a fierce, dragonlike monster who gobbled the flesh of children and then crunched their bones. While he was sleeping, Tilly had to tiptoe past him and touch his nose without waking him. He always leaped from his chair and grabbed her just as she thought she had won. He would roar and growl ferociously, and she would laugh until she cried. But now her mother was the Kraken it wasn't fun anymore. It wasn't a game; it was real. Tilly carefully cut her fish fingers into neat little rectangles and chewed each piece five times before swallowing. She put her knife and fork straight like soldiers on either side of her plate while she counted each five chews. She dipped each piece of fish finger once in the blob of tomato ketchup on the edge of her plate and ate five baked beans on each forkful. Every time she took a drink from her beaker of orange squash, she replaced it on the table in exactly the same place, with the picture of the dog on the beaker facing her. Tilly thought that if she concentrated really hard on what she was doing, she wouldn't do or say anything that might accidentally upset her mother and awake the Kraken. It was like weaving a magic spell, but instead of using toads and bat's blood, she was doing it with fish fingers. For dessert it was banana custard. It was cold.

Just as Tilly was chasing the last piece of banana around the dish with her spoon, and wondering what would happen next, Auntie Wendy arrived like a rainbow in a storm-sooty sky. Tilly felt as though the piece of elastic that was being stretched to breaking point, and which tied her to her mother, had been cut. Auntie Wendy laughed uproariously at her mother's smoking.

"Good God, Gracie! Who do you think you are— Marlene Dietrich?"

Auntie Wendy's cheeks were glowing, and despite her billowing cotton dress awash with pink cabbage roses on a clotted cream background, and her kitten-heeled, strappy sandals, she looked hot and thirsty.

"Put the kettle on, love. I could murder a cup of tea."

Her mother got up to make the tea, managing a weak smile. Tilly's attention wandered back to Auntie Wendy's sandals. She loved grown-up ladies' shoes like these. She loved their clippety-click heels, their pointy toes with bows on top, and their dainty heel straps. Her brown leather T-bars from Clarks were so ugly and clumsy in comparison, and she was only allowed to wear her red ones for best. Auntie Wendy smiled at her and reached inside her handbag for her purse.

"Here you are, Tilly," she said, handing her some coins. "Why don't you pop down to the shop and buy yourself an ice cream?"

This could mean only one thing. Auntie Wendy was going to talk about things that she didn't want Tilly to hear. Just this once, Tilly didn't really mind. She was glad to escape her mother's crushing sadness and simmering temper. She knew that something was badly wrong, but she didn't know how to make it better. It was the mummy's job to make things better, and she wasn't a mummy. And the banana custard had had skin on it, and lumps that weren't banana, and it wasn't a proper dessert anyway. An ice cream might go some way to making up for it. Even so, Tilly couldn't resist hanging around by the back door after she had closed it, just long enough to hear Auntie Wendy shout good-naturedly, "And don't you be standing there listening, young lady!"

Tilly could still hear her laughing as she closed the garden gate. The shop was three streets away, with no main roads to cross, but Tilly was rarely allowed to go on her own. Since her daddy had gone, though, things had changed. While she was with her, her mother minded everything she did and said closely. The slightest wrongdoing was picked up, and any mention of her daddy was greeted with silent disapproval, angry shouting, or vague dismissal. Tilly didn't know where she was. It was as though someone had changed the rules and forgotten to tell her. The uncertainty scared her more than the shouting. And she still didn't understand why her daddy had gone away. On the day he left, he had swung her up into his arms, told her to be a big girl and to look after her mother. She had begged him not to go, but he had kissed her on the top of her head and replied, "Somebody has to earn the pennies." She offered him all the money in her piggy bank to stay and his eyes were wet with tears as he shook his head and waved good-bye. These days, when Tilly was allowed out to play, or went to school, it was almost as though she was forgotten about. If she was late home it was barely noticed, and her mother never asked her where she had been or what she had been doing. Tilly was sure that the soap powder mummy wouldn't forget about her children like that. Still, the new way of things had its advantages. More freedom meant that the edges of Tilly's world were sneaking outward like a pool of spilled milk, and she was ready to make the most of it. As Tilly tried to decide what flavor ice cream to have, suddenly and unexpectedly her eyes flooded with tears. She always had an ice cream on the way home when her daddy took her to the cemetery to see Granddad Rory and Grandma Rose. Tilly didn't see them very much because it was a long way away, but she loved them dearly. Grandma Rose was a loud, happy woman who wore deep pink lipstick and tight skirts that made her walk with a wiggle. Granddad Rory smoked a pipe and was always telling jokes with swear words in them. They would sit on a bench while Tilly arranged the flowers on their graves where they were buried side by side, and she always had an ice cream on the way home. Her mother never came with them to the cemetery. Tilly went with her daddy on the bus, and he told her that it must always be their special secret. He said that her mother wouldn't see Granddad Rory or Grandma Rose, so it was better not to tell her. Or anyone else. Now that her daddy was gone, she realized that she couldn't get to the cemetery on her own. She might never see them again.

She dawdled down the street, sniffing back the tears and tightly gripping her ice-cream money. Her thoughts returned to Auntie Wendy and how she was a lot like a smiley, slightly bossy fairy godmother arriving just in the nick of time when there was trouble. Lassie was a bit like that too, but she was more serious and could talk to adults by barking, even though Tilly never really knew what she was saying. Come to think of it, Uncle Bill was more like Lassie. He was very calm and always knew the right thing to do. He came from a country called Newcastle, and Tilly could never understand a word he said either. Tilly watched her feet, trapped in her ugly brown sandals, as she walked along being careful not to tread on the cracks in case she broke her mother's back. Her mother seemed to have enough problems as it was, even if Tilly didn't know exactly what they were. She tried a bit of hopscotch-style hopping and jumping, but it was too hot for that, so she went back to staring at her feet.

If you step upon a crack,
You will break your mother's back.

It was making her dizzy now, all that staring and being careful. Tilly crossed her fingers and spat on the pavement as a signal that she had finished playing that particular game, and if she should tread on a crack now it wouldn't count. She didn't know exactly who was in charge of these things, and who made up the rules. At first, she thought it might be God or Jesus or Noah, but because they were most famous for being really good and holy and, in Noah's case, having a really big boat, it wasn't very likely that they would approve of a game that involved crippling your own mother. Tilly had seen a cripple once when she was shopping for a new watering can with her daddy. He was a big fat jelly of a man, with red cheeks, sitting in a wheelchair that was being pushed by a pale, scrawny-looking woman who Tilly thought must be his wife, and who would surely end up a cripple herself, if she carried on pushing her great lump of a husband everywhere. Her daddy told her not to say "cripple' because it wasn't very nice, but Tilly thought that the man seemed to be having a fine time of it. Anyway, if it wasn't God or Jesus or Noah,

Tilly concluded that it must be a sort of kraken in the sky (but obviously not the same bit of sky where God lived) who looked down on you to make sure you stuck to the rules.

Tilly raised her eyes from her shoes in search of something more interesting to look at, and found Mrs. O'Flaherty, resplendent in lime green polyester, just coming out of her gate.

"Good afternoon to you, Miss Tilly, and where are you off to this fine afternoon?"

Tilly loved that Mrs. O'Flaherty called her "Miss Tilly" and spoke to her as if she were a grown-up. Mrs. O'Flaherty had a funny way of speaking because she came from an island, but Tilly thought it was pretty and sounded a bit like singing without the music, and anyway she could understand her a lot better than she could Uncle Bill.

"I'm going to the shop to get an ice cream."

"And would you give me the pleasure of walking with you?"

Tilly's face lit up as she grinned her agreement, and Mrs. O'Flaherty's big, warm Irish heart flinched with pity. Mrs. O'Flaherty knew about Tilly's daddy, and her mother's illness. It was that kind of neighborhood, where secrets were as hard to keep as pennies on pocket-money day, and other people's business was everyone else's entertainment. But it wasn't meant unkindly, and Mrs. O'Flaherty worried that Tilly's obviously fragile mother was struggling day to day to preserve what was left of her broken family home. And she felt sorry for Tilly. She seemed like such a singular and solitary little girl. Not at all like her own boisterous offspring whom she had left in the charge of her eldest, Teresa, while she slipped away for half an hour's peace.

"Are you going to the shop too?"

Tilly skipped along next to Mrs. O'Flaherty to keep up with her surprisingly nimble pace.

"No, Miss Tilly, I'm going to Confession."

"Where's Confession?"

Mrs. O'Flaherty smiled.

"It's not a place; it's something I have to do."

Tilly thought for a moment.

"Well, where do you do it?"

"In church, Miss Tilly, under the watchful eyes of our Lord."

"Can I watch too?"

Mrs. O'Flaherty hesitated. Sure, what harm could it do? The sight of Tilly's eager face made up her mind.

"If you're sure your mammy won't mind?"

"She won't even notice."

Sadly, thought Mrs. O'Flaherty, that was probably true. The church was at the end of the street, on the corner. A huge building, it seemed to Tilly, with pointy turrets and arches and colored glass windows, like a castle or a palace. It had a tall steeple pointing straight up to heaven. Tilly liked this church much better than the one where she had been to Sunday school, which was a modern, concrete box with no steeple at all and a car park. Mrs. O'Flaherty's church looked much more like the sort of place where God would live with his angels, even though Tilly hadn't been inside yet. Mrs. O'Flaherty strode up the stone steps leading to the massive wooden doors, Tilly trotting along beside her. She twisted the great metal ring that served as a handle, and opened the door into the still, cavernous coolness that was God's house on earth. Tilly stood and stared in amazement. She had never seen anywhere so beautiful. The rows of flickering candles shimmered in the shadows like fairy lights. Everywhere she looked there were rich, glowing colors, burnished gold and silver, and sparkles, glitter, and twinklings. The breath of magic hung in the air. Tilly thought it was as though someone had put a fairground, a fairy tale, and Christmas in a box, shaken them all together, and tipped them out again. The only thing missing was the noise, but somehow the silence made it seem even more beautiful. She could quite see why God and his angels wanted to live here. She wouldn't mind living here herself. Mrs. O'Flaherty did a funny little curtsy toward the altar, and sat down in one of the dark, wooden pews. Tilly sat down next to her, relieved that Mrs. O'Flaherty's knees hadn't given way, which was her first thought before she realized it was deliberate. The cold, smooth surface of the wood felt good against the back of Tilly's legs, but the best thing was the peace and quiet. It was quiet at home, most of the time, but not like this. At home the silence was stretched and tight, like holding your breath until you felt your chest might explode. Here, the silence was soft and deep and Tilly sank into it as though it were a pile of velvet cushions. Mrs. O'Flaherty loved the quietness here too. Heaven knows, there was precious little of it in her busy days. She glanced at Tilly, lost in her own world, staring openmouthed at her surroundings, and for a moment Mrs. O'Flaherty was envious of her innocence and wonderment. The silence was broken by the clacking of brisk footsteps as a man in a long black dress with a white collar walked through the church and into a little wooden hut to one side of the aisle and shut the door. Mrs. O'Flaherty stood up.

"Now, you wait there for me, Miss Tilly. I shan't be long."

Mrs. O'Flaherty followed the man into the hut using a different door, and silence crept back into every corner of the church once again, and Tilly was alone and spellbound. But she didn't feel alone. She couldn't see them yet, but she knew that there were others here. She closed her eyes and breathed deeply, sucking in the scent of polished wood, burning candles, and incense. This place even smelled of magic. She wondered who had the marvelous job of lighting all the candles and how many matches it would take. When she opened her eyes again Tilly had company. An elderly couple was sitting quietly together, holding hands. They looked up at Tilly and smiled. She leaned forward and whispered, "Hello. I'm Tilly."

The old man lifted the hand that he was holding.

"This is my beautiful wife, Gloria Bow, and I'm the luckiest man in the world, Albert Bow."

"And very handsome you are too, my love," his wife whispered.

In the pew in front of them, a young woman was writing furiously in a tiny notebook, and farther back, toward the door, a little boy was playing with a toy car in the aisle. But the silence remained unrippled by their presence. Mrs. O'Flaherty, true to her word, wasn't very long. After only a few minutes with the man in the hut, she came back and sat down again next to Tilly. She pulled the hem of her lime green dress firmly down toward her knees, and bowed her head. In her hands was a pretty necklace made of sparkling red beads that rattled softly against one another as she moved them through her fingers. Mrs. O'Flaherty began to talk quietly to herself while counting the beads. She seemed to be saying the same little poem over and over again, as though she was trying to learn it. It was something to do with two ladies called Mary and Grace, and their fruit. And then came something Tilly recognized. It was "Our Father." Mrs. O'Flaherty was saying her prayers. Tilly joined in. It seemed like the polite thing to do. She muttered the Mary and Grace one under her breath, trying to pick it up as she went along, but when it came to the "Our Father' her voice rang out in clear, confident tones around the empty church. When Mrs. O'Flaherty had counted all her beads, it was time to stop praying. She looked a bit red in the face, and a bit wet round the eyes, as though she had been laughing or crying, but Tilly thought it was probably just the effort of all that praying and counting at the same time. Mrs. O'Flaherty slipped the necklace into the big brown handbag that was wedged into the crook of her elbow. She turned to Tilly and smiled.

"Well, Miss Tilly, I'm sure that will have made our Lord sit up and listen. You've a fine voice for praying."

"Can I come back again another day?"

"Miss Tilly, our Lord's house is always open, and I'm sure he'd be pleased to see you any time."

As they got up to leave, the big wooden doors opened from the outside and more people came into the church. Several of the women greeted Mrs. O'Flaherty warmly.

They looked at Tilly and then back at Mrs. O'Flaherty as though posing a silent question, but Mrs. O'Flaherty chose not to answer, other than with a very slight shake of her head. Outside, the sun was still shining, and it felt even hotter after the coolness of the church. Tilly's thoughts turned to ice cream. She thanked Mrs. O'Flaherty for letting her watch "Confession," and Mrs. O'Flaherty said she was as welcome as the flowers in May, which Tilly didn't really understand but thought sounded lovely anyway. She set off in the direction of the shop, but had only gone a few yards when she turned and called, "Mrs. O'Flaherty, what kind of soap powder do you use?"

Mrs. O'Flaherty laughed at Tilly's strange question, but answered nonetheless.

"Daz."

That explains it, thought Tilly.

She skipped off to the shop and bought a strawberry ice cream, which dribbled all over her hands, melting before she could eat it. She was still sucking her fingers as she walked up to the back door. She didn't go in straight away but sidled up to the window to see if Auntie Wendy was still there. Her mother was seated alone at the kitchen table. A cigarette was burning in an ashtray at her elbow, and her mother was bent low over the table, writing in a small blue book. Tilly turned away from the house and wandered down the garden toward the shed where the matches lay waiting for her. Nestled in the bottom of her pocket was the key.

8

Tilda

I knew somehow that the small brass key would fit the lock of the walnut box, but I had no clue as to what I might find inside. The lifted lid reveals piles of notebooks, neatly stacked. My mother's diaries. I had no idea she kept a diary. But then, why would I? It seems, after my afternoon tea with Miss Dane, that there is probably a great deal I don't know about my mother. The books lie before me now like another box of matches. But would these ones light a candle to guide me, or a bonfire to burn my memories on? The answer is almost certain to be both. From childhood, I have always loved playing with matches, but now they have become one of my rituals. Some people cut themselves. I light matches. I flirt with the flames, but their fire is under my command. I could conjure black and blistered skin or catastrophic conflagration. But I choose not to. So far. The books are all different colors and sizes, but the one on top looks as though it has been placed there deliberately. It is a small blue notebook containing entries that begin in the year of my seventh birthday. My heart is pummeling my chest as I flick through the pages. This is not merely a record of appointments and a reminder of birthdays and anniversaries. This is the full story, chapter and verse, of my mother's secret life, a life I had lived alongside, crossing over and bumping up against, but never really sharing. Until now, perhaps. Each page is crammed with my mother's elegant handwriting. Words like "love," "hate," and "Tilly' shout out to be read, but the woman who wrote them is a stranger to me, and I am now more scared than excited about what I might discover. The book slips from my hands and drops back into the box with a soft thud. I am sitting on the floor with the open box in front of me, and as I look up I meet the steady gaze of the deep, dark eyes that have long been my solace and my sanity. Eli is sitting just the other side of the box. He rarely comes this close, but when he does his presence is like a cool breeze on a sunburned face; a warm blanket on a bitter night; a nice cup of tea on the heels of disaster. No matter what is wrong, he always makes it better. He is my strength. I shall, of course, read the diaries, every word. But not just yet. I have some clearing up to do first.

As I sweep the pieces of the little blue and white pot into the dustpan, I wonder if I could glue them together again, but what's the point? I only want the pot because of the memories it brings with it, and perhaps, by now, they are as cracked and broken as the pot itself. Or if not now, they might be soon, when I have read the diaries. It occurs to me that perhaps my mother kept the key in the pot precisely because of these memories. Perhaps she kept it there because she wanted me to find it. I have always had the suspicion that some of the early pages of my life story have been ripped out and torn up. That some things have slipped away from me. I sometimes catch a glimpse of the ghostly blacks and grays of a faded negative softly printed on my mind, or hear the dying notes of a once familiar tune, but the photograph is gone and the song forgotten.

The smashed glass in the sink has made a dreadful mess, and I have cut myself twice trying to clear it up. I can almost hear my mother saying, "Serves you right." These grand gestures of rant and rage are all very cathartic and gratifyingly theatrical at the time, but if you have to do your own clearing up afterward, it's very tedious and completely ruins the effect. Outside, it is dark and raining by the time I have finished, but I need to do something to dampen the volatile cocktail of emotions that are fizzing inside me and I have already used up my self-imposed quota of matches. I feel like a small child who has been stuck in a stuffy classroom on a windy day. I need to get out. Instead of my heavy winter coat, I drag on a lightweight trench coat that is hanging on a hook in the hall. It is mine, one of the few things I left here between infrequent visits to Mother. It is entirely inappropriate for the weather outside, but perhaps that's why I choose it. The front door to the building is slammed shut by the wind before I can close it. Eli stays on the other side of it. He hates the rain. I head off down the street toward the sea, always back to the sea. It's like an addiction to a fairground ride that thrills and threatens in equal measure. It has a hold over me from which I can't escape. Maybe I don't really want to. Almost at once I am drenched and freezing. My hair is plastered to my face and my coat is sodden. I may as well have gone swimming with my clothes on, but already I'm beginning to feel more in control of myself, safer. I march on defiantly, stomping over the wet pavements toward the promenade. By the time I am face-to-face with the sea, I have been lashed and battered into a state of calm. Even my eyelashes are dripping and all I can make out of the pier are higgledy-piggledy stings of bright lights smudged onto the darkness. The promenade is all but deserted. The windows of the bars and cafés drop squares of light onto the pavements like shadows in reverse. Inside, the people look warm and happy, talking and drinking. Being normal. Outside, I look like a mad, wet tramp lady, a banshee, washed up by the sea. The idea makes me smile, which probably only compounds the mad-lady image.

I should really like a drink. Now that I am safely calm, I have no further need to be cold and wet, and I am very much both. I am particularly tempted by one café that looks warm and clean, and a little shabby round the edges. I have passed by it several times, when I was visiting my mother, but was never brave enough to go in. It stands in the exact spot where Ralph and Ena's shop used to be when I was a child. The neat shelves full of seaside souvenirs, postcards, flags, and toys have been replaced by red Formica tables with chrome legs, and old film posters on ice-cream-colored walls. Behind the bar, old-fashioned milkshake and knickerbocker glory glasses stand in rows, and a gleaming silver coffee machine hisses and steams on the counter. In the corner, a curvaceous 1950s jukebox is playing an old Roy Orbison song. The door is closed, but the music is drifting out through the air vents in the windows. I know all of this, because I have walked past four times now, trying to decide whether or not to go in. I was always welcome here as a child, but what about now? The man behind the bar is watching me with unabashed and amused curiosity. The café is almost empty, which is good in one way; not many people to notice me, stare at me, or interact in any way with me. Bad in another; I am therefore more noticeable to the man behind the bar, who may feel obliged to talk to me. God, I wish I wasn't so out of practice at being with people. It's a dance I've forgotten the steps to. These days when the music plays, I end up tripping over my own feet or treading on someone else's toes. I'm much more comfortable being a wallflower, standing on the edge of the floor, watching other people dance. My life has gradually evolved into a largely solitary existence. University was a social minefield for someone like me, a place where fitting in was sacrosanct. Of course, individuality was considered a merit, and certain anomalies and eccentricities were acceptable, even encouraged. But not mine. I could do something that scared the bejesus out of some and provoked cruel ridicule from others, and so I learned to hide it. I chose a career that meant I could work from home and did my shopping online. My occasional and fearful attempts at some sort of social life always ended in disaster. Eventually I gave up altogether. As I turn to walk past the café for an embarrassing fifth time, the door opens and the man from behind the bar stands watching me. He smiles and sings along with the song that is still playing inside.

"*But wait, what do I see*

Is she walking back to me?"

I hesitate for just a moment, and he steps to one side, holding the door open.

"Come in before you drown."

I follow him inside and stand, dripping, uncertain what to do next.

"Will I take your coat before you flood my floor?"

The water dripping from my coat is pooling into a puddle around my feet, and creeping across the scarlet linoleum. I unbelt and unbutton the sodden garment and hand it to him. He looks familiar.

"Now, what would you like to drink?"

For the first time, I look into his eyes, and for the first time in a long time, I'm not wholly uncomfortable being this close to a person I don't know. I think I may even like it.

"A cup of tea and a cherry brandy, please."

9

Tilly

The empty cherry brandy bottle was lying on its side on the kitchen table like a lost boat washed up on the shore, and what used to be a tumbler was strewn in a sparkle of smashed glass across the floor. It was Tilly's seventh birthday, and this was definitely not how it was supposed to be. She fetched the dustpan and brush from the cupboard under the sink, and began to sweep up the mess, but the broken glass was tricky, and flicked and skittered away from the dustpan across the tiled floor. Tilly was hungry, and as it was her birthday and there was no sign of her mother, she decided to make her own breakfast. She hadn't learned very much cooking yet, and her small fingers still struggled to get to grips with the tin opener, so her options were pretty limited, but Tilly was determined to have something special to mark her birthday properly. Having searched the shelves in the pantry, she decided on a mashed jam tart and cornflake sandwich. The idea tasted lovely in Tilly's head, but the actual sandwich in her mouth was not so good. Still, at least she had made the effort. She left the remains on a plate on the draining board, in case her mother felt like some breakfast when she eventually got out of bed. She would have given it to the dog, but she had never seen him eat anything. Tilly had woken up one morning a few weeks ago to find him sitting at the foot of the bed, watching her. He was a serious-looking dog, completely black, and one of his ears stood up and the other flopped over. Tilly didn't know where he had come from and he wasn't wearing a collar or a name tag. She would have liked to stroke him, but he never let her touch him, moving just out of reach every time she tried. But he listened when she spoke to him, tipping his head to one side and occasionally wagging his tail. A week after he had first appeared, Tilly decided that she had better give him a name. She remembered her daddy telling her that he had had a dog when he was about her age called Eli. He had explained that in the Bible, a priest called Eli took care of a little boy, and that his dog looked after him, so it seemed like a good name. Tilly hoped that her Eli would look after her too. At first, she thought that perhaps her mother had gotten the dog for her, but when she asked her, her mother said she didn't know what Tilly was talking about, and that of course she hadn't brought a dog into the house. She even said he wasn't there, when Tilly could quite clearly see him in the room. Now, she got really cross if he was even mentioned. Tilly thought that perhaps her mother was afraid of dogs or going a bit mad, or maybe both. Anyhow, she was very happy to have Eli as a new friend. She felt as though, somehow, he was on her side.

Tilly wondered if the postman would come before she had to set off for school. It seemed a shame to have to go to school on her birthday, but she didn't really mind, because today they were making pictures of Bonfire Night and fireworks, and had been promised glitter and glue, and, of course, when she got home, her daddy would be here. Nothing had been said, but she knew that he wouldn't miss her birthday. She wondered what presents she would get. When her mother had asked her what she would like, Tilly had asked for a packet of Daz. She had planned to secretly swap the contents with her mother's usual soap powder to see if it would make any difference, but her mother had told her not to be so silly, so Tilly had asked for a flashlight instead. She had seen a program once on television, where a girl had read books at night under the bedclothes using a flashlight, when she was supposed to have been asleep. She liked the idea of that, and also of holding it under her chin and switching it on in the dark when she was pulling a horrible face, to frighten people. And, if there was an emergency, she could use it to signal S.O.S., something she had learned to do while watching an old war film with her daddy. A flashlight had lots of possibilities. She had also asked for a doll, to keep her mother happy. She could always cut its hair off and bury it in the garden later. She poked around in the kitchen junk drawer for a bit, pinging a couple of elastic bands across the room and rummaging in the button tin to see if she could find any ha'pennies. She looked up at the clock on the wall above the fridge. It was half past eight. She would have to leave in five minutes. The quiet clut of the letterbox was followed by the flutter of envelopes falling onto the doormat. There were several cards for Tilly, and one brown envelope addressed to her mother. Tilly shoved the cards into her satchel and left the house to walk to school. She would open them on the way. She didn't bother calling out to her mother as she left; she knew she wouldn't get an answer. Tilly had woken in the middle of the night needing to use the toilet. As she padded carefully across the landing, she had heard her mother downstairs talking to herself and crying. She sounded angry and upset. It frightened Tilly, but made her sad at the same time. She wanted to go and give her a hug and tell her that everything would be all right. But she couldn't because she didn't know what was wrong, and if it was something really bad, then maybe it wouldn't be all right. And anyway, her mother didn't seem to like hugs very much. Since his mysterious appearance in her bedroom, Eli walked with Tilly to the school gate every morning and was waiting for her there every afternoon at going-home time. Today he trotted along beside her, occasionally glancing up at her as though something was bothering him. Tilly tore the envelopes open as she wandered along, and read the cards inside. One of them worried her. It had a picture of an elephant holding a balloon in his trunk on the front, and inside someone had written:

"Happy birthday to the queen of the land!"

Tilly didn't need to read any further, because she already knew who had sent it and it made her doubt the one thing that she had started the day believing to be an absolute truth. It nagged away at her all day, like a tiny piece of grit in her shoe, pricking and chafing and spoiling the fun of glitter and glue and firework pictures. Her favorite lunch of shepherd's pie, and pink sponge and custard was curdled by the lurching in her stomach each time she remembered the words that were written in the card. She managed to raise a smile when her class sang "Happy Birthday' to her, but by going-home time she felt sick.

"Her eyes they shone like the diamonds,
You'd think she was queen of the land,
And her hair hung over her shoulders,
Tied up with a black velvet band."

It was a song her daddy used to sing to her, and it was the only time she had heard those words. He had promised that he would buy her a black velvet band for her hair, but he hadn't gotten around to it before he left. The card was from him. So, that must mean that he wasn't coming home, because if he was, wouldn't he have just brought it with him? How could he do this to her? How could he miss her birthday? It was a mystery, like a clue in a Famous Five story, but Tilly had a horrible feeling that this one was not going to end up with smiles all round, a slap-up tea, and a biscuit for Timmy.

Tilly dawdled home with Eli trailing at her heels. She went round to the back of the house, and saw through the window a group of people standing in the kitchen. A cruel jolt of hope quickened her step, but it was dashed as soon as she opened the door. Her mother was standing by the kitchen table, which was laid out with a birthday tea, looking like an understudy for the soap powder mummy; almost believable, but just missing something. Auntie Wendy was there with Karen, and even Mrs. O'Flaherty had popped in with a card and a little present in a box tied with a ribbon. Tilly had been to church several times now with Mrs. O'Flaherty, who had insisted that she ask her mother's permission first.

Tilly's mother had seemed surprised that she wanted to go, but had raised no objections. As Tilly walked through the door, they had all shouted "Surprise!" and then sung "Happy Birthday." She blew out the candles on the cake and tried to look as happy as they expected her to be. Tilly could see that her mother had really tried. The cake was chocolate and covered with Smarties. There were egg and cress, and fish-paste sandwiches; little sausages, and cheese and pineapple, on sticks; and a big bowl of crisps. Her mother was smiling, a frail, anxious smile, but a smile nonetheless. Tilly too presented a grin that far outshone her mother's in appearance, but was bolstered by even less real happiness. What Tilly really wanted to do was cry. Her daddy was, of course, nowhere to be seen.

She opened her presents. There was a shiny red flashlight from her mother and a doll. The doll looked like a baby, and you fed it water from a bottle into a hole in its mouth, then it came out through its eyes like tears. The doll also weed the water out of a hole in its bottom. It was the most pointless thing that Tilly had ever seen, and was definitely heading for a short back and sides and a shallow grave, but she managed to coo over it enthusiastically by pretending to herself that it was a puppy. Eli was sitting under the table looking very unimpressed. There was a toy hairdressing kit from Auntie Wendy, and some coloring pens and a drawing book from Karen. The box from Mrs. O'Flaherty contained a smaller version of the necklace that she played with in church, only Tilly's was made from pretty white beads of mother-of-pearl. It was Tilly's favorite present, but young as she was, something told her that it would not be a good thing to say so. They all ate sandwiches and things on sticks and crisps, and Karen and Tilly drank fizzy pop while the grown-ups drank tea. Karen and Tilly inspected the presents one by one, and giggled about the doll that weed out of its bum.

"Didn't your daddy send you anything?"

Karen's question hit Tilly like a hammer on a thumbnail. The grown-ups all started talking at the same time, about nothing at all, as if to rub the question out, but it was too late. The fragile mood of jollity had been blown away like a dandelion clock in a puff of wind. Karen looked at her mother in bewilderment, an indignant "What?" etched on her pretty features. Auntie Wendy's reply was a stern look that firmly discouraged any further mention of the subject.

Auntie Wendy and Mrs. O'Flaherty cleared away the tea things, and Tilly's mother went into the garden to smoke a cigarette. Mrs. O'Flaherty was the only one brave enough to speak directly to Tilly. As she wiped her hands, still soapy from washing up, on the tea towel, she bent down and gently spoke to Tilly.

"Miss Tilly, wherever your daddy is, you know he loves you very much, every day, and not just on your birthday. And that matters more than all the presents in the world."

Tilly was grateful for Mrs. O'Flaherty's kind words, but worried for her knees. She struggled enough with the curtseying business at church, and she had bent much lower to cup Tilly's face gently in her hands as she winked at her. When she was safely upright again, she smoothed her skirt down and met Auntie Wendy's mildly irritated expression with a pleasant smile but defiantly raised eyebrows. Tilly was a quick child who saw that something had passed, unspoken, between the two women, but as was often the case with grown-ups, she had no idea what it meant. Mrs. O'Flaherty busied herself getting into her heavy winter coat, said her good-byes, and thanked Tilly's mother, who had just come back in, shivering, from the garden, to drink the rest of her tea.

"We must be going too, Gracie, love," said Auntie Wendy. "Bill will be wanting his dinner."

She bundled the still rather puzzled Karen into her duffle coat, and kissed Tilly's mother on the cheek.

"Happy Birthday, Tilly. I hope you like your presents."

"Say 'thank you' to Auntie Wendy and Karen," her mother reminded her, with forced brightness.

After all the bustle of hasty departures, the house felt still and cold, despite the flames of the gas fire and the cheery voices coming from the television. Tilly spent the rest of the evening quietly examining her presents, running the beads of her necklace through her fingers; counting the curlers and hairpins in the hairdressing kit; and trying out the coloring pens in the front cover of the drawing book. Her mother sat staring at a comedy program and drinking something brown. When the program finished she finally stirred and told Tilly to go and change into her nightdress. But as Tilly scrabbled to feet, her mother did something strange. She opened her arms and asked her daughter to give her a hug. Tilly stood hesitating by the door, awkward and uncertain. Such displays of affection between them were rare, and never normally initiated by her mother. Tilly's bedtime was normally accompanied by a perfunctory peck on the cheek. She approached her mother reluctantly, warily, before placing her arms carefully around her neck. Her mother squeezed her so tightly that she thought her bones might break. Eventually released, Tilly was glad to go to bed.

Later, she did not know how much later, Tilly woke in her bed with tears pouring down her cheeks. Everywhere was quiet and dark, so it must have been very late. She moved around the familiar landmarks of her room without needing to turn on the light, and fetched something from behind one of the books on the bookshelf. She opened the door and crept downstairs. Eli padded silently behind her. The tiles on the kitchen floor were ice cold, but Tilly walked across them in her bare feet, unflinching. She could feel nothing but the gouging hurt that had woken her. It was worse than a million Chinese burns. Tilly thought she might be dying. She picked up her new flashlight from the kitchen table, unlocked the back door and stepped into the garden. The bitter November night snatched the air from her lungs. Her face was as white as her thick, cotton nightdress, and her lips were blue. Her fingers, crippled by the cold, struggled with the key in the lock of the shed door. Once inside, she switched on the flashlight: three quick flashes, three long, three quick. Over and over again. No one came. He wasn't coming. Tilly opened the drawer where the matches were kept. There was one left. Tilly had been coming to the shed ever since he left, once, maybe twice a week. Every time she came, she lit a match, and now there was only one left. That's how long he had been gone. She put the flashlight down carefully, and took the match in one hand and the box in the other. She was shivering so much that she could barely control her hands, but this was one thing that she was determined to finish. The whiff of sulphur bit the air; a flash and then a flame, left to flicker for just a second before Tilly dropped it into the drawer full of seed packets, brown string, and old newspapers.

The shed was just a broken silhouette, engulfed in crackling and spitting orange flames, by the time the shouts of the neighbors and the fire engines' sirens had woken Tilly's mother and brought her stumbling and panic-stricken into the garden. The sight of her daughter, standing as pale and still as a statue in a graveyard, drove the last remains of drink and sleep from her with the force of a lightning bolt. Tilly was clutching her flashlight, which shone upward onto her tear-streaked face, frozen into an expression of pitiful despair. She was staring at the huge plume of gray smoke, glowing sparks, and embers that was floating up into a black sky glittering with stars. Beside her, as close as he could be without touching her, sat Eli. Her mother ran across the lawn and gathered Tilly in her arms. Her touch broke the spell, and Tilly's face melted into a wailing scream.

"Daddy. I want my daddy!"

Her mother hugged her tightly, rocking her back and forth and tenderly wiping the tears from her cheeks.

"Oh, Tilly. My darling, darling Tilly, Daddy's dead."

10

Tilda

The tiny, tatty teddy wearing a child's rosary beads stands beside the lead horse who has lost his soldier. Next comes the Edwardian glass eye, the wooden walking stick top in the form of a terrier, whose mouth opens when you press a lever, followed by the sheep with three legs and the brooch in the shape of the Eiffel Tower. The lineup is completed by the postcard of Jesus whose eyes move, and the china angel with a broken wing. I have given them all names. Except Jesus, who already had one. Now they are with me and standing in the right order I feel much better. I left the diaries—unread—in the flat, and went home to my small terraced house, in its quiet, unremarkable town to get some of my belongings. The house seemed cold and strange, and somehow less of a home, less my home. I feel as though I am in some sort of limbo, hovering and uncertain where to land. I collected some more clothes, my laptop so that I can work, and my special things that are now lined up on the mantel shelf alongside several boxes of matches. These are the lucky charms that protect me. I can manage without them for a while—a week, a holiday—but any longer and I feel exposed. I wish I didn't need them—the charms and the rituals. I could get help to banish them from my life; maybe try cognitive behavioral therapy. But I daren't. The voice inside my head that says something bad will happen without them also tells me that if I deliberately try to get rid of them (and it)—something equally bad will happen and it will be my fault. It's a consummate catch-22. That voice is such a smartass. The whole thing is ridiculous and embarrassing, I know, but I'm stuck with it. I need ritual and order in some things, and chaos in others. It seems as though my life has evolved into a random pattern of regimen and free-fall, like a military two-step crossed with St. Vitus's dance. Take the diaries; I am desperate to know what's in them but as of yet, I haven't actually read a single page. I have never been one of those people who rips the wrapping paper from presents. I always unwrap them slowly and carefully, like a bomb disposal expert dealing with a dangerous device; and so it must be with the diaries. I have a horrible feeling in the pit of my stomach that they need to be handled with care. This is not just me having a touch of the vapors, like a delicate young lady in a Jane Austen novel faced with an unexpected naked male torso. This is about the card. I took all the diaries out of the box when I found them, to see how many there were, and lying in the bottom of the box was a small white envelope with the word "Tilly' written on it in black ink. It was my mother's handwriting again. My mother hasn't called me "Tilly' since I was a child, in fact, since the summer she sent me away. Inside the envelope was a plain white card; a thick, good-quality, deckle-edged card from an expensive stationer's. It was inscribed with just two words: *"Forgive me."*

She had obviously intended me to find it, but presumably, from where she had placed it, after I had read the diaries. Once again, I shall have disappointed her. But why is it addressed to "Tilly," and what in God's name does it mean?

I came back to the flat last night. Eli accompanied me on my trip home and is now asleep on the green sofa, looking very comfortable. Chivvied along by Queenie, I have packed in boxes some of the things that I think the charity shops in town could sell; unworn nighties still in their cellophane wrappings, kept for best or hospital stays, but kept too long as it turned out. New towels and bed linen kept for guests who never came, and starched linen tablecloths and napkins kept for tea parties that were never given. It's only a token gesture so far, but it's a beginning. I am going to use the best cutlery, the best crockery, and the best glasses every day. I am not going to die with my best party dress still unworn on its hanger. I have cleaned and dusted the flat and moved things around; random things to random places, but with a purpose, a sort of "fuck you' feng shui. It's my place now, not hers.

My laptop is sitting on the kitchen table ready for action. I'm a proofreader. I read for a living. But today I'm going to start reading about my mother's life, and maybe mine too, in the diaries. But not here. The box is still in the bedroom, kept closed like a box of fireworks, to keep the contents from catching a stray spark and exploding. "Remove one firework from the box at a time, and replace the lid." I remember the safety code. I take the small blue book from the box and shut the lid. Eli stirs from his cozy nest on the sofa and trots into the hallway where Queenie is already waiting impatiently. She has decided that the man in the café might be an ideal "gentleman friend' for me.

"I promised your mother that I would keep an eye on you," she said, "and it's about time you found yourself a good man."

But I'm not quite ready to leave yet. First, I light three matches from one of the boxes on the mantel shelf. Only when the smoke has completely cleared do I join Queenie and Eli and shrug myself into my big coat, cursing when I realize that I have not brought from home a replacement for my hat that was stolen by the wind. Outside, the sky is dirty gray, the color of old men's underpants, but it's dry and the halfhearted wind barely troubles the naked treetops. Even the sea looks weary, its waves too tired to crawl up the stony beach. But I am completely at odds with all this lethargy, like a Tigger in a townful of tortoises. Excitement tinged with trepidation is pumping my blood faster and driving me on, and I arrive at the café before I am ready to be here. There are a few people inside, chatting and drinking coffee, and the man behind the bar is drying cups with a tea towel. As soon as he sees me, he stops what he's doing and comes to the door where he finds me shuffling uncertainly from foot to foot.

"Get in here now, before you wear a hole in the pavement. I can't have strange women loitering outside a respectable establishment such as this."

He shoos me inside with a flapping tea towel, quickly checking my face to make sure I know that he is teasing me. Queenie slips in behind me and seats herself at a table far enough away to be discreet, but close enough for her to hear what's being said. He offers to take my coat, but I refuse, remembering that the diary is in the pocket.

"I'm not going to steal it, you know, like the wind stole your hat. Although it looks as though it would fit me a lot better than it does you."

I take the book from my pocket and meekly hand over my coat. So, this was the man who tried to rescue my hat. I was right about his face. It's handsome too, in a comfortable way, as well as kind. He seats me at a table on my own and asks me what I should like.

"Tea and toast, please."

"Coming right up. Now you sit there and behave yourself. I don't want any trouble from you."

I can't help but smile as he wags his finger at me in mock severity. I'm trying hard not to like this man too much, in spite of Queenie's encouragement, but I'm not doing very well. I place the blue diary carefully in front of me on the table. I brought it to the café to read because here, no matter what it says, I will restrain myself. Here, in public, I will rein myself in. I will not abandon myself to extreme emotions, succumb to hysterical behavior and make like a mad lady. And if I do, at least there will be someone to call the men in white coats to take me away. The man I am trying, but failing, not to like brings my tea and toast and goes back to his cup drying. But he is still watching me as I perform my toast ritual, carefully spreading the butter and dividing the square into four neat triangles before placing the knife to attention, like a soldier. A puzzled frown flits across his face, but thankfully, he says nothing. The bell above the door clangs, heralding the arrival of another customer, and the broad, welcoming smile of the cup dryer prompts me to turn to see the new arrival. He is a sight worth seeing: a man who is dangerously handsome, despite being comfortably past his sixtieth birthday. His skin is deeply tanned, and his charcoal gray hair is thick and shiny and hangs loosely down his back, well past his shoulders. He is wearing an ancient leather jacket, cracked and battered like rhino skin, dark jeans and a pale blue shirt. On his wrist is a heavy silver bangle, on his head a black trilby, and on his face a smile like Father Christmas with a Casanova chaser. He strides through the café in his fancy cowboy boots, and slaps both hands down on the counter.

"How are you, Danny boy?"

He addresses the cup dryer with a voice as rich and rough as Guinness laced with gravel.

"I'm grand, thanks. And yourself? What can I get you?"

Without replying, and much to my horror, excitement, and bewilderment, he turns and heads straight toward me. By the time he reaches my table, I feel like an awkward teenage girl hugging the wall at her first school disco, desperate and terrified in equal measure to be asked to dance. My cheeks are the color of pomegranates, and there's not even a glimpse of his naked torso in sight.

"By the way, I let your dog in. It's starting to rain."

"Dog, what dog?"

Now it's Daniel's turn to be bewildered as he glances round the café, his brow once again crumpled with a puzzled frown.

"I'm only joking," says the newcomer, laughing softly to himself.

But he isn't. Although Daniel clearly can't see him, Eli is now sitting next to the jukebox looking very pleased with himself. The man winks at me and smiles, and I'm thrilled that already we share a secret. His handsome face tells the tale of a full life, lit by joy and adventure, and shadowed by hardship and loss. His eyes are kind, but there is defiance there too. He offers me his hand.

"Joseph Geronimo Heathcliff O'Shea; my mammy liked the films. I'm very pleased to meet you."

"I'm Tilda."

His hand is warm and strong, and the skin is rough. He smiles at me again and, pausing briefly to tip his hat to Queenie, goes back to the bar where a large mug of steaming dark brown tea is waiting for him. My concentration has scattered like a bowlful of marbles tipped onto a polished floor. I have finished my tea and toast before I have gathered myself sufficiently to concentrate on what I came here for in the first place. I pull the diary toward me and tap my fingers across its pale blue cover. A thin band of gold sits loosely on the ring finger of my right hand. My mother's wedding ring. She gave it to me just before she died and it was the first time that she had taken it off since her wedding day.

"Whatever's written in there won't change however long you sit there."

Daniel has brought me another cup of tea. He's right. And anyway, I've waited long enough. I want to know the truth.

11

Tilly

The truth, the whole truth, and nothing but the truth." Tilly had heard them say it on the television when a bad man was taken to court, and lots of people came to stand in a little box and tell tales about him.

It sounded perfectly simple, but now Tilly was beginning to think that the truth was a bit like cat's cradle; it was easy enough at the start, but lose your grip for a second and soon there would be knots and tangles all over the place. Tilly was sure that her mother was telling the truth when she had said that her daddy was dead. She might be a bit mad, but even she wouldn't lie about a thing like that. A lie like that would definitely make your tongue turn black and fall out, and your eyeballs bleed as though they had been stabbed by a million needles. God and his angels would drop a thunderbolt on you, and your head would splatter open like a squashed melon. Tilly didn't know exactly what a thunderbolt was, but she knew God dropped them on people who did a really big sin, and that sort of lie would definitely count. Even if you did a confession in church, your rosary beads would break before you could say "sorry" enough times to make things right. You could never make it right.

But when it came to the whole truth, that was a slightly different matter. Tilly had learned that telling only some of the truth could be a good way of avoiding trouble. A big truth told could often distract from the little truths kept secret, and sometimes it was the little truths that made all the difference. It was like drawing a picture of a zebra and leaving out the stripes; it ended up looking like a horse. Her daddy used to take her to the pub called The White Horse and she would sit and drink lemonade through a straw and eat salt and vinegar crisps while her daddy drank beer and talked to people who had died. Sometimes he used cards, but mainly he just looked at someone's hand, or held something like a piece of jewelry or a letter. On the way home they would buy a present for her mother, sweets or cherries in a brown paper bag, or sometimes a bunch of flowers. Her daddy would always tell her mother that they had been for a walk to the shops. He never mentioned the bit about the pub.

When her mother had first told her that her daddy was dead, Tilly could only think of how much it hurt. The pain roared through her again and again until she was sick. And she was sick until there was nothing left but spit, and then she slept. But later, only days later, Tilly wanted to know the whole truth. She wanted to know the "how," "when," and "where." But her mother did not want to tell. She said he had drowned in the place where he was away working. He had been walking back to the pub at night along the promenade and had gotten too close to the edge and slipped. The sea had carried him away. Tilly wanted to know why she hadn't been to his funeral, and her mother said that he had never been found and so there hadn't been a funeral. Her voice was choked with anger or sorrow, but Tilly didn't know which. Then her mother had started to cry and said that she didn't want to talk about it anymore. But Tilly couldn't leave it there. Her mother's tears didn't seem real. They were "get out of trouble" tears. Rosemary Watson was always doing them at school. Rosemary Watson was a very pretty, neat little girl with long blond plaits and big blue eyes. She had a new pencil case at the beginning of every term and her socks were always very white and pulled up straight. She was also what Auntie Wendy called "a right little madam." She was always causing trouble and blaming someone else, and if she was ever caught, she would produce the most convincing tears as soon as the first harsh word was fired in her direction. Tilly hated her, but really wished that she could do the crying thing half as well, as she could see that it might come in very handy. She had tried it once at school when Mrs. Mould had caught her flicking little balls of chewed-up paper at Billy Ellis, who had pulled her hair in the playground. Her melodramatic performance of sobs and shudders had been seriously weakened by frequent hiccups and giggles, and had quickly reduced the rest of the class to helpless laughter. Tilly had to stand in the corner for the rest of the lesson, and wash the paintbrushes and pots after school for a week. Her mother's tears were more convincing, but Tilly still thought that she was hiding something.

One night after tea, Tilly began her questions again.

Even though she was afraid of what her mother might say, she was more afraid of never finding out the truth.

"How do you know that my daddy drowned if you weren't there?"

Tilly's mother, steadied by half a bottle of Scotch, was teetering on the tightrope between mellow and monster. She twisted the gold wedding ring on her finger round and round and sighed.

"Because, Tilly love, there were other people there who did see it happen."

The tears were already shining in Tilly's eyes and threatening to spill down her pale cheeks.

"What people? Who were they?"

Her mother didn't answer, but stroked the rim of her glass lovingly.

Tilly was tumbling downhill fast now and couldn't stop.

"Who were they?" she shouted. "And why didn't they try to help him?"

Her mother's grip tightened on her glass. Her balance was beginning to tip.

"They did. Of course they bloody did! But it was dark, and the sea was rough. God, Tilly, do you honestly think that people just stood around and did nothing?"

Tilly shuddered at the thought of her daddy alone in the dark, struggling to keep his head above the waves.

"I don't know," she sobbed, "and you don't know either, do you? Why don't you know? Why didn't you ask someone?"

Her mother didn't reply. She topped up her glass and drained it angrily before slamming it back down on the table.

"Do you think I really want to talk about this? Don't you think that I miss him? You're not the only one who's hurting. I lost him too! I loved him too!"

Tilly's tongue was too quick for her own good.

"No, you didn't. You were always shouting at him."

"And for good reason, my girl! You think he was so perfect, but you don't know the half of it!"

Her mother refilled her glass. The bottle was almost empty.

"Go to bed."

It was said quietly, but the threat was loud and clear. Tilly knew that she was about to push too far and that she only had to go to bed to be safe. But she couldn't. She needed to know if it was a zebra or a horse. It turned out to be the Kraken.

"But how do you know he's really, really dead?" unleashed a maelstrom of such dark fury from her mother that it left Tilly cowering on the floor as slaps and threats and curses rained down on her. Crouched frozen in terror, Tilly did something that she hadn't done since she was three years old. While her mother raged herself dry, a hot, wet stream coursed down Tilly's leg and soaked into her sock. Her mother's final words were spat so closely into her face that Tilly could feel the warmth of her sour breath.

"You'll be the death of me too when you break my heart and then what will you do?"

Her mother's tears this time were real, but whether of sadness or madness it was impossible to tell, and while she sobbed as she spilled herself another drink, Tilly crept upstairs to clean herself up as best she could. She lay in bed in the darkness, terrified and ashamed, trying to breathe as quietly as she could, thinking about what her mother had said. Even the constant guard of Eli could not comfort her. If her mother died as well, what would happen to Tilly? She wasn't the soap powder mummy that Tilly wanted, but she was all she had. If she died too, Tilly would probably end up in a children's home where she would have to sleep in a dormitory and eat porridge for every meal like Oliver Twist. She made a promise in her head never to talk about her daddy again and *her* heart broke. But if it kept her mother alive, it would be worth it. Her last thought before she fell asleep was *Please God, don't let me kill my mummy.*

The following day, when Tilly got home from school, her mother behaved as though nothing had happened, but she had cooked Tilly's favorite tea, and there was red fizzy pop.

The following week, Tilly's Advent calendar had been fixed to the wall with a drawing pin, and two doors were open revealing a robin and a snowman. Tilly was busy chasing spaghetti hoops around her plate with her fork. She needed five hoops on each small square of toast to eat alternately with a mouthful of scrambled egg. Although her mother was being extra nice to her at the moment, Tilly sensed that this was a fragile and temporary state of affairs. It was her rituals that were a constant and would keep her safe. Her mother had pushed away her plate, food only half eaten. She had lit a cigarette and was drinking Scotch from a tumbler. Tilly had noticed that her mother was much better at cigarettes now. She had bought herself a gold-colored cigarette lighter with her initials engraved on it, and she pulled the smoke deep into her lungs and then blew it out in a thin stream, through lips softly pursed, as though for a kiss. It was a shame about the lighter, because it meant that now the only box of matches was the one kept in the kitchen to light the cooker, and Tilly could only risk taking one occasionally or else her mother might notice they were disappearing. Tilly placed her knife and fork neatly in the center of her plate.

"Have you ever seen a dead person?"

Eli, who was sitting next to Tilly, lifted his head and looked straight at her mother, just as though he was waiting to see if she would answer. Her mother didn't even hesitate.

"Yes, I did, once, a long time ago."

"Was I there?"

"It was before you were born."

"Who was it?"

Tilly's mother flicked her ash into the cut-glass ashtray and sipped the golden liquid in her tumbler.

"It was a little girl who was knocked down by a car."

She stared out at the darkness that was the view from the kitchen window, as though trying to picture the scene. She shuddered as the heat and blood, the scent of lilac and the noise of the traffic swept through her like the echo of a nightmare.

"She was holding a red balloon."

Tilly tried to picture it.

"Was she on her own?"

"No, her daddy was with her."

Her mother bit her lips as she recalled his broken frame slumped helplessly in the gutter as his daughter died.

"Was she covered in blood?"

Tilly's mother ignored her final question and took another deep gulp from her tumbler. She seemed to be somewhere else. For some reason she couldn't explain, Tilly felt suddenly afraid, as though she was standing on the edge of a deep, dark hole. One more step and she would fall. She waited. Eventually her mother noticed the silence.

"Go and put your things in the sink, and then you can do the washing up."

Tilly did as she was told, ever afraid of rousing the Kraken. Besides, she liked washing up. She loved all the swooshing and sploshing of water and bubbles, and the little mini-mop for cleaning the dishes. She squirted an overgenerous arc of green liquid into the plastic bowl, and turned both taps on full blast so that water splashed up all over her chest and all over the draining board, and bubbles quickly multiplied into a wobbling mountain of foam. Tilly's approach to the task in hand was enthusiastic rather than skillful, and she wielded the mini-mop more like a conductor's baton than a domestic utensil. By the time her performance was completed, the floor and draining board were awash with water and bubbles and Tilly's sweater sleeves were sodden. She glanced across at her mother to gauge her mood. She had lit another cigarette and refilled her glass from the bottle on the dresser.

Tilly decided to risk one more question.

"Where do people go when they die?"

Her mother swirled the liquid in her glass round and round.

"Nobody knows."

Tilly was surprised. In her experience, grown-ups knew pretty much everything, or at least they pretended to.

"Don't the good ones go to heaven, and the bad ones to hell?"

Tilly's mother didn't lift her eyes from her glass.

"That's just what people tell themselves to be less afraid of dying."

Tilly didn't understand how this would make the bad people feel better about dying. According to Mrs. O'Flaherty, hell was a really horrible place to end up, full of flames and demons, and people screaming and writhing in agony. Still, if Rosemary Watson carried on the way she was, there was a good chance that she would end up there, which would certainly make Tilly feel better. Rosemary Watson had started saying things about Tilly's mother in the playground. She said that her mum had told Mrs. Dawson at the Co-op when she was paying her money into the Christmas club, that Tilly's mother was a "mental case' and "far too fond of the sauce." When Tilly had confronted her about it, Rosemary had said that she'd better watch out because she'd probably turn out the same way.

"Like mother, like daughter!" she sniped, as she flounced away with a prissy swish of her silly plaits. The name-calling troubled Tilly, perhaps all the more because she didn't really understand it but knew that it was intended to be cruel. It was like being scared of the dark; it wasn't the darkness itself that you were afraid of, but the unknown monsters it concealed. And anyway, Tilly's mother didn't even put tomato sauce on her chips.

Later that night, cozily tucked up in bed, with Eli asleep on the rug, Tilly thought about the dead little girl her mother had seen. She had never really thought about children dying. She knew that poor, starving children died in hot countries far across the world. To help them, she had once saved pennies in a little cardboard money box she was given at Sunday school. But she had never really imagined children like her dying. She wondered what it would be like if she died; what it would feel like, where she would go, and who would have all her clothes and toys. Tilly thought that tomorrow she might make a list saying who she wanted to have what, just in case. Perhaps Rosemary Watson could have her doll that weed out of its bum, and then she would feel bad about being horrid to Tilly, and the doll might wee all over Rosemary's skirt. Tilly lay very still and straight, with her arms by her sides, and held her breath. Perhaps if she could make herself stop breathing for long enough, she could get an idea of what it would feel like to be dead. Instead, she fell asleep.

12

Tilly

The next morning was cold and bright. Tilly drew circles with her finger in the condensation on her bedroom window as she looked out at the back garden below, which sparkled with frost. She was glad that she hadn't overdone the "not breathing' and died in her bed, but she was still going to make the list today. After breakfast, she was bundled into her warm winter coat and red knitted beret.

"Where are your gloves?"

Her mother was scrabbling through the drawer in the coat stand that stood in the hall. Tilly pulled the red mittens from her coat pockets like a magician pulling rabbits out of a hat.

"Ta-dah!"

Her mother tutted impatiently as she tied a woolen scarf around her own neck, and pulled on matching gloves in an elegant shade of cornflower. Tilly remembered that they had been a present from her daddy, and not for a birthday or Christmas, but "just because my lovely wife deserves to be spoiled."

Her mother had wiped her flour-dusty fingers on her apron and shushed away his compliments. But Tilly also remembered her smile as she unwrapped the tissue paper and stroked the soft blue wool. She looked at her mother with pride. Whatever else she might be, she was very beautiful, and always nicely dressed. She didn't look like a mental case to Tilly. It was Saturday, and they were going shopping at the Co-op. Normally Tilly liked this type of shopping with her mother, but today she was worried that Mrs. Dawson might be rude, or whisper or stare at them because of what Mrs. Watson had said.

Her mother walked briskly along the glittering pavement, her back straight and her head held high, gripping Tilly's hand firmly in her own. Tilly trotted along beside her like an exuberant Shetland pony and Eli followed behind. The shopfront of the Co-op was decked in Christmas fare and framed with colored paper chains. There was a small pyramid of Christmas desserts and several iced Christmas cakes. Shiny round tins of sweets and shortbread stood on their sides like wheels rolling across the front of the windows, interspersed with square boxes of crackers. A large—and very obviously plastic—turkey and a lurid pink leg of ham squatted side by side on a huge foil platter. Standing guard was a rather cross-eyed reindeer under a silver tinsel Christmas tree.

"Goodness me, Mrs. Dawson's very early with her Christmas decorations." Tilly's mother peered warily at the strange-looking reindeer.

"I think it looks really lovely and 'Happy Christmassy,'" said Tilly decisively, ignoring her mother's reservations.

Her mother clasped the handle of the shop door

with a blue-gloved hand, and Tilly, still firmly held by the other hand, felt her mother's brief hesitation before she pushed the handle down, and the bell jangled to announce their arrival. Tilly needn't have worried. Mrs. Dawson greeted them with her usual, friendly smile. Whatever she had heard, Tilly thought she must be keeping it to herself, or perhaps Mrs. Dawson didn't care what her customers did at home, so long as their money ended up in her till. The shop was busy as usual for a Saturday, and women with wire shopping baskets hooked in the crooks of their elbows stood chatting to one another, or browsed the aisles looking for something tasty for Sunday tea. Small children stood aimlessly next to their mothers, bored by the domestic chitchat, or chased one another up and down the aisles until they knocked into something or someone and were shouted at by Mrs. Dawson, or their mothers, or both. As well as the festive window display, the shelves on the end of one aisle carried a range of "specials" seductively billed as "Christmas gourmet treats." On the top two shelves there were tins of chestnut puree, maraschino cherries, blocks of marzipan, paper cake frills decorated with sprigs of holly, and boxes of dates. Lower down in the display sat tins of red salmon, cooked ham and crabmeat, and jars of potted shrimps, pickled onions, pickled walnuts, and piccalilli. Shopping on a Saturday was a social occasion and nobody seemed to be in any hurry. A few of the other women smiled briefly at Tilly's mother as she moved through the shop, and a couple even murmured "hello," but the economy of their greeting made it clear that they did not consider her to be one of them, and nobody stopped her to chat. Tilly was relieved therefore to spot Auntie Wendy inspecting a tin of chestnut puree with a mixture of suspicion and disdain.

"Auntie Wendy!"

Auntie Wendy looked up from the offending tin and greeted them a little more extravagantly than usual, a greeting that could not be missed, nor its intention misinterpreted by the other women in the shop.

"What in heaven's name are you supposed to do with chestnut puree?" she exclaimed as she replaced it on the shelf with a thump. She took Tilly's mother by the arm, and they wandered around the shop together filling their baskets with less exotic but more appetizing fare. By the time they were ready to pay for their shopping there were long lines at both tills. Her mother and Auntie Wendy set their baskets down on the floor and Tilly smiled sweetly at the young woman who was standing in front of them jiggling a plump, gurgling baby on her hip. When they eventually reached the till, Tilly helped her mother unload the shopping onto the counter. The cashier, a ruddy-cheeked woman with a sturdy shampoo and set and gold hoop earrings nodded approvingly at Tilly.

"What a helpful young lady you are. And what do you want to be when you grow up?"

"A virgin."

The silence that followed was immaculate. The cashier, whose face was bravely resisting a grin, continued.

"And why's that?"

"Because I like bananas."

An amused splutter escaped from someone in the

other queue, but was immediately stifled and Tilly continued into the expectant silence:

"And apples, and oranges, and grapes. I don't really like apricots, but I love raspberries."

The cashier nodded again, but this time because she hoped the movement would distract her from the eruption of laughter that threatened to destroy her composure. Tilly's mother hastily packed away their shopping into her bag and paid the cashier. She then helped Auntie Wendy to do the same. The expression on her face and her manner were calm and assured, but Auntie Wendy's lips were pressed together so tightly that her mouth had become little more than a crease on her face. Once they were safely outside and several yards down the road, Auntie Wendy gave in to the laughter and wiped the tears from her cheeks. She looked at Tilly, who was completely oblivious to the fact that she was the cause of such amusement.

"Tilly, do you know what a virgin is?"

"It's a bit like a greengrocer."

"And what makes you think that?"

Tilly rolled her eyes in exasperation. Sometimes grown-ups could be very dim.

"Like Mary the Virgin in Mrs. O'Flaherty's prayer: 'blessed art thou among women and blessed is the fruit in thy room.'"

Tilly was fed up with all this now. The grown-ups were being inexplicably silly and their laughter had wounded her dignity. She wasn't even sure if she wanted to be a virgin anymore. She thought she might run off and join the circus.

13

Tilda

As I open the blue cover of the diary, the hubbub of voices and the clatter of cups and saucers in the café are sucked into the background. The diary is a doorway to another world.

July 27

Stevie has gone and I'm glad. Perhaps that is a wicked thing to say, but it is the truth, and the truth is sometimes an ugly thing. The doctor says that my nerves are bad again. Perhaps it is just me that is bad. He says that it might help if I write things down like I did before. Now I have Tilly all to myself and perhaps she will love me, because I am all she has left. Of course, Stevie will be back. But not for a while.

I know I can't compete with him. He is her clown, her knight in shining armor, her playmate, her partner in crime. But I am her mother. She misses him so badly, she goes into his shed and touches his things. She thinks that I don't know about the key. But she doesn't know why he had to go. She has no idea that he was stupid enough to lose the only proper job he's had in years. The one that meant we could finally settle down and make a real home. And that after he was sacked no one else would employ him. She doesn't understand the shame, the gossip, and the worry about where the money's coming from to pay the bills; the fear that comes with each brown envelope that falls through the letterbox. If it wasn't for his cousin's friend's broken hip we could've been out on the streets by Tilly's birthday. I'm sure Stevie will be like a kid in a sweetshop running the pub while the landlord recovers. And no doubt he'll be giving readings to anyone who's taken in by his sweet talk. But at least he'll be earning enough to pay our bills. He didn't want to leave his precious daughter, but I bet he couldn't wait to get away from me. He is afraid of my illness and would rather not see it. He still wants to be a father, but not a husband. He promised "in sickness and in health," but Stevie is better at making promises than keeping them.

Before Tilly came, it was different. Stevie and I were in love. We loved each other: proper love, when all the time not spent together is wasted and just to be endured, got through somehow. The kind of love that makes you utterly invincible and utterly vulnerable. Stevie made me forget about my awkwardness. He charmed me. His love protected me and made me normal. It made me believe in "happy ever after." But I was wrong. I gave up everything for him. Mum and Dad said that I had a choice: him or them. Him or God. I chose him. I went with him when he moved from job to job, town to town. I thought that Stevie would be enough. I made him my whole life. When Tilly was born, she became his life and a part of me died. It wasn't meant to be like that. We were supposed to be a circle of love, we three.

I fed her, changed her nappies, dried her tears, soothed her fevers, and paced the floor exhausted, night after night, rocking her in my aching arms until she fell asleep. He worshipped her. She was perfect, and he loved her absolutely. He had nothing left for me and I'd never felt so alone.

My eyes are awash with unshed tears, and I can hardly breathe. I need someone to thump me on the back before I choke on her words. I feel a soft, warm weight on my knee. Eli's head is resting there. I barely have time to register the feeling before he moves away, but I know it happened. I have never felt him before. My breath shudders through, resuscitated by his touch. My mother's words are rewriting the childhood that for so long I have claimed to be my own. The people and the places are still there, but the perspective has slipped so far out of focus that I barely recognize the story that was once, and ought to remain, so familiar. I never knew that my dad had been sacked. What the hell for? I never knew that they had ever been so in love. I never even thought about it, not once. The Grace and Stevie I knew, my parents, lived as man and wife under the same roof and cared for each other, but I don't remember many hearts and flowers. There were secrets, fights, days of bitter silence and occasionally a truce. And yes, sometimes he would slip his arm around her waist, or kiss her on the cheek, but it was the fights I remember most. Had I really robbed them of their precious love for each other, and stolen him away from her? I think about my mother, softened by love and truly happy. I can't remember her like that. My tears splash onto the open pages of the diary, smudging the black ink, as though trying to wash the words away. But they have been written and read, and now nothing can wash away what I know. Thank God I have long hair. It curtains my face and hides my embarrassment. I never cry. I am blinking furiously to stop the tears, but I badly need to sniff or risk a snail trail barely excusable on a three-year-old. Eli sighs loudly. I have a feeling that he is telling me to get a grip as I fumble in my pocket for a tissue. A soft wad is pressed into my other hand.

"They're napkins really, I'm afraid, but they're not too scratchy."

I peer up through my hair into Daniel's green eyes. His kindness threatens to undo me completely, and I blow my nose as though my life depends on it, which is such an attractive thing to witness for the man you are trying to seduce. He hastily retreats to his place behind the counter. Oh God, am I really trying to seduce him? In the midst of this emotional Armageddon, am I seriously contemplating romance? In spite of everything I have just read, I'm still worried about him seeing that I have a red, snotty nose and smudged mascara. I really like him. I have been trying to keep this a secret, even from myself. But now I know. I am ridiculous. When I have finally finished my impersonation of Nellie the elephant, Daniel returns with a glass of cherry brandy.

"I know it's a bit early, but it'll be good for your cold."

This time I am just about able to meet his smile with one of my own. He returns to the counter and his conversation with Joseph Geronimo. After a swig of brandy, I return to the diary.

August 13

I am worried about Tilly. She is such a funny little thing; so singular and stubborn, so determined to follow her own path. But I am worried that she will end up like me. Or worse. She already has her own strange little ways. She cuts up her food into squares and counts her forkfuls. She insists on using the same plate, the same glass and the same knife and fork for every meal. She's always listening at doors and sometimes I catch her looking at things that I can't see. Things a little girl shouldn't be able to see. With Stevie, she was learning things she shouldn't know, and meeting people she shouldn't meet. Ungodly things and ungodly people. I know he takes her to see Rory and Rose. He denies it, but I know when he's lying. He will ruin Tilly like he's ruined me. Unless I can stop him. Tilly is too young to be afraid. She seems to welcome them and acts as though it's a game. Or even worse, normal. She doesn't understand how much trouble and pain it will bring her. I haven't said anything to her. She won't hear a word against her daddy. God won't listen to me anymore, but if he did, my one prayer would be "don't let Tilly be punished for her father's sins."

I have started smoking. I don't really care for it, but I shall persevere. It is an act of rebellion. Stevie hates to see a woman smoking. Of course, it's fine for him to smoke his roll-ups in that damn shed of his. Wendy came round today and caught me. She thought it was hilarious. But she is a good friend to me, even though we have practically nothing in common. The other women talk about me behind my back. I can see the disapproval on their sneering faces. Sometimes I envy

Wendy for her cheerful, straightforward, sensible life; her satisfaction in the mundane, her contentment with routine. But more often, it sickens me and I feel trapped. Is this really all there is? Is this what I needed a grammar school education for? Perhaps it is my illness that makes me want something else for me and Tilly, and perhaps it is wrong. But I need more. I need a bigger life than this. Wendy says that I shouldn't worry about Tilly; that she's as bright as a shiny shilling and will find her own way. I hope she's right. The tablets the doctor gave me make me muddled and so tired. Sometimes I sleep for hours in the middle of the day, and then I can't sleep at night, so I drink to help me sleep, and then I can't wake up the next day and mostly I don't want to. I'm living in a fuzzy-felt world. My head is never clear. I'm trying so hard to be a good mother to Tilly, to prove to her how much I love her, but it's not as easy as I thought it would be. She keeps asking about him. I've told her that he's had to go away to find work, but I get the feeling that she thinks it's my fault. I just wish that she would forget about him for a while and try to love me. Why can't I be enough?

August 27

I miss him. God, how I miss him. I never thought that having whatever scraps of love from him that were left over from Tilly would be better than nothing at all. I hate myself for having no pride and self-respect, but if he were to walk through the door right now I would go down on my knees and beg him to stay. I would do anything to make him love me again. But I am stupid and unlovable. My husband,

God, my parents. Even my own child does not love me. She prefers to go to church with some fat, Irish Catholic housewife who already has too many children of her own than spend time with me.

I was so stupid to think that Stevie ever really loved me. He only wanted me to have a child, but he is a child himself. I used to feel like a stranger in my own home, while the two of them would sit together giggling and laughing, keeping their secrets. He was her hero, she was his princess, and I was the wicked witch. I used to watch them in the garden. Part of me was desperate to join them, but they would not have wanted me to. She would cling on to his hand and listen to his every word. He would show her how to grow the fruit and vegetables and flowers, and she would copy his every move. They would take raspberries into the shed and eat them, and then bring in barely a handful in a bowl. They were laughing at me. So why do I miss him so much? I want to sit and cry and rock and cry and rock until the world disappears. Until I disappear. I am pathetic. What kind of monster is jealous of her own child? I hate them both, but not as much as I hate myself. And most of all, I just want him to come home.

August 28
I hope he rots in hell.

I am not crying now. I'm dumbfounded by her desperate words. I sit staring at the page in front of me, while scrabbling frantically through the memories of my distant past to see if any of it can be true. Certainly, her feelings must have been true. Her pain and loneliness scream out from the pages as real now as it was then. But so does her illness. She loved us, she hated us. She wanted him gone, she wanted him back. But most of all, she just wanted to be loved. I don't think that I ever once told her that I loved her. I just assumed she knew.

I am done. I cannot read any more today. My body feels as stiff and frozen as my mind. Eli shuffles into a sitting position at the sound of my chair scraping along the floor. I stand up slowly, stretching my arms in front of me. The café is almost full of people eating their lunches. I didn't notice any of them coming in, sitting down or placing their orders. I have been locked in my own little world, or rather my mother's. I need to get outside and stoke myself into life again. I need to walk by the sea. I take my glass back up to the counter where Daniel is busy preparing orders. There is no sign of Joseph Geronimo Heathcliff O'Shea or Queenie. I thank Daniel and ask for my bill.

"Oh, this one's on the house." And as I open my mouth to protest, he continues, "As long as you promise to come back soon."

It is an easy promise to make.

14

Tilly

Tilly thought that the baby Jesus looked more like a garden gnome than the son of God. She had opened the last door on her Advent calendar and was rather surprised to see that the baby in the manger had a very red face, big ears, and what looked like a rather pointy head. The Mary and Joseph looked a bit more normal, with the usual tea towel hats, accompanied by a very fat lying-down cow and a fluffy white sheep.

"Is that the lamb of God?" Tilly asked her mother, pointing to the sheep.

"I expect so," her mother answered without much conviction. She was heating a pan of milk for Tilly's breakfast. As it was Christmas Eve, Tilly was allowed her cornflakes with warm milk as a special treat.

"How can Jesus be the son of God, when Joseph was Mary's husband and Jesus's daddy?"

"Why don't you ask Mrs. O'Flaherty? I'm sure she'll be able to explain it much better than I can."

Tilly's mother smiled to herself, glad to be off the hook while hanging Mrs. O'Flaherty firmly on it. She was grateful for her kindness to Tilly, but the woman was filling Tilly's head with all sorts of religious mumbo jumbo. Tilly had insisted that she was going to church with Mrs. O'Flaherty and her family later that afternoon because "Christmas without God and Jesus was like an angel without any wings." Tilly's mother had almost laughed, but Tilly was more serious than a seven-year-old should know how to be. She had tried to persuade her mother to come with them, but was secretly glad when she refused. She might do the wrong sort of curtsey or not pray at the right time and upset God. Tilly was trying really hard to keep in God's good books at the moment so that he would look after her daddy and not send him to Bermondsey. At least she thought it was Bermondsey, but it was sometimes tricky to understand Mrs. O'Flaherty's way of speaking. Mrs. O'Flaherty had told her all about how when people die before all their sins are forgiven, they must stay in Bermondsey until their friends and family have done enough praying and lit enough candles to get them out and up to heaven. If the sins were really big, like killing someone or calling God a rude word, it could sometimes take years to get out. Tilly always lit a candle and said a prayer for her daddy when she went to church, just in case. She would have loved to talk to Mrs. O'Flaherty about her daddy, but she had made a promise and she couldn't break it. But perhaps Mrs. O'Flaherty had guessed that he was dead anyway because of all the candles that Tilly lit, and she always said a prayer with Tilly to keep him safe.

The question about who was really the father of Jesus probably wasn't that difficult to answer. Tilly thought that perhaps Mary had just forgotten who the real daddy was, and so had told them both that they were so that no one was disappointed.

After breakfast, they were going to decorate the Christmas tree. Uncle Bill had dropped it round yesterday after work. It wasn't very big, and its branches were a bit crooked, but Tilly thought it was beautiful. It smelled of Christmas. She had been a bit worried that her mother might not bother with a tree at all, but she had been surprisingly enthusiastic when Auntie Wendy had suggested that Uncle Bill get one for them. Before, it had always been her daddy who was the one who got excited about Christmas, "like an overgrown child," her mother had said. Once, he had come home with a bunch of mistletoe and chased her mother round the kitchen holding it over his head and demanding a kiss. It was one of the few times Tilly remembered seeing them laugh together. They had seemed happy for once, and her daddy got his kiss. It must have been a long time ago.

While Tilly was spooning the mush that was cornflakes and warm milk into her mouth, her mother fetched the battered cardboard box from the cupboard underneath the stairs. The box contained the tree decorations wrapped in crumpled newspaper, and strands of silver tinsel, and the colored fairy lights. Tilly climbed down from her chair at the kitchen table, put her breakfast bowl and mug into the sink, and followed her mother into the sitting room, Eli trotting along behind her. Tilly's sweater was beginning to make her itch. It was bright red with a row of reindeers galloping round the middle of it. Tilly's mother had laid it out ready for her that morning, thinking that she would love to wear reindeers on Christmas Eve. It was one from a generous bundle of clothes that Karen had outgrown, and that Auntie Wendy had passed on for Tilly. Karen was very pleased to see the back of it. Tilly's mother wasn't very keen on the idea of Tilly wearing hand-me-downs, and had picked out only a few items that she could wear in order not to seem ungrateful. Tilly put the sweater on to please her mother, but thought it looked a bit scratchy. And she was right; it was. She stood pulling at its neck and cuffs as her mother unpacked the decorations, first from the box, and then from their newspaper wrappings. Each delicate bauble was a familiar treasure, a beloved part of Tilly's Christmas; the goldfish and the fat robin, each with silky tails; the three little white birds with silver glitter sparkles; the apple, the orange, and the pineapple; the silver moon and the golden star; and finally, the rather tired and tatty-looking fairy for the top of the tree. Her white lace dress was grubby and torn, her golden hair was missing in places and what remained was full of tangles, and her silver wand was bent. She was missing a slipper, and her tinsel crown had lost its sparkle. Last year, Tilly had said that she looked like Cinderella with her missing slipper, and her daddy had laughed and said that she looked more like the barmaid at The White Horse the morning after the night before.

"The night before what?" Tilly had asked, but her mother had said that he was just being silly and not to pay any attention to him. This year, as the fairy emerged from her newspaper shroud, Tilly's mother looked at her disapprovingly.

"We shall have to get a new fairy, or perhaps an angel this time."

Tilly was horrified.

"We can't. She's our fairy."

"She's too old and scruffy now. She doesn't even look like a fairy anymore."

"I can brush her hair, and we can get her a new dress."

"Honestly, Tilly, there's no point. We'll just get a new one."

Tilly was desperate.

"But she's not ready to go to heaven yet."

"Old fairies don't go to heaven. They go in the bin."

Tears pricked the back of Tilly's eyes. She knew that the fairy was really just a shabby little doll, but she was one of the many single bits and pieces that made the whole that was their Christmas. And every single thing that was left was precious and had to stay the same, because the most important thing had already gone. Her daddy.

Her mother was completely oblivious to Tilly's distress as she retrieved the fairy lights from the bottom of the box and was trying to unravel them.

"Goodness me, it looks like the mice have been doing their knitting with these. Tilly, come and help me with this muddle. Here, you hold this end, and I'll try and untangle the rest."

Tilly rubbed her tears away with the back of her hand, and sniffed more loudly than she meant to.

"Tilly, don't sniff; use your hanky. What's the matter?"

Her mother looked up from the fairy lights to see a lost and miserable-looking little girl. Tilly didn't want to talk about her daddy with her mother, so she told a different truth.

"This sweater's scratchy."

She yanked at the neck to underline the point.

"I thought you'd like it. The reindeers are very Christmassy."

"I do like it. It's just too scratchy. It feels like spiders crawling with spiky feet."

Her mother shook her head dismissively and handed Tilly the plug end of the lights to hold. She worked through the green flex, untying and untwisting, until the lights were tangle-free. Tilly's mother took the plug from Tilly and pushed it into the socket. Nothing.

"Damn and blast!"

It was exactly what Tilly had expected. If her daddy had been here, at least he would have known how to fix them.

Tilly's mother once again looked at her daughter's disconsolate face and her mood seemed to soften.

"Don't worry, Tilly. It's probably only a loose bulb."

She then began checking each one to make sure it was screwed in properly. Tilly's hope, as fragile as one of the glass baubles waiting to go on the tree, was almost gone by the time her mother reached the last bulb, but then suddenly the room was washed with colored light and a smile finally broke across Tilly's face. She was astonished and impressed that her mother had been able to perform such a small but significant miracle. Together, they wound the lights round the tree, followed by the tinsel, and then carefully hung the decorations on the tips of the branches. Even the fairy earned a reprieve, and was allowed to take her usual place, on the grounds that it was too late to get a replacement for her this year. Tilly began to feel a bit more cheerful. Perhaps Christmas wasn't going to be as bad as she had thought. By the time they finished, Tilly couldn't stop fiddling with the neck of her sweater. Her skin felt as though it was on fire.

"Tilly, for heaven's sake, leave that sweater alone!"

"But it really hurts."

Tilly was usually a stoic child, not given to whinging when it came to minor aches and pains and childhood ailments. When she had had measles, she still wanted to go to school because she didn't want to miss sports day. She rarely cried when she fell off her bike, and only a little when she had been stung by a wasp last summer. Her mother finally paid attention to what she was saying and inspected Tilly's neck. Tilly was delighted to see the look of concern that immediately clouded her mother's face.

"Quickly, Tilly, take it off!"

Her mother grabbed the hem of the dreadful scratchy sweater and began yanking it up over Tilly's wriggling torso. The neck was tight, and Tilly's head stuck fast until one final desperate tug from her mother released her from the evil sweater's stranglehold, and Tilly staggered backward across the room, landing hard on her bottom. Tilly's pain was considerably lessened by the look on her mother's face. She knew she could risk it.

"I told you it was too scratchy," she said, with just the right amount of petulant insistence. She followed her mother through to the kitchen where she began searching in the cupboard for the bottle of calamine lotion and some cotton wool. Tilly trotted into the hall to inspect herself in the mirror.

"I look like I'm wearing a red necklace and two bracelets."

She continued admiring her wounds for a moment.

"Or people might think that you keep me tied up with a lead and handcuffs."

Tilly thought that this was a very good joke, but for some reason, her mother didn't seem to think that it was funny.

"Tilly, come here and stand still while I put this lotion on you."

Tilly did as she was told, and was immediately grateful for the coolness of the soothing lotion on her burning skin. Her mother gently dabbed her neck and wrists with cotton wool dipped in the chalky white liquid, until all the livid red patches were covered. Eli sat on the kitchen floor, watching, with a quizzical expression on his face.

"Now, just wait there a minute until it's dry."

Tilly stood in the kitchen with her arms outstretched, shivering in her winter undershirt while the lotion dried. Her mother stood watching Tilly jiggling from foot to foot and pulling faces, and she began to giggle.

"Oh, Tilly, you look like some sort of mad scarecrow."

Tilly thought how much prettier her mother looked when she laughed.

"Can I have red fizzy pop with my lunch today?"

Her mother laughed even more. But she nodded.

15

Tilda

I kept my promise to Daniel, much to Queenie's delight. I went back to the café the next day; and the next, and the next. And today I am going without my comfort blanket. I am not taking the diary with me to hide behind and use as a reason for being there. I am just going for breakfast. And to see Daniel. I might as well be naked. These are dangerous waters for me. I really like him, and that means I'm in trouble. He always seems pleased to see me; no, more than pleased. He comes out from behind the counter to meet me and take my coat. He talks to me and teases me, but kindly. He makes me laugh. He even makes me feel almost normal. Yesterday, he gave me a hug. I'm in *real* trouble here. A small, but persistent, voice in my head is warning me to get out while I can. But I don't want to. It's not as though I'm a virgin. I have *had* relationships before. I've known the rapture (and on one occasion, revulsion) of first dates, and the exquisite thrill of dizzying first kisses. I've wasted minutes, hours, even days just marking time until I next saw the one I thought I loved. I've known the fear and fire of physical intimacy; of breath on breath, mouth on mouth, and skin on skin. But afterward I always want them gone. Sometimes in minutes; sometimes days; sometimes weeks. But eventually, I always want them gone. Self-preservation always wins. If they stay too long, they will find out about me, and then they will leave anyway. One of them said I had no trust, and he was right. Without trust, love is a frail, hollow thing, easily frightened away. I haven't really trusted anyone. Not yet. Whenever I think of Daniel and his green eyes, it makes me catch my breath. Sometimes I do it on purpose just to feel it. Other times, he slinks into my thoughts like a cat through a door left ajar. But the effect is just the same. People will think I'm asthmatic.

Eli trots along beside me on the rimy pavement as I wonder for the umpteenth time if Daniel really likes me or is just being polite. We are so very different. He nods and smiles and chats to his customers as he glides easily through the intricate patterns woven by social interactions, balancing plates and cups and saucers like a circus juggling act on ice skates. I'm more like the clown with too-big shoes, who gets squirted in the face with water from the fake flower. I can see the café now. The lights are on inside, but it's still early. I don't want to be the first customer and look too keen. But I do want to be the first customer and have Daniel to myself for a bit. Oh, for heaven's sake, woman! Get over yourself! My hand is on the door handle now. I hesitate for just a moment, but Daniel looks up from behind the counter and waves me in. We are alone. Together.

"Right, my lovely but mad friend! Give me your coat and sit yourself down."

I make toward a table in the corner, but Daniel shoos me away from it with my own coat.

"Oh no you don't. No hiding over there. I want you close by where I can keep an eye on you."

I can't help but smile. I stand and wait, a little awkwardly, but willingly nonetheless, while he hangs up my coat and returns to seat me at the table nearest the counter.

"Now. What can I get you?"

I suddenly realize that, so far, I haven't spoken a single word.

"No. Don't tell me. I'll surprise you!"

Not a single word. Maybe that's why I'm beginning to feel so comfortable with him. I don't have to say anything if I don't want to. The bell over the door jangles and two sharp-suited young men burst in from the cold, breathing steam and rubbing their hands together. Daniel greets them warmly and, whistling, prepares their takeaway coffees. They venture back outside, their hands cradling the paper cups full of scalding liquid.

"Right then. And now for you . . ."

He winks broadly and disappears behind the counter. From my chair I am too low to see what he is doing, but it involves a lot of banging and clattering of pots and pans. It reminds me of the old kitchen at Queenie's. Oh God! I hope he's not cooking boiled eggs. Ten minutes later he presents me with a face on a plate. The eyes are fried eggs; the nose is a mushroom with stalk still attached; a large grilled tomato has been cut to resemble a pair of pouting lips and the creature's hair is an ocean of baked beans.

"You don't have to eat it all if you don't want to. There's toast as well." And a pot of tea.

"Thank you. It's lovely."

Daniel cups his hand to his ear in mock surprise.

"What's this? She speaks."

He makes a low, sweeping bow and rushes off to attend to the other customers who have been gradually filling the café. Once their orders have been taken and served, he returns and watches me in a silence he is obviously completely comfortable with, as I spread my toast with butter and cut it with my usual obsessive precision.

"Why do you do that?"

It's merely a request for information. There is no judgment in his tone.

I think before I reply. But I realize that, just for once, my hesitation is not an attempt to conceal or to think of an excuse. I'm trying to be truthful.

"I have to. It makes me feel safe."

He tips his head to one side and raises his eyebrows, considering.

"Fair enough. But eat your mushroom. It's good for you."

16

Tilda

Over the past week I have eaten a tree, a dog, a boat, a lighthouse, and an umbrella. Every time I go to the café, Daniel presents me with a food picture on a plate. Some have been more successful than others. The chocolate brownie dog with whipped cream spots was delicious; the sausage and broccoli tree wasn't. Yesterday's creation was a heart-shaped pink sponge pudding in a swirl of custard. That was my favorite.

But this morning I am not going to the café. I am going to see Miss Dane for coffee. I haven't read any more of the diaries yet. I need time to make the shift from what I thought was my childhood to another version that is dark and unfamiliar. At the moment, I'm not sure which is fact and which is fairy tale, and so I'm going to see Miss Dane for clues. It seems she got to know my mother well while they were neighbors. She probably knew her better than I did, so perhaps she can tell me something about the diaries. I light two matches before I go. Once outside the door of the flat, I need to go back inside to check that the spent matches I know are floating in a saucer of water are out. At least today I only feel compelled to check once. Eli follows me downstairs, as though he knows that he is included in her invitation this time. As I ring the doorbell, I am still nervous, but for a different reason than on my first visit. I am nervous about what I may discover. I need to know everything. Miss Dane opens the door and greets me with a smile of genuine welcome. She ushers us through to the sitting room, where a tray of coffee things is waiting. I sit down in one of the chairs next to the fire.

"Did you bring your dog with you this time, my dear?"

Eli is sitting right next to me, looking intently at Miss Dane.

"You can't see him?"

"Oh no, my dear, but your mother told me all about him."

"And you believed her?"

"Of course. There are a great many things in this world that we can't see, but that doesn't mean they don't exist. I trusted your mother, and at my age, I have faith in a whole world I cannot see. Would he like a biscuit?"

"He doesn't really eat much."

Miss Dane pours the coffee and hands me a cup. The trepidation I felt on my first visit seems barely comprehensible now, as I settle back in my chair ready to gently interrogate Miss Dane. Already I am a different Tilda.

"Why did my mother tell you about Eli?"

"Because she worried about you, and she said that perhaps he would always look after you, the way he had once looked after her."

"You mean she could see him?"

"Sometimes she could. But he was your father's originally."

I had come here searching for clues, but it looked like I was going to get bombshells instead.

"But she always denied that he existed. When he first came to me, when I was a little girl, she said I was just making him up!"

"As I said, she was worried about you. She was always worrying about you. Your mother was a highly intelligent woman capable of great compassion, loyalty, and love. But she also had a devastating illness and so she lived much of her life in fear, which sometimes led her to act in a way that she deeply regretted afterward. She wanted so much more for you."

"I'm not sure I understand."

Miss Dane's expression is sympathetic, but her words unflinchingly direct.

"I think that you probably understand much more than you are willing to admit."

This time I am not offended by Miss Dane's frankness, merely puzzled. What is the elephant in this sitting room that I'm simply not seeing? Sensing my confusion, Miss Dane relents.

"Unless I'm horribly mistaken, Tilda, you see things, don't you? Things that most other people can't see. Ghosts, dead people; call them what you will, but you can see them, can't you?"

"Yes."

There. I've done it. A single word spoken before a cautious thought could silence it. I've taken a risk, and a huge one at that. I have never, in my adult life, told anyone that before. Not a soul. The relief is monumental. I feel as though I have been holding my breath forever, and have finally exhaled.

"Well, so could your father."

Never mind bombshells; this is turning into the Blitz. In the ticking away of little more than sixty seconds, however, I swing from dumbfounded surprise to hazy recognition. Miss Dane is right. This truth is not as unexpected or unfamiliar to me as I want to believe. It just seems a long way away.

"How much do you know about your maternal grandparents?"

"Very little. They died before I was born."

Miss Dane raises her eyebrows in mild surprise and breathes a gentle sigh.

"Your mother's parents disowned her when she married your father. Cut her off like a sucker from a rose. The estrangement was immediate, absolute, and irrevocable. They were very religious, you see. Baptists of some sort, I believe. They viewed your father's ability as dabbling with the occult, tantamount to consorting with the devil. Your mother's marriage to him was, in their eyes, the route to certain damnation. It was a horrible choice for your mother to make. And a brave one too. But her love for your father gave her the courage she needed, and her life with him at its center was a very exciting place to be for a young woman from such a sheltered background."

"But how could they bear to lose her? She was their only child. They must have loved her. How could they not?"

Miss Dane shook her head sadly.

"I'm sure they did. But they feared God more. And it would seem that theirs was a most unforgiving god."

"So why did she never tell me the truth? Why did she say they were dead?"

"I can't answer that, my dear, but perhaps she was trying to protect you. It certainly seems to have been her life's work."

Miss Dane pours me another coffee. I need it.

"Miss Dane, did you know about her diaries?"

"Penelope, please. Call me Penelope. 'Miss Dane,' from you, makes me sound like a schoolmistress. Yes, I knew she kept them, but not much more than that."

"I've started reading them."

Miss Dane, or rather Penelope, makes no attempt to fill the silence, and calmly waits for me to continue.

"I'm finding out things that it's hard for me to know—or even believe."

"Tilda, if your mother left those diaries where she knew you would find them, then she wanted you to read them. You must trust that she had a good reason."

"But I'm afraid of what might come next and once I know these things, I can't un-know them."

"I'm sure you are, my dear, but because of your mother, you are not your mother. You are greater than your fear. Read them, and then go on and live your life. It's what your mother would have wanted."

I hope she's right. We chat about other things, more comfortable things, like how I'm settling into the flat, and what her niece brought in the shopping this week (artichokes—they went straight in the bin). After a while, Eli begins to fidget. He knows I have work to do. I thank Penelope for the coffee.

"You are both very welcome. You know where I am if you need me."

Back upstairs, I try to settle to some work. The cursor on my laptop blinks at me accusingly, highlighting how little progress I have made. If staring blankly at the screen counts as work, I manage a good couple of hours. My brain is occupied elsewhere, dragging Penelope's revelations back into my past and seeing where they fit. I wish Queenie were here.

When I have had enough, my thoughts turn to what I am going to wear tonight. I'm going to the café to surprise Daniel and I want to look nice. Well, not just nice, gorgeous actually. For Daniel. Iceberg ahead. The "Tilda trying to look gorgeous' outfit turns out to be a clean pair of close-fitting dark jeans, an emerald green silk tunic top, and a velvet tasseled scarf. The green glass drop earrings I am wearing flash and sparkle in the light, and even my hair is behaving itself. Perfume and a slick of lip gloss add the final touches. After four matches and two checks to make sure they are out, I close the door behind me for the final time and set off to dazzle Daniel with my gorgeousness. Make ready the lifeboats.

My stomach is tumbling over and over, and my heart is banging in my ribs as I walk along the promenade toward the café. I have to stop this ridiculousness. I'm not a teenager, and it's not a date. He doesn't even know I'm coming. We're just friends. So far. But I have allowed a small but shiny hope to creep into my heart. I am out of puff from walking too quickly and not breathing enough. I stop for just a moment to compose myself, before continuing at a more sensible pace. As the café comes into sight, I check myself again. A shadow flits over me like a cloud blown across the moon. It is a feeling as familiar as it is unwelcome: doubt. Man the lifeboats. I want to turn back, run home to the flat; give in to the fear. But I won't. As I reach the café, instead of going straight in, I stand back, a little to the side, and look through the window. I want to see him first. I want the sight of him to make me catch my breath. And it does. Daniel is standing by the jukebox with a truly stunning young woman with long red hair wearing a short black dress. She has the air of someone who knows her own beauty and the effect it has on men. Someone I will never be. They are laughing and standing very close to each other. I feel sick and stupid. She reaches up and strokes his face tenderly, and Daniel, my Daniel, looks at her with his green eyes and smiles. Except that he's not my Daniel, and he never was. Stupid, stupid, stupid. How could I be so stupid? He was only being kind to me. Nothing more. I turn away, and march along the promenade clenching my fists until my knuckles turn white. The pain of my nails digging into my palms is a welcome distraction. I will not cry. Hope has humiliated me. My ship has sunk just yards from shore. It wasn't meant to be like this. Not today. Today is my birthday.

17

Tilly

Tomorrow it was going to be Jesus's birthday and inside St. Patrick's there were more candles than Tilly had ever seen in her life. It looked as though all the stars in the sky had flown in through the window and scattered themselves inside the church to twinkle and dance while everyone sang carols and said their prayers. St. Patrick's was packed tighter than the number 9 bus on a rainy afternoon at going-home time. Tilly was squashed into one of the pews with Mrs. O'Flaherty and her seven offspring, and was firmly wedged between Mrs. O'Flaherty herself and Declan, the second youngest of Mrs. O'Flaherty's brood, who had brought along his pet earwig, Margaret, in a matchbox for the outing. Mr. O'Flaherty had just been setting off for The Star and Garter when Tilly had arrived at their house, but she heard him promising to go to midnight mass on his way home. He was a big, tall man with a fuzz of ginger hair that was almost always covered by a dark green cap. He seemed to overfill whichever room he was in, like a grown-up in a playhouse, but his voice was soft and low, like a cat purring. Tilly supposed that if you were as big as a giant, like Mr. O'Flaherty, you wouldn't ever need to shout to get people to mind what you said. Tilly liked him. He always ruffled her hair and winked at her whenever she saw him, and tonight he had wished her "a very merry Christmas with bells on."

Her mother had given Tilly a small bottle of perfume in a very pretty box to give to Mrs. O'Flaherty, and a tin of chocolate-covered biscuits wrapped in Christmas paper for the children. Tilly was very pleased and very surprised. She hadn't really thought about her mother as being a kind person, but it looked as though she must be. Tilly knew that giving presents was supposed to be as lovely as getting them, but as yet she wasn't completely convinced. She was really happy, though, to have something nice to give to Mrs. O'Flaherty, who was, apart from Karen, her best friend. She had proudly presented the gifts to her when she stopped by the house to join the family on their way to church, and Mrs. O'Flaherty's cheeks flushed with delight as she accepted them. She said that she had something for Tilly too, but that she could pick it up on her way home.

As the expectant congregation whispered and fidgeted in their pews, Tilly was craning to see the Nativity scene that was set out under an enormous Christmas tree near the front of the church, to one side of the altar. From what she could see, and much to her relief, the baby Jesus looked much more like a proper baby than the one on her Advent calendar. He didn't at all give her the idea that he might look more at home in boots and a green tunic clutching a fishing rod, than wearing a rather baggy diaper and sleeping in a manger. Although she did think he might be a bit cold, and wondered why Mary hadn't thought to knit him a nice blue short jacket with matching bonnet and bootees. Perhaps it was because of her having to ride on the donkey, which must have been quite wobbly, and she would have dropped too many stitches. Somewhere upstairs, near the beautiful, gold-painted ceiling of the church, the part where God and his angels most likely lived, the great organ began to breathe music into the air. Softly at first, its huge pipes puffed out sweet, gentle notes, but gradually the sound began to swell, and soon the pipes were blasting and booming until Tilly could feel the music echoing inside her chest. It was lovely. It was like sucking a flying saucer; the soft, fuzzy feel of the sugar paper slowly melting on your tongue, followed by the sharp lemon trill and fizz of sherbet buzzing inside your mouth. Tilly recognized the tune as "Hark the Herald," and as they all stood up to sing, leafing through the pages of their hymn books to find the right page, Father Damien marched slowly down the aisle followed by his assistants and the choir. Tilly had realized after her many visits to the church that the assistants, who were both boys aged around twelve, were really only there to make Father Damien look more important. They handed him things that he could perfectly well fetch for himself, but because he was so important and worked for God, he just didn't have to. Over their long dark dresses, the assistants wore white lacy apron things that Auntie Wendy would call "a bugger to wash." When Tilly had first started coming to St. Patrick's with Mrs. O'Flaherty, she had been very worried when she had thought a swear word in church, in front of God, by mistake. But with a bit of concentration, creative thought, and a little practice, Tilly had managed to persuade herself that thinking a swear word completely accidentally (even if it was in church, in front of God), particularly if it really belonged to someone else, couldn't count as a sin because that wouldn't be fair, and God had to be fair because he was perfect. So Auntie Wendy's "bugger' didn't count.

"Sailed in fresh, the cod said, 'See!'"

"Hail in the garden, David's tea!"

Tilly liked "Hark the Herald' and sang with gusto, even though she wasn't too sure what a talking fish had to do with Christmas. She hadn't bothered with a hymn book, as she knew the words by heart. Tilly was a child who had to get things straight in her head, and she had asked Mrs. O'Flaherty about Jesus being both the son of God and Joseph, as her mother had suggested. Mrs. O'Flaherty's answer had been immediate and beyond question. She had leaned forward and placed a hand on each of Tilly's shoulders before saying, almost in a whisper, "God moves in mysterious ways his wonders to perform," followed by a firm nod and a wink, which placed a perfect full stop on that particular conversation. It did occur to Tilly that having "mysterious ways' gave God quite a lot of chances to get away with things that he didn't have to explain, but then he was God, after all, and in charge of everything, so she supposed you just had to trust him.

A magician could perform tricks that fooled the people who saw them, but everyone knew that really they were just clever tricks with a clever explanation. Her daddy used to pretend to swallow a penny and then pull it out of Tilly's ear. Tilly always tried to look impressed, but she knew it wasn't real. The penny wasn't even wet. Perhaps the reason why God didn't have to explain anything properly was simply that his magic was real, and if he wanted talking fish in his Christmas carols, Tilly was happy enough to sing about them. The hymn finished with a resounding chord from the organ, followed by one wrong note when the organist knocked the sheet music onto the keys with an overenthusiastic final flourish. Tilly and Mrs. O'Flaherty's six younger children giggled and spluttered, but were fiercely shushed by Mrs. O'Flaherty and Teresa, who was looking very grown-up in a smart navy blue coat and a pout of scarlet lipstick. Teresa's attention was divided between keeping the younger children in order and pretending not to notice a rather good-looking young man several pews in front of them, who kept turning around and smiling at her. Declan, who was a lively little chap and missed nothing, quickly spotted Teresa's admirer and her feigned indifference to him, and began clutching both hands to his heart and making kissy-kissy noises that quickly earned him a clip round the ear from his mother. Tilly was torn between finding his antics funny and upsetting God for not being holy enough and not taking things more seriously, especially on Christmas Eve. She decided that she wouldn't look at Declan for the rest of the service, in case she got distracted again. Even when he let Margaret out of her matchbox for a little stroll down the pew to stretch her legs, Tilly only allowed herself a brief glance, and anyway, that was at Margaret and not at Declan.

As Father Damien climbed the steps to his wooden turret and spread his bits of paper out in front of him, ready to give one of his speeches, Tilly looked round for something to keep her amused for the next twenty minutes. She knew that what he was going to say was probably quite important, and was intended to give her a few tips on how to be a better person and get God to be proud of her, but more often than not she didn't really understand a lot of what Father Damien said. It didn't help that he got really excited and spoke so quickly and in such a shouty voice, that Tilly sometimes thought he sounded more like he was describing a horse race on the television than telling people how to get in God's good books and what some of the strange stories in the Bible actually meant. Tilly studied the row of heads in the pew in front. The first was a shiny bald dome, ringed with coarse white hair, like an egg wearing a grass miniskirt. The next was a pom-pom of tight brown curls sitting on a short fat neck, wrapped in a silky scarf covered in roses. Tilly thought that the pom-pom was probably married to the egg. Then came a small, bobbing-about head, crowned in waves of golden thistledown topped by a pale blue bow almost large enough to serve as a hat on a head that small. Tilly thought that it was probably the weight of such an enormous bow that was causing the head to wobble and bobble about so much. Number four was a shapeless brown tea cozy of a hat, with a yellow flower attached to one side of it, which looked as though it had gotten there by mistake; "self-seeded," as her daddy would have said, Tilly thought with a sudden pang. The glamorous mane of blond waves that was number five belonged to a very pretty lady who Tilly sometimes saw in Mrs. Dawson's shop. Tilly had once heard Mrs.

Dawson describing the pretty lady's blond hair to another customer as "not the color God gave her," but Tilly thought that Mrs. Dawson was just jealous and being horrid because the blond lady was as beautiful as an angel, and Mrs. Dawson had bushy eyebrows and a wart on her chin with a hair growing out of it, which God had probably given her for a very good reason. Next came a sleek, black slick of hair with an immaculate side parting, above a pair of large ears that stuck out just a bit too far for Tilly to consider their owner to be handsome. Mr. and Mrs. Bow were there, holding hands as usual, and finally there was a beautiful, soft white bun, shaped like a round loaf of bread. Tilly knew that this belonged to the old lady with the kind smile and the brown lace-up boots who normally sat right behind Mrs. O'Flaherty. Tonight all the pews were full, so perhaps she had arrived too late to get her normal seat.

There was a loud bang as Father Damien slammed both hands down in front of him to emphasize the final point of his sermon, which woke up those parishioners who had managed to drop off in the muzzy warmth of the crowded church. The next hymn was "Away in a Manger," during which Declan sang "Teresa and Seamus asleep on the hay' loud enough for Teresa's admirer, Seamus Milligan, and the rest of his pew, to hear, causing the young man to grin and giggle very inappropriately, and earning Declan a double-sided ear clipping from both his mother and Teresa. Tilly managed to keep a straight face. But only just. A nervous middle-aged woman in a sensible beige suit and pearl earrings read out the story of Mary and Joseph and the donkey getting to Bethlehem very late at night when all the hotels were shut, or full, or both, and having to make do in a stable, where Jesus was born and shepherds came to visit him. Tilly loved this story, no matter how many times she heard it, but was always puzzled that his grandparents never came to visit Jesus, as well as the shepherds. She knew that after a few weeks the three kings came with gold, Frank, and scent, and more, but there was never any mention of the grandparents. Maybe they were dead. The final carol was "Once in Royal David's City." Tilly wondered vaguely if the city belonged to the same David whose tea was in the garden, but before she could decide, Father Damien had passed them by, and members of the congregation were spilling out from their pews and shuffling toward the great wooden doors to go home and drink beer and snowballs, hang stockings and wait for Father Christmas. Outside it was cold and clear, and a glittering frost was already icing the roads and pavements. The stars had all flown back to print their proper patterns on the blue-black inky map of the sky. Tilly's daddy had told her that this was the map that Father Christmas used to find his way, so she was glad that it was a clear night.

When they reached the O'Flahertys' home, Tilly was invited into the front room to fetch her present from under the Christmas tree. She had only been in as far as the kitchen before, and was surprised to see that, despite having to accommodate so many occupants, the room was neat and tidy, but still warm and cozy, with bright curtains and cushions, and a gleaming sideboard covered in pretty ornaments and photographs in frames. A familiar face shone out from one of the pictures: the old lady with the round loaf bun. Tilly pointed to the picture and said, "That's the lady who always sits behind you in church."

Mrs. O'Flaherty smiled at Tilly's mistake but said nothing; instead she fetched two small parcels from under the tree and handed them to Tilly.

"There's one for you, and one for your mother. Now, Miss Tilly, you have a very happy Christmas, and wish your mother the same from all of us."

She bent down and kissed Tilly on the cheek as Tilly thanked her for the presents.

"Now, Teresa, you walk Miss Tilly home, and the rest of you hang up your coats and wash your hands for tea."

Left alone for a moment, in peace, Mrs. O'Flaherty picked up the photograph of her much-loved and long-dead mother and kissed the cold glass.

"Merry Christmas, Mammy."

18

Tilda

The winter sky outside scowls gray. It matches my mood as I return, once again, to my mother's diary.

October 14

It was so long ago, and since then I have forgotten so many things: names, places, things that have happened, but nothing about that day has been smudged or softened by the time that has passed. That day still has all its sharp edges, bright colors, scents, sounds and silences frozen perfectly in my mind. It was a beautiful spring day, full of promise, and I was wearing my new dress as I knelt in the road holding in mine the still-warm, tiny hand of a dead child. She looked like a broken doll lying in the gutter. Her face was perfect, framed by soft, blond curls, and her eyes were closed as though she was sleeping. But her legs were all wrong, and the back of her head was smashed. Kneeling beside me, her daddy was gently cradling her head in his lap, his hands cupping and pressing as though to stop the life from slipping out of her, but I could see the blood, and bits of flesh and bone on his trousers. And I felt so sick. Silent tears were streaming down his ashen face but I knew that inside he was screaming. A few minutes earlier, she had been skipping toward me wearing a frilly pink ballet skirt, smiling and holding her father's hand. He stopped to buy her a balloon and the next moment she lay crumpled in the road. Every time I think of her, I see that red balloon.

As I knelt there with her father, I could hear the traffic around us, and beyond that, the sound of the waves on the beach. In the public gardens across the road, a blackbird was singing and I could smell the lilac blossom. But it all seemed very far away as we waited and waited there in helpless, hopeless silence, her father and me. The ambulance took forever but it didn't really matter because I knew she was already dead. I remember the driver of the car that had hit her, standing on the pavement shaking and shouting, and telling everyone who would listen that it wasn't his fault. I remember the faces of the people who just stood watching, horrified, but still too morbidly curious to move on. But most of all, I remember her father's desperate, silent sobbing, and the feeling of her hand in mine. It was still warm when they took her away. Afterward, I sat on a bench in the gardens, listening to the blackbird. The sun was still shining and the heavy, sweet scent of lilac filled the air. There was blood on my new dress.

Somewhere in the next room, my mobile is ringing. I ignore it. I remember the little girl with the red balloon. I remember asking my mother if she had ever seen a dead person, and she had told me about her. She had probably been drinking, and the drink allowed things to sneak out that sobriety would have kept a secret. I was young and so curious, and desperate to know about everything, especially the things that grown-ups didn't seem to want to tell me. And I could be very determined if I wanted to know something badly enough. Knowing things made me feel safer back then. Now, I'm not so sure. As a child, I always wanted the details, the what, who, when, why, and how. The synopsis was never good enough; I always wanted the complete works. I can remember my childhood very well, but the proper sequence of events is sometimes harder to get right. Did I learn to tie my own shoelaces before I could make myself go cross-eyed, or was it the other way round? If I'm right about where these pages fit into my past, I had a very good reason to be curious about dead people. But reading her words, written so long after it happened, it's obvious that she was haunted by that day. It must have felt to her as though I was kicking a bruise. The coffee in front of me has gone cold, and I shudder as the unexpectedly tepid liquid fills my mouth. I'm tempted to spit it back into the mug but manage to swallow it. I get up and tip the rest into the sink and pour myself a glass of wine as compensation before returning to the diary that lies waiting for me on the kitchen table.

I sat on the bench. I couldn't move and I couldn't think what to do next. Everything had changed and it could never be put back. Suddenly everything all seemed *so* completely pointless. Perhaps that was the day when my illness really started. I don't know how long I would have sat there if the dog hadn't come to take me home. He was completely black, and one of his ears stood up and the other flopped over; Stevie's dog. I recognized him from a tattered photo that he always kept in his wallet. He was supposed to be a family pet, but he was only ever interested in Stevie. He was fifteen, the same age as Stevie, when he died. That day, he came right up and sat just inches away, staring at me with his solemn eyes. He led me home to Stevie. I had some news for him. That morning I had been to the doctor. I was pregnant.

I never saw the dog again after that day, but now he's come back, and this time it's Tilly who can see him. She couldn't be happier. She always wanted a dog. At first, she thought that I had gotten him for her, but I have denied him. I have told her that there is no dog. The irony is that I would love to give her something that brings her so much happiness, but as usual, it's Stevie's doing. And now, I'm afraid; afraid that the dog means something bad is going to happen. He is here to protect her, I'm sure. But from what?

I drain the rest of the wine from my glass, and take a match from the box. Once struck, the flame twists the wood into charcoal and I drop it into the saucer of water that is beside the box. And again. And again. I get up to refill my glass. Eli is watching my every move, and raising each eyebrow alternately as I slam the fridge door and bang the chair on the floor as I sit down again.

"You may well look at me like that. You knew all about this, didn't you?"

He plonks his head down onto his paws with a huge sigh, as if it has suddenly become too heavy for him. I sit at the kitchen table and slap the diary shut. I want to bang and crash about to relieve my frustration, but resist the urge to go and hurl pots and pans around the kitchen. I'll only have to clear them up afterward. I sometimes wish I had a set of drums. I have no idea what it is exactly that I am feeling, but a red warning light is flashing inside my head that I know I can't ignore. She lied to me about Eli and her parents. And if she lied to me about them, what else did she lie about? What else did she "protect' me from? I have already used up six of my matches today and I like to keep some for the nighttime. Just in case. I kick the table leg. Hard. It hurts. I forgot that I have no shoes on, and it really hurts. But at least the pain is a distraction.

I read the last lines of the diary entry again. Eli first came to me just a few weeks before my dad died. My mother always denied his presence. Did she have a premonition about my dad's death, or did she have something to do with it? Both options seem equally ridiculous. My mother was a fanatical pragmatist; she would have had little truck with premonitions and the like. Was she a murderer, then? She had some sort of breakdown when I was about three, and spent several weeks in a psychiatric hospital. She had even had electric shock treatment. I was too young to remember much about it, but I do remember thinking that she must have done something naughty, because some-body, maybe it was my dad, said it was "for her own good' when she went away, and grown-ups only ever said that when you were being punished for something. I must have heard him talking to someone else about it, because nobody told me anything, and when she came home it was never mentioned in my presence. And she never spoke of it to me until one day, about a year before she died. We were sitting on the promenade, drinking coffee and watching the gulls swoop and glide on the wind, when she told me that she had sat waiting on a wooden bench in the hospital corridor with another woman, wearing only a gown that tied at the back, and it was chilly. The other woman was crying, so they took my mother in first, and when they strapped her to the bed they placed a gag between her teeth so that she wouldn't bite her tongue. It had tasted of rubber and disinfectant. And that was it, like a snatch of conversation caught when changing stations on the radio. So, could she ever have been mad enough to kill him? I need to get out more. My imagination is beginning to mess with my head. I am about to get up from the table when the realization hits me like a swallow of turned milk; the day my mother found out that she was pregnant with me was one of the saddest days of her life.

An hour later, I am standing on the pier, staring out across the endless, gray sea and thinking of Daniel. I haven't been back to the café since my birthday. What's the point? I have tried to convince myself to go back, act cool as though I only ever thought of him as a friend, and possibly stick my foot out at an opportune moment and trip up the red-haired beauty as she swans past me. But I'm no good at acting cool. I'd be like the clown again in the too-big shoes. The only one who'd fall flat on her face would be me. Queenie thinks I should go back. She says that fear can play havoc with the eyesight, but I have 20/20 vision. I know what I saw. I pull out a cigarette from the pack in one pocket of my coat, and fumble for a lighter in the other. A click, close to my face, followed by a flame comes from a brass Zippo held in a deeply tanned hand. A heavy silver bangle spins on the wrist of the lighter's owner as he snaps the lid shut.

"I didn't know you smoked."

I drag deeply on the cigarette, pulling the smoke into my lungs.

"I don't."

"Well, you're doing a mighty fine job of pretending to be someone who does."

I offer him a cigarette that he takes with a grin. Joseph Geronimo Heathcliff O'Shea rests his elbows on the railings next to me and blows the smoke from his cigarette out to sea. He is standing very close and I am glad. Eli, who is sitting on the other side of me, is gently wagging his tail. It seems that he is pleased to see Joseph Geronimo too.

"I haven't seen you in the café recently."

"No."

"Daniel's been wondering where you are."

"I bet he has."

Joseph Geronimo takes my hand and begins walking me down the pier. The wooden slats clack beneath our feet and my hand feels small, like a child's, in his.

"I was there that night, you know. I saw you outside and I know why you turned away, and why you haven't been back since."

I can't trust myself to speak. I don't want to think about Daniel, or my mother, or anything else for that matter. I just want to throw myself at this man and hide in the embrace of his strong, warm body. I want him to be my shelter from a world where I feel like an outcast. Instead, I kick a discarded drink can with petulant venom, sending it scuttering down the pier. Joseph Geronimo stops and turns to face me.

"What is it, exactly, that you're afraid of?"

"Boiled eggs."

He laughs and we continue walking hand in hand.

"Nice try. But you're not getting out of it that easily."

He leads me to a wooden bench facing out to sea and we sit down.

"You're a smart woman, Tilda, so don't take me for a fool."

We sit in silence for a while, Joseph Geronimo waiting for an answer, and me trying to find the appropriate words to construct one. My reflex response of evasive bullshit clearly isn't going to cut it with him. Finally, in exasperation, he answers his own question.

"The thing you are most afraid of is yourself. Of who you are. Am I right?"

He leaves no pause for an answer because he doesn't need to. We both know he's right.

"You sneak around in the shadows pretending to be like everyone else, but like it or not, you never will be. What you have can be a blessing or a curse, but the choice is entirely yours. It is what you make of it. You can spend the rest of your life skulking or you can find your swagger."

And with that he kisses me. Not a peck on the cheek, like a friend, but long and full on the mouth like a lover. I don't stop him. I don't pull away.

"My man, Daniel, will disembowel me with his bare

hands if he finds out about that," he declares, leaning back on the bench and grinning.

"I doubt it!"

"Look at me, Tilda."

He cups my chin in his hand and forces me to look into his dark blue eyes.

"Tilda, you are a fine-looking woman, and you are magnificent in more ways than you know, but in affairs of the heart you've shit for brains. Pardon my language."

He can see I am about to argue, and he silences me with a finger across my lips.

"Sometimes, we see what we fear most, instead of what's really there. Sometimes, we have to learn to trust. That redhead—she's been after Daniel for months, purring and pouting and wiggling her ass. But he's not interested. It's you he's set his cap at, damn him. He's friendly because she's a customer and so are her friends. But that's it. And if I didn't know it to be true I'd be chasing you to church for myself. But I've seen how you look at him, and he's the man for you. Now get up off your bony backside and come with me. I'm going to buy you a mug of tea and a cherry brandy."

He takes my arm and we head off back down the pier toward the café.

"Come on, dog, keep up."

19

Tilly

Eli stood in a patch of gossamer winter sunlight next to the lilac tree, gently wagging his tail. Tilly loved the lilac tree. It was just a collection of bare brown sticks now, but in spring it would be a haze of blossom and fresh green leaves. Tilly thought that the flowers looked like fluffy, purple pine cones, but her mother said that their perfume gave her a headache. She would never have lilac in the house, and one year she had tried to persuade Stevie to chop it down and replace it with an ornamental cherry tree. But when Tilly had found out what was planned, she had been heartbroken, and made such a hullabaloo that her mother eventually relented and the tree was left in peace. Tilly was playing tag with Eli, but she knew that she could never win. She flung herself this way and that, her hair flying wildly behind her and her coat flapping open, but she could never quite touch him.

Auntie Wendy was watching from the back gate in complete bewilderment. She was glad to see that Tilly was enjoying herself so much, as things had been hard enough for her lately, but she seemed to be sharing her game with someone else, and yet she was com-

pletely alone in the garden. Auntie Wendy closed the
gate behind her with a deliberate clunk, so that Tilly
would be sure to hear her. Tilly looked up at her and
waved, and then returned to her game. Auntie Wendy
was prickled by a vague worry that something wasn't
quite right.

"Who are you playing with, Tilly?" she asked.

"My dog. But he's too fast for me to catch him."

Tilly looked to her side as if to indicate his presence.

"That's lovely, sweetheart, but it's just pretend, isn't
it? He's a pretend dog?"

Tilly looked up at Auntie Wendy, her eyes completely
clear with truth.

"No, he's not pretend. He's dead, like daddy."

Under normal circumstances, Tilly was quite pleased
when something she said provoked such a shocked
expression from a grown-up, but almost as soon as the
words were out of her mouth, she remembered her
promise. Auntie Wendy's face looked exactly like her
mother's when she had first tried a big gulp of the
whisky that was kept in the sideboard. Tilly clamped
her hand over her mouth to stop any more words escap-
ing. Her tummy lurched with fear and she hoped that
her promise wasn't broken.

Auntie Wendy's face didn't move. Tilly wondered if
she might have to poke her to get her going again. It
was like being at the cinema when the film gets stuck,
and the picture freezes on the screen. The appearance
of her mother at the back door jolted Auntie Wendy
back into motion. Auntie Wendy smiled weakly at Tilly,
and turned toward the house. Tilly hoped she wouldn't
say anything. Tilly lay flat on her back on the frozen

lawn and squinted up at the sky, watching the tiny flecks of black pitch and wheel across the bright, blue space. Tilly wondered if the birds could see heaven from where they were, and if her daddy could see her from wherever he was. Something tickled her neck, and her fingers touched the fine gold chain, searching for the heart-shaped locket that Father Christmas had brought her. It was engraved with a "T" in a tiny circle of flowers. It had come in a lovely red velvet box that now stood in pride of place on her dressing table, next to the white china angel that had been Mrs. O'Flaherty's Christmas present to her.

Tilly's daydreaming was soon interrupted by the sound of raised voices coming from the house. The angry shouting made Eli sit up very straight, and Tilly's tummy pitch like the birds in the sky. In the weeks before he went away, her daddy used to shout like that, and her mother would scream back at him. Tilly never heard the actual words, just the anger, because as soon as it started, she would run to the bottom of the garden, or at night, pull the covers over her head and hide under the pillow. She had never heard her mother and Auntie Wendy argue about anything. Auntie Wendy was always on their side, no matter what, so this must mean serious trouble. Tilly got up and crept a little closer to the house to see if she could hear what they were saying.

"The poor kid's obviously disturbed and it's not surprising after what you've done to her. I ought to report you to someone."

Auntie Wendy was fuming, but her mother's voice was surprisingly calm.

"She's my daughter and I think I know what's best for her. I'll thank you not to interfere in something that's really none of your business."

The back door burst open, and Auntie Wendy marched out into the garden. Her face was cross and very red, and she looked as though her head was going to explode. Her mouth was still moving, but she had run out of words, and Tilly could tell by the quick, clackety-clack of her heels on the path and the fierce grip that she had on her handbag that she was very, very upset about something. Her mother followed Auntie Wendy, but only as far as the doorway, where she stood watching her. She looked like someone who had made up their mind about something that no one would ever be able to change. As Auntie Wendy reached the gate, she hesitated for a moment and looked toward Tilly.

"Wendy."

Her mother's voice was quiet, but heavy with warning. Auntie Wendy left without saying a word.

After she had gone, Tilly hung around in the garden for a bit, even though her fingers and toes were beginning to go numb with the cold. She was dying to go and ask her mother what had happened, but more than a little bit afraid to know the answer. Tilly loved Auntie Wendy. She was like a hot-water bottle, chocolate sponge and custard, Black Beauty, a go on a helter-skelter, and Milk of Magnesia. She could make Tilly feel happy and excited, warm and safe, and when something was wrong, she could always make it a bit better. Now Tilly was worried that she might not see her anymore. She couldn't understand it. Auntie Wendy was her mother's best friend, her only real friend. Something really bad must have happened.

"It's just a bit of a misunderstanding," her mother said, when Tilly eventually plucked up the courage to go inside and speak to her.

"Is Auntie Wendy still our friend?"

"Of course she is. She's just got the wrong end of the stick about something. Everything will be back to normal in a couple of days."

Tilly was unconvinced. Auntie Wendy usually had the whole stick, and not just one end of it, let alone the wrong end. Tilly didn't know anyone who was more organized, or who knew more about what was going on around them. Auntie Wendy always knew if someone had new curtains or was having a baby, and what was on offer at Mrs. Dawson's and if the coalman didn't fill the bunker right up to the top. Tilly wasn't fooled for a minute. Her mother was trying to pass off a zebra for a horse.

"Why don't you write a letter to Daddy? You haven't written one this week."

Tilly recognized the diversionary tactic and was even more suspicious. She had begun writing to her daddy again just before Christmas. When he first went away, he had written to them every week—sometimes letters, sometimes postcards with pictures of the seaside on them—and Tilly always wrote back. But as time went on, they heard from him less frequently. Her mother said that he was very busy running the pub, and he didn't always have time to write. After her daddy died, starting to write the letters again had been her mother's idea. One day, when Tilly had been feeling really miserable and missing her daddy so much that it made her cry even when she was watching *The Clangers*, her mother had suggested that she could write him a letter and if they left it in the right place, an angel would find it and take it to him. Tilly thought it was a stupid idea, even more stupid than kissing boys or having bosoms, but she knew that her mother was trying to cheer her up, so she went along with it. Each letter was left on the kitchen windowsill, at night, just before Tilly went to bed. They would say a little prayer for her daddy, and ask an angel to come and collect the letter and take it to him. Sometimes Tilly nearly laughed during the prayer because it seemed so silly, but her mother took it all very seriously. Tilly was certain that it was her mother who took the letters, but she kept writing them. Just in case.

Later, after the letter was written, Tilly sat at the table dividing her fishcake into eight equal pieces and crowning each piece with three peas while her mother sat smoking and searching through a shoebox full of old papers and Christmas cards. Tilly ate a piece of fishcake, and then a piece of carrot, and then had a drink of orange squash. She kept going until her plate was empty except for one piece of carrot, and her glass was drained.

"I'm not eating this carrot. It's got a brown bit. I think a maggot must have pooed on it."

"Hmm."

"Or weed on it, or been sick on it."

"Probably, dear."

"I'm having a hysterectomy."

Tilly had no idea what one was, but if it was good enough for Mrs. O'Flaherty, it was good enough for her.

"That's nice."

"Muuuuuuummm!"

Tilly's exasperated whine was accompanied by her feet drumming against the chair legs.

Her mother looked up, finally.

"I'm sorry, Tilly, what is it?"

"I've finished. Ages ago. Except for the carrot with maggot poo on it."

"Don't say 'poo' at the table."

It was a good job she hadn't heard the rest of it. Her mother returned to the shoebox and pulled out an old Christmas card. She opened it, read it, and smiled.

"Let's go to the seaside."

"But it's winter."

"It'll be lovely," her mother replied, smiling.

Tilly thought it would be lovely too. But she still wasn't going to eat the last piece of carrot.

20

Tilda

Danny boy! I found your woman wandering on the pier. Smoking cigarettes she was too. If you don't come and claim her, I'm keeping her for myself, and we'll run away together to Roaring Water Bay. And I'm taking the dog too."

Joseph Geronimo has marched me into the café, and makes his declaration with all the swash and buckle of a pirate in a Hollywood film. I don't know whether to laugh, cry, or hide under one of the tables. Daniel, who is clearly not good with surprises, stares at us both openmouthed and forgets to stop filling the coffee cup that he is holding, so that it overflows and the scalding liquid runs down his leg.

"Shit! Shit! Shit!" he shouts while struggling frantically to remove his jeans, having thrown the coffee cup and its contents all over the floor. Now I know what to do. I'm helpless with laughter at the sight of Daniel bunny-hopping behind the counter, his jeans round his ankles. Two elderly ladies with very sturdy handbags, who are sitting at a table in the corner, and who look as though they may have come into the café by mistake, are watching with shocked disapproval.

"Language! Language!" tuts one of them.

Queenie is sitting alone in the corner, grinning from ear to ear.

"Right, Danny boy, I'm counting to five."

Joseph Geronimo nods toward me and raises his eyebrows at Daniel. Daniel, who is now without his trousers or any vestige of dignity, hesitates for just a second before he strides out from behind the counter, with as much swagger as a man wearing only his underpants and socks in a public place can muster. He grabs me by both arms and kisses me passionately on the lips. It's not exactly *Love Actually*, but it's a start. And they are very nice underpants. Of course, if this was a film, there would have been a spontaneous round of applause from the customers in the café at this point, but in real life, there's a rather embarrassed and very English hush, followed by one of the old ladies remarking, "That's all very well, but when's he going to take our order?"

A little while later, Daniel and I are sitting at one of the tables drinking tea and cherry brandy. Daniel is wearing a clean pair of jeans and he is holding my hand. Having flattered and fussed over the two old ladies, and given them free tea and crumpets, Joseph Geronimo is in charge behind the counter and I suspect that Eli is behind there with him. I'm explaining to Daniel how I've ended up here and why I've been reading little books in his café.

"So, have you had any surprises so far?"

"A few. But I think there's probably worse to come."

He squeezes my hand.

"Well, I always thought you were as mad as a box of jumping jacks anyway, so feel free to come here and read whenever you like. If you read anything that makes you even more peculiar than you normally are, I promise I'll either ignore you or lock you in a cupboard."

I can't stop smiling. Maybe I am mad, and yes, maybe I will get hurt, but isn't it about time to take a risk? I'm sick of being careful and hiding who I really am. I'm fed up of waiting for my real life to begin. I'm going to get my party dress out of the wardrobe and start dancing. If it gets ripped or stained, so be it. At least I'll have worn it.

"Hey, you two! Don't get too mushy. It's only the first date."

Queenie has gone and Joseph Geronimo is getting bored of serving teas and wants some company.

"How about you make me a chip butty? I think I deserve it."

I go and sit at the counter, and Joseph Geronimo comes around and sits on the stool next to mine, while Daniel sorts out his order. I place my hand over his.

"Thank you."

Joseph Geronimo turns to me and winks.

"You're as welcome as the flowers in May."

Part 2

*Divas, doughnuts,
dating, and dancing*

21

Tilly

Tilly had never been in a taxi before, but her mother had said that they were treating themselves because they were on holiday. Tilly didn't think it was much of a treat. Although she had felt quite posh and important when the driver had opened the door for her and called her "miss," she still preferred to ride on a bus with its prickly velvet seats, a friendly conductor and lots of other people to watch. But as they drove down the hill from the station, past the shops and the bank, several pubs and a large post office, Tilly felt a fizz of excitement starting in her tummy. It had something to do with the strange light at the bottom of the road. Tilly felt as though she was about to emerge from a long, dark tunnel. All at once, the brown and gray of bricks and concrete fell away, and the whole wide world was filled with bright light, sand and sea and sky. Tilly bounced with joy and pointed and shouted.

"The sea! The sea! I can see the sea!"

The taxi driver glanced back in his mirror at Tilly's beaming face. He had seen it hundreds of times before, but it still warmed his heart like a lover's kiss. Tilly craned her neck at the window, desperate to gather in all the sights and sounds and smells. The sun was high and shining brightly on the sparkling waves, and she could taste the sharp, salty tang of the sea in the air. Children swaddled in hats, scarves, coats, and gloves ran along the beach chasing footballs and flying kites, and men in tweed coats walked along the promenade arm in arm with ladies wearing silk scarves to keep their hairstyles safe from the whirling wind. An elderly couple ate fish and chips from newspaper, huddled in a bus shelter facing out to sea, while hungry gulls stood guard, hoping for scraps. A man, walking alone, with one hand on his hat and the other in his pocket, looked so familiar that for a tiny breath Tilly thought it was her daddy. But the truth pulled her back by her pony-tail before she could blink. Her mother took her hand and squeezed it gently.

"Look, Tilly, the pier."

The pale blue metal tentacle stretched out to sea, strewn with colored lights and fluttering flags. The golden minaret that crowned the ballroom at the end of the pier glinted in the sunlight, and the fairground rides whirled and spun and raced just like Tilly's heart when she saw this magical world spread out before her. This was definitely Tilly's idea of a treat. The taxi carried on past the pier and then turned left, and began to climb one of the long roads lined with tall Victorian houses, many of which boasted colorful signs declaring them-selves to be hotels or bed and breakfast establishments. The taxi pulled up outside a splendid-looking house, with a green and white sign hanging on an ornate metal bracket over the door. The Paradise Hotel was a burst of high summer in a bleak midwinter street. The front of the house was bedecked with hanging baskets of roaring red geraniums, purple and white petunias, and pink fuchsias. White troughs on the windowsills were over-flowing with trailing lobelia, more fuchsias and jewel-hued violas, and two huge pots either side of the very grand-looking front door contained a riotous display of snapdragons, marigolds, and busy Lizzies. Tilly thought that whoever lived here must be very special indeed to make such beautiful blooms grow in winter. Her mother thought that the person who lived here had spent an awful lot of money on plastic flowers. The sign proclaimed this person to be one Queenie Malone, and just below a first-floor window a huge Union Jack was waving from a diagonal flagpole. Tilly was impressed.

"Do you think the queen stays here on her holidays?"

Her mother pushed open the first of the two front doors, and once they were both inside the lobby and she had checked her appearance in the glass, she rang the doorbell on the inner door. Tilly was jiggling from one foot to the other in excitement, peering through the glass door panels to see if anyone was coming.

"Tilly, do stand still. Anyone would think you've got ants in your pants."

Tilly knew that they must be on holiday for her mother to be saying "pants' in a public place, so she couldn't resist pushing the joke a little further.

"Or nits in my knickers."

A sentence containing both the words "knickers" and "nits," and so bringing together the rude and the repulsive was, in Tilly's eyes, a recipe for the knicker-bocker glory of all jokes, and she collapsed into a fit of giggles at her own comedy genius. Even her mother was trying not to laugh. At the sound of footsteps coming from inside the house, her mother grabbed Tilly's hand and shook her, as though to throw off the giggles, and they both stood to attention, although the shadow of a grin was still dancing across her mother's face. The woman who opened the door was unforgettable in every way. Her hair, which was the color of Parma violet sweets, was swept into an immaculate candyfloss bouffant. Her matching eyeshadow, lipstick, and nail polish were a toning shade of frosted lilac, and on her bosom shelf rested several strands of pearls and an enormous sparkling brooch in the shape of a peacock. The rings on her fingers twinkled like the crown jewels. She was wearing a tight-fitting, plain cotton dress that was a striking shade of fuchsia. Her perfume smelled of gardenias. Tilly thought she was beautiful.

"Good afternoon, ladies, and welcome to The Paradise Hotel."

She swept them through into the hallway where she hugged Gracie hard, like a mother welcoming a long-lost child home.

"My God, Queenie! You look so different. You look amazing."

Gracie's face was lit by a smile brighter than Tilly had ever seen on her mother before.

"Is that why you've got the flag over the door? Because you're called Queenie?" Tilly asked.

"It most certainly is, young lady. That, and to show people that The Paradise Hotel is fit for the queen herself."

Tilly knew already that she was going to love Queenie. Once the greetings and hugs were over, Queenie said that she would take them to their room. It was up three flights of stairs, almost at the top of the house. The stair carpet was a deep maroon and cream pattern, and almost every step creaked when it was walked on. Queenie said that the creaky stairs were a good way to deter guests from creeping about in the middle of the night to indulge in "clandestine canoodling." Tilly had no idea what she was talking about, but made a mental note to ask Queenie about it later. Perhaps when her mother wasn't listening. Every landing windowsill was adorned with gleaming brass plant pots which sprouted huge, feathery ferns or lush green aspidistras. On the walls were little signs made of varnished wood saying things like "Home, Sweet Home," "Bless this House," and "No Swearing," and framed pictures of the queen. The real queen. Queenie unlocked the door to their room and handed the key to her mother.

"Now, once you've unpacked and settled in, come downstairs to the guests' sitting room and I'll bring you a nice cup of tea." And with a fragrant waft of gardenias she was gone.

Their room was full of light that streamed in through the big bay window facing the seafront, and it even had a little balcony. The twin beds had matching eiderdowns covered in pale cabbage roses, and beside each bed was a little cupboard with a lamp and a small jug of water and a glass, set out on a lace doily. There was a wooden wardrobe with coat hangers covered in pink and blue quilted padding, and right next door was a tiny bathroom with pretty flowery wallpaper and yet another picture of Her Majesty on the door facing the toilet.

"I don't think I'll be able to wee if the queen's watching."

"I'm sure you'll manage," her mother replied as she lifted their suitcase onto her bed and snapped the lock undone.

Tilly gazed out of the window toward the sparkling sea and the magical pier, and was enchanted.

"I want to stay here forever."

22

Tilda

I'm looking for something to keep me occupied until it's time to get ready. Tonight, I'm going on a proper date with Daniel. He's taking me out for dinner and I don't want to get ready too early and then have nothing to do but wait. God, I'd forgotten how slowly time goes when you're so looking forward to something. It's like playing a 78 rpm at 33 rpm; I want to crank the handle to make the time go faster. I'm trying really hard to quit the matches. I've only lit two today and that was this morning, because I don't want to have to come back into the flat and leave Daniel standing at the door while I check that any more recently spent matches are still dead and floating in the water. There is, however, one thing that might distract me for a while. The little blue book is lying on the kitchen table. I pour myself a glass of wine. I could just read a few more pages.

November 3
Stevie still hasn't replied to my letter. Until now, I've been happy enough that he's away from Tilly. I need to protect her. It's my duty as her mother. I told him that he's got to change; be more responsible and act like a

grown-up. And stop teaching Tilly things she shouldn't know. I wanted her to have time to forget and perhaps learn to love me the way she loves him. I thought that if she had only me, then maybe she would. But who was I kidding? He is still her hero, and although she tries not to show it in front of me, that bastard is breaking her heart. She thinks I don't notice her watching for the postman, desperate for a letter from her daddy. I know I wanted this. But we needed the money. It was only meant to be for a few months. Has he given up on both of us so soon? I wrote to him asking him to visit us. I can't bear to see Tilly so desperate for him and not do anything about it. I will never be enough for her. Besides, if I'm honest, I'm not sure I can cope for much longer on my own. Well—I'm not on my own, am I? It's me, the drink, and the pills; the unholy trinity. God help us. But I love my child more than my own life, and I know now that I need him to come back. It'll be Tilly's birthday soon, and he must be here for that. I'll beg if I have to.

November 10

He's not coming. Tilly's seventh birthday and he won't be there. He's working, he says. Can't get the time off. He'll lose his job. He works in a pub, for Christ's sake; and that's more important than his daughter's birthday? I'm supposed to be the bloody drunk, but at least I'm here. I pleaded with him, for her sake, and God knows it hurt. But never, ever again. He can go to hell.

I don't seem to have much luck with birthdays. But at least, in the end, my dad had a bloody good excuse for standing me up on that one. My eyes fill with tears at the memory of one of the worst days of my life. The chime of the doorbell pierces the silence like a hatpin into a balloon. Instead of a bang, there is a crash as my toppled wineglass spills its contents across the table before rolling off the edge and onto the floor. If I carry on breaking them at this rate, there will be none of my mother's best wineglasses left. Daniel is early. Eli watches my confused dithering and I swear he is smiling. Do I clear up the mess first or answer the door? The bell rings again and answers my question for me. Daniel is standing in the hallway, grinning broadly and shuffling from one foot to the other.

"I know I'm early, but I was ready and just hanging around, so I thought I'd come and hang around with you."

Just the sight of his face is enough to dispel the darkness contained in the pages I have just been reading. I stand awkwardly in the doorway, smiling like a toothpaste advertisement.

"I think this is the bit where you ask me in."

"Oh God! I'm so sorry. Please do. Come in."

"I don't mind if I do," he laughs, and he does. Then stands in the hallway waiting patiently for me to turn into a sensible person again and show him where to go. I take him through to the sitting room. Eventually.

"I'm not ready or anything. Would you like a drink?"

"No, I'm fine thanks. You look ready enough to me. Come on, get your coat. Let's go. We'll be late!"

"Late for what?"

"For everything!"

His enthusiasm is reassuring and contagious.

"I was going to get changed. Where are we going?"

"You're lovely as you are. Just put on something warm. And hurry up!"

On my way to the bathroom for an emergency make-up, hair and perfume pit stop, I make a very slapdash and perfunctory effort to clear up the mess in the kitchen. This involves extravagant swaths of kitchen roll, and the inappropriate and largely ineffectual use of a newspaper and a tea towel as a makeshift dustpan and brush. When I have spread the mess around sufficiently, I chuck the whole lot in the bin. Five minutes later I am wearing my big coat and my neck is swaddled in a soft, cream cashmere scarf that I found hanging on the coat rack in the hall. Daniel is standing with his hands in his pockets, pretending that he has not been poking around my things that are lined up on the mantel shelf. But he has put the glass eye back in the wrong place. I wish I could just leave it where it is. Simply turn my back on it and walk away. But I can't. The things have to be in a precise order. The threat of some unspecified catastrophe is still too strong for me to abandon all of my safety rituals and so I restore it to its proper place.

"Aha! You caught me!"

Daniel is smiling, but clearly slightly puzzled.

"I'm sorry, it's just . . ." I trail off lamely.

How could I even begin to explain something so nebulous and complicated?

"Right, that's enough. I'm hungry and we're going. Now, this minute!"

Daniel grabs me and spins me round to face the door. Eli climbs onto the sofa and nestles himself into the cushions for a cozy night in. He obviously trusts Daniel to look after me and is standing down for the night.

Daniel takes me to the pier.

The sky is blue-black velvet scattered with diamonds, and the lights strung along the length of the pier twinkle like stars threaded onto a wire. Waves rise and crash beneath us, and then splash and burble their retreat across the pebbles speckled with flecks of white foam. The smell of hot doughnuts and fish and chips wafts in warm currents through the cold night air and mingles with the snatches of music from the fairground rides. I love the pier. At least here I feel safely inconspicuous. Maybe because it is a world of smoke and mirrors. It's a good place to hide. There is magic here, even if some of it is only make-believe. Daniel could not have chosen better. Now I'm the one who's grinning.

"Where are we going to eat?"

"Right here. Sit down, and I'll be back in a sec."

"Right here' is on a wrought-iron and wooden bench facing out to sea under a little wooden shelter, on the middle of the pier between the amusement arcade and the fairground rides. Daniel returns with two parcels of fish and chips wrapped in white paper, and a black duffel bag from which he produces a chilled bottle of pink champagne, two glasses, two white linen napkins, and a single red rose. It's plastic.

"God, it's awful, isn't it? But I don't want you getting spoiled, so I borrowed it from the amusement arcade on the way back from the chips shop."

I'm dumbfounded.

"What's the matter?"

"Why this? Why here?"

"Don't you like it?"

The disappointment on Daniel's face hits me like a punch in the stomach. Why am I so awkward at this?

"It's perfect. I just can't understand how you got it all so right."

His grin reappears.

"Well, judging by how long it took you to cross the café's threshold for the first time, I figured that if I took you to a restaurant the chef would be having a smoke and the kitchen would be closed for the night by the time I actually got you inside."

The champagne is cold and delicious. The fish and chips are hot and delicious. And so is Daniel. But I'm not going to tell him that bit. Not yet, anyway.

After dinner we repack Daniel's duffel bag and stroll down the pier toward the fairground rides. Daniel is holding my hand and swinging it gently backward and forward. Despite the champagne, I am silenced by a sudden shyness, but Daniel doesn't appear to notice.

"So—which ride are we going on? Which one's your favorite?" he asks.

"The galloping horses. But it's closed."

The ride is in darkness, the brightly painted horses still and silent. Even though it's midwinter, some of the rides are still half full of passengers, screaming with fake fear on the ghost train and squealing as their stomachs lurch and their heads spin on the roller coaster. The slot machines rattle and ring all year round, swallowing money with appetites as insatiable as baby birds'. But the galloping horses are all asleep.

"Well, let's just pretend."

Daniel drags me over to the horses.

"Which one do you want to ride?"

With anyone else, I would just feel silly, but with him, somehow, it's all right. We climb up onto the carousel and I inspect the horses. Each has a name painted in swirling gold script along its neck.

"I want Jim."

He has a wild eye and his mane is twisted and curled as though by a stormy wind.

"Hop on and hold on tight."

My hands grip the golden barley-sugar-twisted pole in front of me, and I can feel the coldness of the metal even through my wooly gloves.

"Now close your eyes."

I hear Daniel walk away. As I sit there in the darkness, I am afraid that he has left me here and gone home. That I have said or done something wrong, and he has taken his chance to escape. Or maybe he has only done all of this for a bet, and I am "stupid Tilda' again, believing in magic where there is none. But then I remember Joseph Geronimo's words. No, more than remember, I can hear them in my head. Sometimes we have to learn to trust. And even though my eyes are still closed, I know that there are bright lights all around me, and I am slowly moving, and there is music. God, maybe I am drunk after all. I dare myself to open my eyes. The carousel is alive. This magic is real. Daniel is in the control booth. For at least ten seconds he manages an expression of cool nonchalance before dissolving into mad excitement. He punches the air with triumphant joy, like a small boy who has scored the winning goal in a game of football in the park. He disappears from the booth and clambers unsteadily across the wooden boards of the moving carousel to mount the horse next to Jim. Molly is a cheerful-looking white mare with blue eyes and a pink ribbon in her mane.

"How on earth did you manage all this?"

Daniel can't stop grinning.

"Joseph Geronimo."

"But how did you know that I would choose the horses?"

"I didn't. But he did. He said it was an absolute cert. And I said I'd bar him from the café for life if he was wrong."

Daniel pauses for a second, and then adds, almost to himself, "But then, he never is."

We are galloping at full speed now. The wind is styling my hair in the same tangled fashion as Jim's, and the lights are flashing past in a kaleidoscopic blur. All I can hear is the bright organ music, and Daniel whooping with joy. I want to stay here forever.

23

Tilly

W hy has Queenie got a dead dog on her poof?"
Tilly and her mother had unpacked and were
now taking in the remarkable splendor of the guests'
sitting room while waiting for their promised cups of
tea. It was clear from their surroundings that Queenie's
style of interior decor was as flamboyant and individual
as her fashion sense. Eli, who had appeared in their
room soon after Queenie had left it, showed little inter-
est in the rather odd-looking Pembrokeshire corgi, but
Tilly was fascinated. She poked at its fur with a tentative finger and then, with more confidence, at one of its
dark, glossy eyes.

"It's stuffed," she pronounced.

The taxidermist must have been having an off day,
for he had condemned the unfortunate little dog to
both an expression and a posture that suggested the
poor creature was suffering from the discomfort of
severe constipation. The dog's face was ruched into an
anxious frown and was staring in the direction of his
own bottom. Tilly had once seen a glass case full of
stuffed animals on a school trip to a museum. The rest
of the exhibits had been very boring: old bits of broken

pottery, funny-shaped rocks that were supposedly ancient tools but looked like stones that you could find all over the place in your own garden, and bits of old wooden farming equipment. The most exciting thing about the whole trip was when Rosemary Watson was sick on the bus. That and the glass case. It had held a fascination for Tilly that she didn't really understand.

"The eyes are made of glass," she said, adopting the manner of someone who was an expert in these matters.

"The real eyes would have gone squidgy and moldy and dribbled out onto the floor by now."

She paused in thought for a moment.

"Which hole do you think they put the stuffing in? His mouth or his—"

Tilly's question was cut short by the grand entrance of Queenie, bearing a huge tray draped in an elaborate lace doily and laden with tea things. Puffing gently with the effort, she set it down on a side table covered in a heavily fringed, red chenille tablecloth, and was just about to pour when the telephone rang in the hallway. Queenie bustled out again, inviting them to help themselves. Tilly was growing more impressed by the minute. First there had been the lovely Queenie and their beautiful room with its view of the pier; and now there was a stuffed dog and a telephone. Tilly didn't know many people who had a telephone inside their own house, or a stuffed dog for that matter. Her mother poured her a milky cup of tea and handed it to her.

"Now be careful not to spill it, Tilly. I think you would have been better off with a little mug," she added, almost to herself. But Tilly was delighted to be treated like a grown-up with a proper cup and saucer for once.

"Can I have some sugar please?"

Tilly's mother raised her eyebrows in puzzled surprise.

"But you don't like sugar in your tea."

"I know, but it's lumps."

"Just one then. Put your cup and saucer down first."

Tilly was desperate to get her hands on the little silver sugar tongs that were hanging tantalizingly from the edge of the cut-glass sugar bowl. She carefully replaced her cup and saucer on the tray, and took up the silver tongs. She almost managed to get the sugar to her cup and saucer, but was squeezing the tongs so tightly in her concentration, that at the crucial moment, the lump shot up into the air and landed on the carpet. Before her mother could say a word, Tilly quickly retrieved it and placed it on her saucer.

"Don't you want it in your tea?" her mother asked.

"No. I don't like sugar in my tea, do I? I just wanted a sugar lump."

There was also cake. Tilly's mother made her sit in a chair next to the table before she was allowed to choose. There were the pastel shades of sponge cake; rich, dark fruit cake; rock cakes knobbly with currants; and tiny jam tarts. Tilly chose sponge—not because she liked the taste, but because she liked its color and construction. Her mother passed her a small slice on a delicate, bone china tea plate decorated with red and gold roses. Once again, her mother rued the choice of such delicate crockery, but this time she did so silently. She didn't want to make Tilly nervous and therefore possibly precipitate any breakages. Crossed fingers would have to do. Tilly, completely undaunted by the best china, peeled off the marzipan that framed the slice and unstuck the four squares of sponge from each other; two pink and two yellow. She then licked the jam from the edges of the squares; first a pink one, then yellow, then pink, then yellow. That was really as far as she wanted to go with that particular cake, and she already had her eye on a green jam tart. But she knew that the chances of her getting it would be greatly improved if she ate the cake she already had first, and as her dress had no pockets in which to hide them, she ate the squares of sponge in the same order in which she had licked them. Just as she was about to make a plea for the jam tart, Queenie returned.

"Now, ladies, how are we getting on? Is everything all right for you? Is the tea hot enough? Do you need any more cake?"

Tilly did, but there was no pause to allow her to make this known. Queenie seated herself opposite her mother, crossed her ankles in a most elegant manner, and poured herself a cup of tea.

"Now, I want to hear everything that's happened since I saw you last. But first I want to tell you all about me and my beloved hotel!"

Queenie's lilac coiffure and sparkling jewels and Tilly's natural sense of curiosity in adults' conversations held her attention for a little, but deprived of the green jam tart and fascinated by her new surroundings, Tilly soon allowed Queenie's voice to drift into the background while she continued her inspection of the sitting room from her chair. A shiny upright piano stood against one wall, crowned with a vase of brightly colored plastic flowers and populated by a collection of china dogs of every size and breed imaginable. Tilly didn't count them, but she reckoned that there must be about a hundred. Or at least twenty. There was a grand marble fireplace flanked by two china statues. One was a young lady wearing old-fashioned clothes and with rather too much of her bosoms on show, who was holding a basket of oranges. The other was a man wearing a big hat and boots, who was smiling at the lady in a very friendly way. Tilly thought that either he must be her boyfriend, or that he was just after her oranges.

On the mantel shelf there was a mirror with a fancy gold frame, and a set of dangly, sparkly glass things that looked like candlesticks wearing earrings but had no actual place to put the candles. In the center of the shelf was an impressive mantel clock decorated with golden birds and fat babies with little wings; it had a very loud tick and an even louder chime, and struck every quarter of an hour. In between the non-candle-sticks and the clock was a selection of ornaments and boxes made completely out of shells. Above the piano was another picture of the queen, and skulking in vari-ous corners of the room was a splendid collection of lush green ferns and aspidistras sprouting from yet more gleaming brass pots on mahogany plant stands.

The curtains in the bay window were a complicated, layered arrangement, firstly of brilliant white lace, and then drawn-back, swagged and tasseled folds of heavy, deep gold velvet. On the windowsill stood a magnifi-cent glazed urn, covered in red, blue, and purple flowers and dragons, which held a bouquet of peacock feathers. In the center of the room was a high-backed Knoll sofa and two matching chairs, all of which were sporting embroidered and fringed antimacassars. Plonked, seemingly at random, in places where they were bound to get in the way, were several other upholstered chairs in various colors and patterns, but all similarly accessorized with antimacassars. Tilly thought that perhaps the guests played musical chairs in here.

"Good grief, is that the time? I must get on. No rest for the wicked."

Queenie's voice tuned back into the foreground, and as she gathered up the tea things onto the tray, she passed Tilly the green jam tart in a paper napkin.

"Keep it for later," she said with a wink.

After their tea and cake, they went for a walk along the beach, Eli trotting along just behind them, and Tilly, scarlet-cheeked and cheerfully bedraggled by the wind, darted back and forth toward the foaming fringes of the waves, squealing in delight each time the freezing water threatened to drench her good winter shoes. By midafternoon the orange sun was slipping down the sky behind the farthest edge of the sea, and Titian streaks shimmered on the distant water. The lights on the pier beckoned and Tilly's mother was unable to resist her daughter's pleading any longer. It was decided that they would not have dinner at The Paradise Hotel on their first night. Dinner there was not until 7 P.M., and they hadn't had any lunch, just tea and cake. They ate fish and chips sitting on a wooden bench on the pier. Tilly loved eating them straight from their newspaper wrapping. It was a rare treat. She smothered her fish and chips in salt, vinegar, and tomato ketchup, and breathed in the delicious vinegary steam before tucking in with the little wooden fork that came free with the chips. Tilly's mouth was soon dementedly lipsticked with ketchup, but her tummy was full and she couldn't stop smiling. Even her mother had managed to eat most of her dinner, and the seagulls were the grateful and greedy recipients of her leftovers. As she watched her mother eating, Tilly thought how her mother looked softer and happier than she had seen her in a long time. The sea air had brought color to her cheeks and a sparkle to her eyes. She looked like she'd been carrying bags of shopping that had been far too heavy, and had finally put them down.

After the fish and chips it was time for the funfair.

"Just one ride tonight, Tilly. Which one will it be?"

Tilly didn't even have to think about it.

"The horses, please."

The carousel of galloping horses was at the far end of the funfair, but Tilly had spotted it as soon as they had arrived. It was the first fair ride she had ever been on, and still the one she loved the best. The first time she had been far too small to ride alone so she had sat in her daddy's lap, her tiny, chubby legs barely long enough to straddle the seat. But she had laughed and clapped her hands in delight, forgetting, in her excitement, to hold on tight as her mother had told her, but she was safe in her daddy's arms. Her mother had stood on the ground watching them gallop round, and had waved each time they passed.

"Are you coming on too?" Tilly asked her mother.

Her mother looked uncertain, but tempted.

"You'll be all right. It doesn't go very fast. Come on. Please," Tilly coaxed.

Her mother gave in. As they flew round and round, and up and down in a whirl of lights, with the music and the sound of the seagulls echoing in their ears, Tilly saw a man standing by the ghost train who seemed to be looking straight at her. He was tall and dark with a neat little mustache, and very smartly dressed, but seemed to be a bit out of place. Tilly thought that he looked rather like a film star. He lifted his hat to her and waved as she galloped past. The next time she looked he had gone.

Tilda

The little blue diary has gone. I last saw it the night Daniel took me to the pier. I have searched for it everywhere, except, of course, the place where it is. I have crawled around on the floor, checked the kitchen cupboards and drawers, my pockets and the fridge. I have emptied the bin full of wine-soaked newspaper and broken glass. But it has disappeared without a trace; vanished into thin air; gone absent without leave. Daniel says it will turn up when I stop looking for it. I hope so, because while it is lost, so am I. I need to know what happened next.

Tilly

Tilly was terrified of boiled eggs. The fear of discovering a sharp, snipping beak and a pair of black, googly eyes staring up at her as she broke through the shell was as scary as an unexpected attack by a dozen grumpy Daleks on *Dr. Who*. And the thought of finding a slimy, green, stinky dead baby chicken floating in a cloudy, snot-like jelly was even worse, and almost more than Tilly's normally robust morning stomach could bear. She could feel the sick rising in the back of her throat and she swallowed hard. She never ate boiled eggs at home, but the one squatting menacingly in front of her had arrived without any prior warning whatsoever. It had been delivered by the magnificent Queenie, who was, this morning, squeezed into an emerald green dress that fit so tightly that Tilly thought it made her look like a zucchini. Her earrings were balls the size, shape, and color of cherry tomatoes dangling from delicate gold chains, and her bracelet of green beads looked exactly like a string of fresh peas. The overall effect, Tilly thought, was that of a rather glamorous vegetable patch.

But however much Tilly admired Queenie, there was still the problem of the egg. Breakfast had started well enough with the snap, crackle, and pop of Rice Krispies. There was a choice of cornflakes, bran flakes, Rice Krispies, or Grape-Nuts, which Tilly had tried once and thought was like crunching bits of grit and gravel. The cereals were kept in large plastic containers on a sideboard covered in an oilskin cloth decorated with baskets of fruit. The milk was in a big glass jug, and although Tilly had been allowed to pour her own Rice Krispies, and had managed to do so without allowing more than a sparse sprinkling to escape across the oilskin, her mother had insisted on pouring the milk. There was also a deep dish of stewed prunes, dark brown and with a sweet, earthy smell. Nobody seemed to be having any prunes. Her mother had managed a couple of spoonfuls of cornflakes instead of her usual cigarette and was now buttering a slice of toast. Tilly wondered if she could get away with just eating the soldiers.

"Now, young lady, don't let your lovely chucky egg get cold," warned Queenie as she sailed past with a plate piled high with sausages, bacon, eggs, and canned tomatoes. Tilly caught the whiff of a diversionary tactic and seized on it like a robin on a worm.

"What's a chucky egg?"

Her mother looked up from her toast.

"It just means a chicken's egg."

"What language is it in?"

"What?"

"Chucky. Is 'chucky' French for chicken?"

"No."

"Well, is it German?"

"No, it's—"

"American?"

The diversion was going well from Tilly's point of view, but she was running out of countries, and she knew that her mother's next "no' would be followed by a full stop.

"Is it Eyetie?" she asked, in desperation.

"Tilly!"

"What?"

"Don't use that word. It's not polite."

"Well, Uncle Bill says it. He says that Mr. Brunetti in the fish and chip shop is an 'Eyetie.'"

"I don't care what Uncle Bill says. You do not say 'Eyetie.'"

Tilly was quiet for a moment.

"What language is 'Eyetie'?"

Her diversion was up and running again.

"It's Italian, but—"

"So 'Eyetie' means 'Italian' in Italian?"

"Tilly, that's enough. Eat your egg."

Tilly stared mournfully at her egg. She touched the top of it very lightly with her fingertip.

"It's cold."

"Well, whose fault is that? Come on, Tilly, eat it up. You don't want to upset Queenie."

"It might bite me. I'm scared."

Tilly's mother rolled her eyes in exasperation. Ever since Tilly had been old enough to understand what eggs were, she had avoided them while they were still in their shells.

"How do you know there's not a tiny chicken in there waiting to peck me?"

"Because I do."

"But you don't. Nobody does until I open it, and then it's too late. I'm sure it moved. I saw it moving a really little bit. Twice."

Tilly's mother looked across at her small daughter's face crumpled into a scowl, and with her chin jutting in determination. She also saw the flicker of genuine fear in her eyes. Without a word, she reached across the table and snatched the dangerous egg. A moment later it was safely trapped in her handbag, and a huge smile of surprise and relief shone on Tilly's face.

With the egg disposed of, and a dollop of marmalade from her mother's plate to spread on her soldiers, Tilly was able to relax and examine both her surroundings and her fellow diners. The dining room was considerably less grand than the sitting room, but very cheerful and definitely made Tilly feel like she was on holiday, even though it was winter. The brightly colored wallpaper was a repeat pattern of a pretty lady wearing a short, flowery dress and a wide-brimmed straw hat, leading a smiling donkey wearing a matching hat and carrying two baskets of lemons. There were ten round tables covered in red, yellow, and white checked oilskin tablecloths, and on one wall a large display of photographs. Tilly thought the people in the photographs looked very interesting. They looked like the kind of people you saw at the circus, in magazines, or at the London Palladium. Tilly had never been to the London Palladium, but she had seen it once on the television. The man in charge talked very fast and was called Bob Monkeyhouse. And all the people in the photographs must be friends of Queenie's, because she was in the photographs too.

On either side of the display stood a small side table.

One acted as a pedestal for a large basket of plastic fruit: grapes, apples, oranges, lemons, cherries, and an impressive-looking pineapple; and on the other was a very pretty wire-work birdcage containing two yellow canaries, both of which were dead. And stuffed, of course. Tilly was desperate to get a closer look at both the canaries and the photographs, but knew better than to leave the table before she had finished eating. So instead, she turned her attention to the other people in the room. On a table in one corner, a middle-aged man in a brown suit with a tired face and dull eyes sat alone eating bacon and eggs. He chewed his food wearily, as though it gave him no more joy than eating a pair of old socks. And he had his elbows on the table. It was a good thing her mother had her back to him. As Tilly cut each of her soldiers in half and lined them up in two exactly straight rows, one with marmalade and one without, her gaze drifted to a couple eating toast and drinking tea. Both had beautiful table manners. The lady, who was very pretty, with blond hair swept into a French braid, was wearing a powder blue skirt suit and dabbed the corner of her mouth with her napkin after every sip of tea. Tilly would have bet her pocket money that she had a clean hanky in her pocket too. The man had neat, dark hair, parted at the side and shiny with hair cream. His eyes were bright blue and a neat mustache twitched jauntily on his top lip as he ate his toast with obvious pleasure. He was wearing a light gray jacket with dark trousers and a very white shirt, with a pale blue silk cravat at the neck. He caught Tilly's gaze and winked at her. Tilly was happy to return the wink with a smile.

There was a family struggling to get through breakfast while waging domestic war in stage whispers. The chubby, red-faced boy, who looked a year or so younger than Tilly, was kicking the leg of the table and demanding chocolate spread for his toast. The mummy was hissing through gritted teeth that there wasn't any, and he'd have to make do with jam. The girl, who was about Tilly's age and had long blond braids tied with pink ribbons, was poking her tongue out at her brother while pushing her scrambled egg from one side of her plate to the other and squashing it with her spoon. The daddy was shoveling huge forkfuls of sausage, beans, black pudding, and fried bread into his mouth as though someone was about to steal the plate from under his nose, only occasionally pausing for breath, and taking the opportunity to hiss at the mummy to "control those bloody children." Queenie wouldn't be pleased with that sort of language at the breakfast table, and Tilly didn't like the way that bits of food sprayed out of his mouth when he was hissing at the mummy. She was sure a bit of black pudding landed on the mummy's chin. Tilly couldn't understand why they were bothering to whisper, because everyone could hear everything anyway. Just as the daddy was cramming the last forkful of food into his already overstuffed mouth, Queenie sailed in and straight over to their table, where she gathered all their plates, including the uneaten toast and scrambled egg, with menacing speed, and swept out again flashing a smile that could chip granite. The family left without another word. Returning once more to the dining room, Queenie came to clear their table. She looked at Tilly's egg cup and plate, and then at Tilly, clearly registering the peculiar absence not only of egg but also eggshell. Tilly willed her not to say anything. Queenie paused for a moment, hand on hip, one eyebrow raised in a question-mark arch, before soothing Tilly with a wry grin.

"And where are you ladies off to today?"

26

Tilly

The lady in the blue suit with the blond hair, and her husband with the neat mustache and the wink were Bert and Effie Perkins. Tilly was bitterly disappointed. They were too posh to be called Bert and Effie Perkins. It was like finding out that the queen's real name was Dolly, and that instead of living in a heavenly palace, God lived in a bungalow. But Bert and Effie were redeemed when Tilly learned that they were amateur ballroom dancing champions. That single fact put them right up there with Black Beauty, the Virgin Mary, and Charlie's Angels as far as Tilly was concerned. Effie had already promised to show Tilly her dresses and paint her fingernails for her. The man in the brown suit, who ate his food so joylessly with his elbows on the table, was called Mr. Rubbing and sold encyclopedias door to door. According to Queenie, he was "just passing through," and not a "regular." Bert and Effie were very regular, and came every time there was a dancing competition in the ballroom on the pier. The family with the daddy who swore and stuffed his food had gone, and "Good riddance!" Queenie had said. After they had paid the bill. Now there was a new family staying, with twin boys called Tom and Jerry. Tilly had laughed very loudly when they told her because she had thought it was a joke. But it wasn't. In fact, she soon found out that the boys were very serious about most things, and especially about collecting tea and cigarette cards. They spent ages looking at the ones they'd already gotten and talking about the ones they needed. Tilly didn't think that they were going to be friends.

So much had happened in just a week. Tilly and her mother should have been going home tomorrow, but now they weren't. They might not be going home at all. That morning her mother had told her that Queenie needed some more help to run The Paradise Hotel, and had offered Grace a job. Her mother had asked Tilly what she thought about staying on. She said that it would mean changing schools and leaving some friends behind, but reminded her of how much she loved Queenie and living so close to the pier, and reassured Tilly that she would soon make some new friends. It would be a fresh start for them both, she had said. Tilly pretended to think about it for a bit, because she thought that was what her mother wanted. She already felt released from the painful knots and tangles of their old life, but most important of all, in Queenie's house she felt safe. It was true that she would miss going to church with Mrs. O'Flaherty. But there must be a nice church here too, and perhaps Mrs. O'Flaherty could come and visit. She was sure that Mrs. O'Flaherty and Queenie would get on like a house on fire. It was also true that she would miss Auntie Wendy and Karen, but she still wasn't convinced that Auntie Wendy was their friend anymore anyway. Eli had already made himself quite at home. Her mother looked happier than Tilly had seen her in a long time. Here, nobody nudged and whispered about them in the street, or looked down their noses at them when they went into a shop. But more important, here they had Queenie. Tilly couldn't believe that all this time her mother had had a friend that she had never even heard about. But now they both had her, Tilly never wanted to let her go. In the end, she decided it was a choice between boiled cabbage with half a fish finger, or a great big plate of chips. Tilly chose chips. Queenie said that they could keep their lovely room at the top of the house, but after tomorrow, they were to eat with the others in the back dining room. Tilly couldn't wait. She had never been in a back dining room and she was very keen to meet the others.

She didn't have to wait very long to meet one of them. It was later that afternoon when her mother was having one of her little lie-downs and Tilly was exploring the house. She thought that if she was going to be living there, it was important that she should get to know the whole house. She also wanted to see the garden. Perhaps Queenie grew her own fruit and vegetables too, although it didn't seem very likely. Maybe she had garden gnomes instead, like Auntie Wendy. Tilly headed toward the back of the house down a long corridor past the kitchen. She was looking for a back door into the garden, but before she found one she came across a funny little staircase not at all like the grand, sweeping affair with all the ferns and brass pots at the front of the house. This one only had four steps to the first landing before it turned and continued up.

On the landing was a door, and it was the door, or rather the music coming from behind it, that caught Tilly's attention. It was dancing music, soft and floating at first like feathers on a pond, but growing faster and wilder, like the wind whorling the leaves into autumn skies.

Tilly stood at the door, rapt. The crackle of a needle skimming across the old record broke the spell.

"Who's there?"

The voice came from behind the door and caught Tilly completely off guard.

"No one."

"Well, there must be someone there to say 'no one.'"

It was a woman's voice, scrattled with old age, but with the tone of a proper lady and not at all cross.

"I only meant no one you know," Tilly floundered.

"How do you know that I don't know you?"

"Because I don't know who you are."

"But that doesn't mean that I don't know who you are."

The voice from behind the door didn't answer back like a normal grown-up; it was much craftier and almost as good at answering back as her. Tilly thought for a moment and then replied.

"Who am I, then?"

"Well, if you come in here, I'll tell you."

Tilly was well versed in children's fairy tales. She knew that talking to strangers usually led to trouble of one sort or another. Look what had happened to Hansel and Gretel and Snow White. But this was Queenie's house, and Tilly couldn't see her renting rooms to people who ate small children, or wicked stepmothers. Besides, Tilly was curious. She couldn't help herself. She turned the brass knob slowly and gently pushed open the door. The woman sitting up in the huge bed looked to Tilly as if she were at least a hundred years old. Her long, gray, wispy hair stuck out from her head like an explosion of cobwebs, and her face was as wrinkled as the pushed-back skin on top of a rice pudding. Her lips were shiny red with lipstick and a slick of sky blue covered each of her eyelids. Her cheeks were overripe wrinkly apples of rouge and she was wearing a black satin evening gown that was cut to display a generous amount of the crack between her bosoms. She wore long white gloves that stretched over her elbows, and a white feather boa. She might be old, Tilly thought, but she certainly hadn't let herself go as Auntie Wendy would have said. But why was she still in bed at gone three o'clock in the afternoon? Tilly looked round the room for the telltale signs of illness, a bottle of Lucozade and a new comic, but saw none.

"Are you poorly?" she asked.

"No. What makes you ask?"

"Because you're still in bed and it's the afternoon."

"Yes. But it's Friday."

As an explanation, it meant nothing to Tilly, but her thoughts had already moved on.

"Well," she said, hands on hips, "who am I then?"

The woman studied her carefully for a moment through a pair of spectacles with a long handle on one side.

"You're a little girl."

"Yes, but which little girl?"

"Well, for heaven's sake, child, if you don't know who you are, then you can hardly expect me to know."

"But I do know. I'm Tilly."

The woman nodded her head as if to acknowledge that Tilly had answered correctly.

"And what precisely are you doing here, Tilly?"

"I'm looking for the garden."

"Well, you won't find it in here, and anyway, that's not what I meant. What are you doing here, in this house?"

"Today I'm on holiday, but tomorrow I start living here."

"In the garden?"

"No . . ." Tilly began to answer but realized from the woman's smile that she was teasing her. Her gaze moved away from the woman's face to explore her surroundings. It was a pretty room, full of light from a large window. Next to the bed, on a small cabinet, was a wind-up gramophone, and by the window was a button-back chair strewn with fringed silk shawls and dressing gowns. A dressing table with a trio of mirrors was littered with beauty creams and potions, makeup, and sparkling glass bottles of perfume. On the floor were several drunken towers of old magazines: *The Lady*, *Vogue*, and *Harper's Bazaar*. And then there were the boxes. Every available space and surface was taken up by music boxes of all shapes, colors, and sizes. Tilly was fascinated. The old woman saw Tilly staring at the boxes and suddenly her mood changed.

"Off you go now. I'm very busy."

It seemed Tilly's visit was over. She desperately wanted to play with the boxes, but she was clearly being dismissed. Reluctantly she turned to leave, but with her hand still on the cold brass doorknob, she turned back for a moment.

"Excuse me, lady, but what's your name?"

"Anita Ekberg."

27

Tilly

A re you sure it was Anita Iceberg?"
Tilly's mother was brushing her hair and putting on her lipstick, guided by the reflection in the bathroom mirror.

"Well, it sounded like 'Iceberg,' and it was definitely 'Anita.'"

Tilly was watching her mother deftly coloring her mouth, two arcs on the top lip and a single sweep across the bottom. She pressed her lips together and kissed the air with a soft "puck' sound. Tilly had tried this once herself with a red felt-tip pen. The result hadn't been quite what she was hoping for. Tilly's mother was wondering exactly who it was that her daughter had encountered during her exploration of the house. Anita Iceberg was only a slip of the tongue away from the film star who had frolicked seductively in the Trevi Fountain in Fellini's celebrated *La Dolce Vita*, but it was hardly likely that Queenie was harboring a famous Swedish sexpot in her very respectable and very British establishment. Tilly's mother smiled to herself at the absurdity of such a notion.

"Come along, Tilly, let's go down for dinner."

*   *   *

The next morning, Tilly was wide awake long before the first feeble light had trickled through the crack between the bedroom curtains. Today was the start of their new life. Today they began living at the seaside, and from today they belonged to The Paradise Hotel, and Queenie became truly their Queenie. Today they would have breakfast in the back dining room with the others. Tilly lay on her back staring up at the ceiling, where she could just make out the faint mark that looked like a penguin riding a bicycle. She wondered who "the others" might be. There would be Queenie, of course, and the old lady with the mad hair called Anita, but who else? Perhaps Queenie had a husband hidden away at the back of the house, who worked in an office all day. Tilly was pretty sure that Queenie didn't have any children, although she couldn't really explain why, but perhaps she had a couple of servants. She looked the sort of person who might have servants. And there was definitely a cook, because Tilly had heard Queenie talking about her with one of the guests at dinner last night. The guest had said that his pork chop was "a bit tough" and Queenie had said that she would "advise cook of your opinion," but Tilly wasn't convinced. Queenie had looked more likely to whack him round the chops with his chop. Eli was sitting at the bottom of Tilly's bed with his chin resting on the edge of the eiderdown, watching her. It was as though he too knew that there was something different about today. Queenie had never mentioned him. Even though he followed Tilly just about everywhere, including into the dining room, she had never said a word. It was as though she couldn't see him. Tilly knew that it was sometimes better not to draw attention to certain things. She didn't always get it right, but she was pretty sure that Eli was one of them. Besides, he seemed happy enough to be living here, and as far as Tilly was concerned, that was the main thing.

After what seemed like a week, she heard her mother stirring. In five minutes Tilly was up and dressed, having washed and cleaned her teeth in record time, and sat fidgeting on her bed while her mother got ready at a more leisurely pace. Each stage of her mother's early morning routine seemed to be taking place in slow motion, as though she was underwater. Her hairbrush wafted through the air like the queen of England waving on a day when she was very tired, instead of at its usual brisk and efficient pace. The decision between a dark green woolen dress and a navy skirt with a camel-colored sweater took longer than Tilly would have taken to choose between chocolate and strawberry ice cream. And they were her favorites. This was worse than waiting to open presents on Christmas morning.

"Come on!" she pleaded, her impatience finally bubbling over like a pan of boiling milk.

"Tilly, Queenie said that breakfast was at six thirty and it's still only quarter past."

"Yes, which means that if we're not there in fifteen minutes we'll be late and make a bad expression on our first day."

Her mother smiled to herself, hearing her own words, or rather a version of them, spoken back to her by her daughter.

"It doesn't take fifteen minutes to walk downstairs to the dining room."

"Yes, but we're not going to the dining room, we're going to the *back* dining room, which is farther away. And anyway, someone may have fallen halfway down the stairs and broken a leg and be blocking the way, and then we'll have to wait for an ambulance."

Tilly paused to assess the effect of her pronouncement of doom.

"They might have broken both legs. And an arm."

Fortunately, the staircase proved to be casualty free, and they arrived at the door of the back dining room with one minute to spare. Before going in, her mother turned to Tilly as though she were going to say something, but instead knocked softly on the door, which immediately flew open to reveal a small, sturdy-looking woman wearing a long apron with large pockets and a pair of black boots that would have looked more at home on a sailor.

"Come in! Come in!" she said, ushering them into the room. "There's no need for knocking here. You're not the bleedin' gas man."

She laughed heartily at her own joke, and as she did so, Tilly noticed that one of her front teeth was missing.

"It's a pleasure to meet you both, I'm sure. I'm Lil, the cook."

Tilly had a feeling that she was going to get on very nicely with Lil.

"Sit down and help yourselves to tea. We don't have no airs and graces down here."

They sat down at the table, and just as Tilly's mother was pouring tea into blue-and-white-striped mugs, the door banged open and a young girl of about seventeen rushed in, breathing hard and red in the face. She threw her battered brown bag on the floor and began frantically struggling to get out of her old navy raincoat as though she was trying to strip off cold wet clothes. In the middle of her desperate wriggling and writhing, she looked up and saw Tilly and her mother and her face turned even redder.

"I'm late," she gasped. "The missus'll kill me."

"And serves you right, my girl." Lil marched through the swinging door that adjoined the kitchen to the back dining room, carrying a heap of toast on one plate and rashers of bacon on another. "You're always bleedin' late!"

She turned to Tilly and her mother as she slammed the plates down on the table.

"This is Cecily. She helps with the cleaning and the housekeeping. When she eventually turns up."

Tilly looked at the scrawny girl who had finally managed to escape from the clutches of her old school raincoat, and thought that she had never seen anyone who looked less like a Cecily. A proper Cecily should have blond curls, blue eyes, rosy cheeks, and a lovely pink dress. And a kitten. This one had tangled, mousy hair that looked like it hadn't seen a brush since last Tuesday, eyes the color of jellied eels, and spotty, flushed cheeks. Tilly didn't suppose for one moment that she had a kitten. She looked more likely to have lice.

Cecily snatched a piece of toast from the plate and held it between her teeth while she grabbed a mug and sloshed tea into it.

"Cecily! Sit down properly at the table and use a plate. We are not savages, my girl, so please try not to behave like one."

Queenie had glided silently through the other door, and on her arm was the mad hair lady who was wearing a pair of black capri pants that were rather tighter than they ought to have been, black pumps, and a cream-colored sweater with a silk scarf tied at the neck. Some of her hair had been persuaded into a French braid, and her eyes were heavily and haphazardly ringed with black eyeliner. Queenie helped the old lady to her seat at the table.

"Good morning, ladies. I should like you to meet my mother, Audrey Hepburn."

Tilly stared at Queenie openmouthed. This was definitely the same old lady that she had met yesterday. So, one of them had told a whopper. Mindful of her new status as belonging to The Paradise Hotel, Tilly got straight to the point.

"But yesterday, you said you were Anita Iceberg."

The old lady peered at Tilly across the table and smiled in recognition.

"I remember you. You're the little girl who's going to live in the garden."

"But you said you were Anita Iceberg," Tilly persisted.

"I said nothing of the sort. I said I was Anita Ekberg, because yesterday was Friday. Today is Saturday."

As an explanation, Tilly found it completely unsatisfactory, but her mother's hand on her arm made it quite clear that it would have to do. Queenie, meanwhile, had poured Audrey some tea in a bone china cup and saucer and placed it in front of her. Audrey poured some of the tea from the cup into the saucer and lifted it to her lips to drink, her eyes scanning the table. Her mother's hand gripped Tilly's arm even tighter, imploring her daughter's silence. Tilly was certain that she would have a bruise.

"And who, pray, is this one?"

Audrey waved her index finger at Tilly's mother as though she was trying to hook a fish.

"I'm Grace. It's nice to meet you." Tilly's mother smiled and stretched her hand across the table toward the old lady, but her answer had not gone down well with Audrey, who had set down her saucer and drawn herself up in her seat, ready to pounce.

"You most certainly are not!" she retorted imperiously. "I'm Grace. But not until Wednesday!"

Lil breezed back in from the kitchen with a plate of sausages and sat down at the table with them.

There was one seat at the table still empty. As Tilly carefully cut her toast and jam into neat squares, she wondered who they were waiting for. As though she had read her mind, Queenie spoke.

"Reg won't be joining us this morning. He had to go in early."

Tilly had to ask.

"Is Reg your husband?"

Lil inhaled some of the tea she was drinking and then snorted it out, almost choking with laughter. Even Cecily paused momentarily from eating as much toast as she could, as quickly as she could, to stifle a high-pitched giggle. Queenie ignored them and turned to Tilly.

"Reg is our permanent lodger and we couldn't do without him. He works at the pier and looks after the ballroom. You'll meet him tonight at dinnertime."

Tilly was thrilled. He sounded perfect. Watching Cecily devour slice after slice of toast and bacon, Tilly wondered where she put it all. Perhaps under that baggy dress of hers she had an enormous, round tummy. Lil drank three mugs of tea and ate three sausages between two slices of bread and butter while smoking a roll-up cigarette. Queenie nibbled at toast and marmalade. Audrey spread a slice of toast with something called anchovy paste from a little tin and dipped it in Cecily's mug of tea. Tilly couldn't remember when she had last enjoyed breakfast so much.

When everyone was finished, Lil and Cecily cleared the table and Cecily washed up while Lil began cooking food for the guests. Queenie helped Audrey up from her chair.

"I'll just take Mother back to her room, and then we'll go upstairs and start taking the breakfast orders."

As Audrey tottered to the door, leaning heavily on Queenie's arm, she turned and spoke to Tilly.

"Come and see me again, little girl, and I'll show you my music boxes."

When they had gone, Tilly's mother turned to her with a hopeful look on her face.

"Well, Tilly, what do you think?"

Tilly grinned.

"I think it's heaven."

28

Tilda

The cinema is a tiny, forgotten jewel hidden among the bric-a-brac buildings of a tired-looking back-street. It belongs to a film club and Daniel has brought me here to see *Breakfast at Tiffany's*.

"Don't think that you're going to have it all your own way," he joked. "Next time it's going to be *The Silence of the Lambs*."

Inside, the cinema is a lavish confection of red velvet and gold leaf. There are just ten rows of red velvet seats and the heavy curtain that is currently hiding the screen boasts extravagant swags and fringing. Plump golden cherubs entwined with flowers and leaves frolic across the ceiling, glowing in the soft light of two ridiculously over-sized but nonetheless beautiful chandeliers. It reminds me of the ballroom where I used to go for dance lessons while I was living at Queenie's. Daniel and I are swapping family histories while waiting for the film to begin.

"My dad was a taxidermist before he retired."

I immediately think of Queenie's corgi.

"Was he really?" I'm intrigued.

"No." Daniel laughs and shakes his head regretfully.

"I'm just trying to make my lot sound more interesting. They've got a bit to live up to in comparison with yours. But my mum does have double-jointed thumbs *and* my eldest sister, Maggie, does a mean impersonation of the soup dragon from *The Clangers*."

"She sounds lovely." I mean it too. "So, what did your dad really do?"

"He ran a café in the East End of London, mainly for market traders and cabbies. My sisters took it over when he retired, and, in his words, 'poncified it up.' Its customers now are mainly city traders and tourists, but a couple of the old regulars still go in there if they see Dad sitting in the corner drinking builder's tea and tutting over the mocha cappuccinos, or 'crappuccinos' as he calls them."

"So how come you didn't take over from your dad?"

Daniel shakes his head with an expression of mock horror on his face.

"God, Tilda, I've grown up in a houseful of women. I've got an Irish mother, three sisters, and more aunties than any man deserves. Much though I love each and every one of them, except maybe Auntie Yvonne, a man needs his own space eventually."

The seats are filling up now, but the lights are still up and the curtain closed.

"What's wrong with Auntie Yvonne?"

"She has an awful funny smell about her. And she wears suspenders on her socks."

Fair enough.

"So, you came here and got your own place?"

"My sisters bought my share in Dad's old café, and I

had always loved the sea. My mum blames the smell of the fishmonger's that used to be on the corner of our street."

"And what about Joseph Geronimo? How do you know him?"

For the first time there's hesitation in Daniel's easy flow of words, and the hint of a puzzled frown flits across his open face.

"He's a bit of a man of mystery, is our Mr. J. G. I remember him coming into my dad's place a few times. Always said he was 'just passing through.' But he's the kind of man you never forget. And then, a few months after I came here, he swaggered into the café and he's been about ever since."

The hesitation returns, and I'm curious.

"What? What is it?"

"I don't know. There's this thing with him. He always seems to be there when you really need someone; as if, somehow, he knows. He's like the big brother I never had."

Daniel squeezes my hand.

"But he's a devil with the women, so you watch yourself. You're spoken for now."

I can feel my cheeks grow hot. I feel like I should have felt when I was a teenager, but never did. Maybe he *is* "my Daniel' now.

"What about you?" Daniel wriggles down into his seat. "We've done mine; what about yours?"

I'm willing the lights to dim and the curtain to open, but it remains stubbornly shut. I take a deep breath.

"Well, as I told you, my dad died when I was seven, and my mother and I were never close." The standard lines trip easily off my tongue. "She sent me away to boarding school and I hated it. I wanted to stay living at Queenie's. I loved it there. It was . . ." I search for the right word. "Magical. It was magical."

"So why did your mum send you away?"

"I don't know but I hated her for it. She said it was for my own good, to get a proper education. But I never believed that was the real reason. It always felt more like some sort of excuse."

"Blimey. Did you never ask her why?"

It seems such an obvious thing, but I have to think about it. I know I did at the time. As a child. "Why? Why? Why?" But I never got a satisfactory answer. But as an adult? I'm not sure I did. Maybe I stopped believing that it would make any difference, that whatever excuse she came up with could never be good enough. Maybe by then the distance between us had become too fixed. Daniel is clearly struggling to understand a family existence so different from his loving, cheek-by-jowl, bustling nest of mum and dad, sisters and aunties.

"And you were never close to your mum? Even before she sent you away?"

I'm so used to saying it to fob people off, to explain away our strange rift; but was it really true? Had it always been like that? I remember loving her until I thought I would burst when she fixed the tree lights that first Christmas after my dad died. And that first night at Queenie's when she took me on the galloping horses. I can still see her hair blowing in the wind and her dress billowing. She was so beautiful, and I was so proud of her. So where did it all go so terribly, irrevocably wrong? Daniel's questions are pebbles thrown into the pond and the ripples are spreading. As the lights dim and the curtain swishes open, it's more than just an old film beginning; it's a new version of an old life. I need to understand what happened. I need to find out the whole truth. But who can I ask now?

29

Tilly

Cecily was honking and gasping and wobbling her head about on the end of her long, skinny neck. Her eyes were bulging and watering and she was holding a cigarette between her finger and thumb as far away from her face as the length of her fully stretched arm would allow. Tilly was rolling around on the grass laughing.

"How can we possibly transform you into an elegant swan when you insist on behaving like a galumphing goose?"

Marlene was reclining languorously in a deck chair with a striped canopy, smoking a cigarette from a ridiculously long ebony holder. She was wearing wide-legged gray slacks, a man's shirt, and a demeanor of exaggerated boredom. Her mad hair was tucked into an odd-looking bob and her face was virtually obscured by a wide-brimmed hat and enormous sunglasses. Marlene was always losing her cigarette lighter, so she had appointed Tilly her "little match girl." It was a role Tilly was more than happy to fulfill, giving her plenty of opportunity to play with the little sticks of magic that Marlene doled out to her like candies.

Marlene was teaching Cecily to smoke, to give her "an air of sophistication" and therefore make her "more alluring to the opposite sex." Cecily had taken a fancy to a young man called Sidney who sold doughnuts on the pier, but her attempts to seduce him had so far only resulted in far more doughnuts than were good for her purse, waistline, or complexion. Tilly was hoping that once Cecily had learned to smoke properly she might be persuaded to teach her. Not that Tilly had any wish to get a boyfriend. She just thought it would be a good trick to know; it involved matches, making it particularly attractive, and it reminded her of her daddy. She had been practicing on her own in her room with rolled-up bits of paper torn from one of her school exercise books, but it wasn't quite the same without the setting on fire bit, which she had so far resisted. She didn't want The Paradise Hotel to meet the same sad end as her daddy's shed. Marlene lowered her sunglasses and peered critically at Cecily, who was still coughing and wiping her nose on her sleeve. She shook her head despairingly and retreated behind her sunglasses.

Tilly lay back on the grass and wriggled contentedly in the hot summer sun. So much had happened in the last few months. She felt like she had been at The Paradise Hotel forever. She had finished two terms at her new school, and one day when she had gotten home her things had arrived in boxes from their old house. She had sent postcards to Auntie Wendy and Mrs. O'Flaherty, but neither had replied yet. That old life seemed so far away now. She still missed her daddy of course. The pain would sometimes buckle her like a stubbed toe. But their new life was such a sea of color and bustle and different people that the pain was quickly washed away by the tide. Her mother was busy all day with Queenie, and seemed so happy, and now Tilly never had to come home to just her mother, wondering if it would be Gracie or the Kraken that she would find. Reg had turned out to be a lovely man with brown eyes, a quiff of black, shiny hair, and a tattoo of a lady in a swimsuit on his forearm. He called Tilly "sweetheart," her mother "Gracelands," Lil "Lily Lilo," and Cecily "Silly." But Queenie was always Queenie. It felt like they were a family, and it was the first proper family that Tilly had ever had. Now it was the school holidays and Reg had promised to take Tilly with him to the ballroom. Bert and Effie were due back next week for a big dance competition and Cecily was taking her for a doughnut on the pier later that afternoon.

The smoking lesson wasn't a great success and ended with Cecily being sick over a pot of purple petunias. Lil, who had been watching through the kitchen window while rolling pastry for that night's steak and onion pie, came into the garden wiping the flour from one hand on her apron and holding a glass of water in the other, which she handed to Cecily.

"Very ladylike, I must say. I'm sure Sidney will be very impressed."

Cecily took the glass gratefully and inspected the petunias from a safe distance.

"The missus'll kill me when she sees that."

Marlene flicked the ash from her cigarette into a half-empty glass of lemonade that was standing on a small tray next to her deck chair.

"Don't be ridiculous, girl! The birds will eat it."

She took a final, deep draw and then dropped the cigarette, still in its holder, into the glass. Tilly was lying on her tummy, propped up on her elbows.

"You should drink all that water, Cecily. Sidney won't want to kiss you with bits of sick between your teeth."

"I don't want him to kiss me," Cecily said, gulping down the rest of the water anyway. "I just want to be friends. I don't know what makes you think I want him to kiss me."

"Maybe it's the year's supply of doughnuts you've eaten in the last two weeks, and the cotton wool you stuff down your bra when you go to buy them," said Lil, who took the empty glass from Cecily and picked up the tray next to Marlene. She looked at Cecily's red face and her manner softened.

"Now go and wash your hands and face and help Gracie set the tea things. I'll give you a squirt of perfume before you go out."

Marlene stirred a little in her chair and looked at the place on her wrist where her watch should have been if only she could remember where she'd left it.

"Is it time for my gin yet?"

An hour later, Cecily and Tilly were strolling hand in hand toward the pier, closely trailed by Eli. Tilly didn't really want to hold hands these days. She felt she was too grown up now. But today she was making an exception. Today she was holding hands with Cecily to make Cecily feel better. Cecily's hand was cold and clammy. She had brushed her hair and scraped it back from her face and then tied it into a ponytail high on the back of her head. It was pulled so tight that Tilly thought it made her face look a bit surprised. She had dabbed her cheeks with some rouge that Marlene had provided rather grudgingly after relentless pleading on Cecily's part, and sprayed herself liberally with some perfume Lil had found that had been left behind by one of the guests. Moonwind by Avon.

"Do I look pretty?" she had asked Tilly, when she was ready. Tilly thought that the honest answer would be "no," and the kind but untrue answer would be "yes," so she chose one in the middle, hoping to avoid both Cecily's disappointment and God sending her to Bermondsey for lying.

"You look much prettier than you normally do. And you smell lovely."

The promenade was crawling with holidaymakers buying buckets and spades for their sandcastles, and postcards, and cheap and cheerful souvenirs for the neighbors who were minding their goldfish and para-keets. The man with the funny accent was mending his fishing nets as usual, with his permanent cigarette flut-tering up and down between his lips as he greeted them. Tilly waved at him and smiled.

"You should get him to teach you how to smoke. He's really good at it," she said.

"Who?" said Cecily with a distracted frown that struggled to wrinkle her ponytail-stretched forehead. Walter's fish stall was doing a brisk trade selling cockles and winkles in little cardboard baskets, and the sharp smell of vinegar cutting through the air made Tilly's mouth water. She would rather have had some cockles doused in vinegar than a doughnut any day, but Cecily said they looked like dead baby birds and made her heave. And, more important, Walter wasn't Sidney. Outside Madame Petulengro's velvet-curtained kiosk, a snake of people wriggled and fidgeted in the hot sun, anxious to know if a big win on the football pools was reflected in the crystal ball, or if a tall, dark, handsome stranger was on the tarot cards. Tilly had brought some pennies with her from her money box to buy yet another windmill for the small area in the garden that Queenie had given her to plant whatever she liked. At the moment, Tilly was planting windmills. Ena saw them coming.

"Let me guess. Is it another windmill you're after?"

She and Ralph sold buckets and spades, sticks of rock, postcards and all sorts of little toys, ornaments and tea towels proudly proclaiming their seaside origins. And, of course, windmills.

"Well, Cecily, you're looking very la-di-dah today. Are you two off anywhere special?"

Cecily was already too red in the face from the afternoon sun and Marlene's rouge for her blush to show, but nerves made her throat telltale dry and her answer was brief and mumbled.

"Just going for a walk."

Tilly chose a red and yellow windmill and handed her money to Ena.

"And to see Sidney at the doughnut stall," she added helpfully.

Cecily's grip on Tilly's hand was a little firmer than was friendly as she dragged Tilly away. Tilly liked that she knew the names of the people in the little shops and stalls along the promenade and that they knew her back. It made her feel as though she belonged, and it made her feel safe. But there was one man whose name she still didn't know. He was the man she had seen on the first night when she was on the galloping horses with her mother; the handsome man with the mustache. He always had the same clothes on, whatever the weather: a dark suit, a gabardine raincoat, and his hat. She didn't think that he was following her, and he never came very near, but he always seemed to be around whenever Tilly was on the promenade or pier. It was as though he were watching out for her. Today he was standing on the pavement of the street above them, leaning over the turquoise wrought-iron railings. He tipped his hat at Tilly and smiled, and she waved back at him. Eli lifted his head, following Tilly's gaze and hesitating slightly before continuing his loping trot at her side.

"Who were you waving at?" Cecily asked, shading her eyes with one hand and looking across the road.

"That man in the hat."

"Do you know him?" said Cecily, still searching.

"Well, not really. But sort of."

"Well," said Cecily, turning her attention back to Tilly and adopting a superior tone of voice, "I don't think that you should be waving to strange men. It's not safe. He might be a pervert or something."

"What's a pervert?"

Cecily floundered, suddenly out of her depth.

"It's a man with peculiar interests."

"What, like stamp collecting?"

Tilly's question went unanswered, as they had now arrived dangerously close to Sidney's doughnut stall.

There was a small line, but Cecily hung back. Tilly peered round the people waiting in line to get a good look at Sidney and saw a short, stocky youth with pale skin splattered with freckles and a fiercely ginger frizz of curls. She tugged at Cecily's hand.

"Come on!"

She dragged Cecily to join the end of the line and fussed and fidgeted in excitement while waiting to see what the two young lovers would do when they finally came face-to-face. At last it was their turn. Sidney barely looked up.

"What would you like?"

"She'd like to kiss you!" The words trumpeted out in Tilly's head, but fortunately didn't get as far as her mouth.

"Four please." Cecily kept her eyes firmly fixed on her purse.

"Righto, luv."

Cecily shoved some coins toward him, grabbed the bag of doughnuts, and marched Tilly away, her "thank you very much' trailing in her wake.

They sat on a bench eating their doughnuts, with a welcome breeze from the sea blowing in their faces. Tilly smiled at Cecily as she licked the sugar from her fingers.

"You've still got a bit of sick on your dress."

30

Tilly

"He's ginger," announced Tilly, while carefully dissecting her steak pie into equal pieces.

Queenie's hand quickly closed over her mother's.

"Hair, dear, not Rogers."

Marlene helped herself to a forkful of peas from Reg's plate.

"Never heard of her."

They were all seated around the table eating dinner, and Tilly was eagerly updating them on the progress of the prospective lovebirds.

Lil was particularly keen to hear more about the object of Cecily's affection.

"And what did he say to her?"

For a moment, Tilly considered making the story more exciting, but ever mindful of the risk of Bermondsey, decided against it.

"He said, 'Righto, luv.'"

"And that was it?"

"Well, Cecily said, 'Thank you very much' but I don't think he heard it."

"Blimey," said Reg, "it's not exactly *Brief Encounter*, is it?" He was gallantly ignoring Marlene, who was stealing more of his peas.

"It's such a shame. She spent so long getting ready, and she seems really keen on him," said Tilly's mother, pouring more orange squash into Tilly's glass.

"Maybe Effie could help her look more beautiful. She always looks lovely, and she's coming this weekend."

"Now, Tilly, you're not to go bothering the guests."

"But Effie said I was welcome to go and see her any time I liked."

"Yes, but she was probably just being polite."

Tilly thought about this as she put the last piece of steak and onion pie, topped with three peas, into her mouth.

"So, being polite is the same as lying then?"

"Ha!" said Reg, grinning. "She's got you there, Gracelands!"

Gracie rolled her eyes and sighed.

"It's not always that simple, Tilly. Sometimes people say that you can do something because they're being nice, but they don't really expect you to do it."

"But that's not very nice if they don't mean it, is it? And it's lying." Bermondsey was going to be very crowded.

"Tell the truth and shame the devil," said Marlene, starting on her own peas now that Reg's were all gone.

Lil was still thinking about Sidney.

"Well, that girl's never going to get anywhere with him if she doesn't try a bit harder than that."

"I never had to try," said Marlene, sipping her gin and winking at Reg. "Men cluster to me like moths around a flame, and when their wings burn, I know I'll get the blame," she wavered like a harmonica short of air.

"Quite right," said Reg, "but then Silly doesn't possess your wealth of womanly charms."

Marlene attempted a seductive smile for Reg's benefit, but the effect was rather spoiled by the bits of pea caught among her dentures.

Lil shook her head and started gathering up the plates.

"It's like living in a bleedin' madhouse, here," she said good-humoredly. "Who wants some dessert?"

Over plums and custard, Queenie entertained them with a story about one of the guests whose false teeth had fallen into the soup of the woman sitting opposite him when he bit into a particularly crusty roll.

"What did he do?" asked Tilly, giggling.

"He fished them out, sucked them clean, and popped them back in his mouth again."

"What did she do?"

"She ordered the shrimp cocktail."

Tilly lined up her plum pits around the edge of her dish. Her daddy had taught her a rhyme that began "Tinker, tailor, soldier, sailor' and said that she could count pits using the rhyme, and that would tell her who she would marry. Tilly wasn't sure if she wanted to get married, but if she did, it wouldn't be to anyone like that. So she made up her own rhyme.

"Pirate, gypsy, Father Christmas, Tarzan, magician, man-in-charge-of-the-galloping-horses." The last one had used to be Doctor Who, but she had changed it when she came to live here. Today it was Tarzan's lucky day. She decided that she would make up a special rhyme for Cecily to use that might cheer her up. It would probably have a doughnut seller in it.

The next day was a Friday. Tilly knew this because Marlene Deeptrick had been replaced by Anita Iceberg. By now, Tilly had learned all the ladies Queenie's mother was, and which days of the week they appeared on. The weekends, however, were more of a lucky dip, and usually one-off performances. They had recently included Carmen Miranda, Doris Day, and Harvey the giant rabbit. Tilly only knew about the last one because she had asked Queenie why it was that the old lady hadn't been out of her room all day, but places had been set and food put out at both the breakfast and dinner tables. Queenie said Harvey was invisible, which Tilly thought was a shame. This Friday was particularly exciting because Bert and Effie were coming and Reg was taking Tilly to the ballroom. Cecily arrived halfway through breakfast, bursting through the door like a jumble sale on legs. The sight of poor Cecily made Tilly determined to ask Effie's advice on making her more beautiful. She might ask God for a bit of help too. She had found a nice new church to go to, just a couple of streets away. Lil went there sometimes, "just so that God doesn't forget my face," and was happy to take Tilly with her. But Lil didn't go to confession. She said it would be too much like painting the Forth Bridge. Tilly wasn't sure what she meant by that, but she was quite sure that God would always remember Lil. Hers wasn't a face that was easy to forget. The church wasn't quite as beautiful as Mrs. O'Flaherty's church, but Father Trevor had made her feel welcome and showed her where she could light candles for her daddy.

Just as Cecily sat down and began piling toast onto

her plate there was an almighty crash in the kitchen followed by a furious torrent from Lil.

"Bugger the bloody soddin' thing! Shit, bugger, bastard! Bugger, bollocks, sod!"

"Would anyone like more tea?" Queenie asked, reaching for the teapot.

There was a further crash followed by the sound of something metal being thrown across the kitchen.

"Bollocks! Shit, bugger, bollocks, bugger, buggery bollocky shit!"

Queenie replaced the teapot on its raffia mat.

"Would you pass the marmalade please, Gracie?"

When Tilly had first heard Lil using so many swear words all joined together, she had been a bit surprised, but very impressed. But she had also expected Queenie to have a blue fit. The varnished wooden signs all over the house made Queenie's rules very clear to the guests, and "No Swearing" was definitely one of them. But the first time Tilly had heard Lil use "language," as her mother called it, Queenie had turned to Gracie and said in a loud whisper, as though she was telling a secret, "She can't help it. It's her affliction."

Tilly had been desperate to ask more about Lil's "language," but her mother's warning look had silenced her. It was still on Tilly's list of questions to ask Queenie when her mother wasn't listening, along with whether or not swear words still counted if you said them very quietly when nobody else could hear, and how do bats wee when they're hanging upside down? Tilly sometimes practiced swearing when she was on her own, rolling the deliciously naughty sounds over her tongue like warm chocolate custard. She only knew five:

bloody, sod, shit, bugger, and basket, but she wasn't sure if the last one was a real swear word. Another question for Queenie. She also needed to know who decided which words were swear ones. She had supposed that it was probably God, but then English was the queen's, according to her teacher, so maybe it was the queen who decided.

Lil strode in from the kitchen, her boots clomping on the tiled floor, carrying a plate of fried eggs and a dish of steaming canned tomatoes. She dumped them on the table and sat down. She grabbed a mug and poured herself some tea.

"Ruddy handle's fallen off the grill pan again," she said, helping herself to an egg.

Gina Anita wagged a crooked, veiny finger back and forth at Lil and tutted.

"Language, language!"

Tilly spent most of the morning hanging around the reception area playing hide-and-seek with Eli, hoping to bump into Bert and Effie. Eventually, Tilly's patience was rewarded by a flurry of cases, perfume, kisses, hugs, and hair cream, as her two very favorite guests swept through the doors. Her ambush worked perfectly and five minutes later she was sitting at the dressing table in Bert and Effie's room carefully inspecting Effie's dazzling array of costume jewelry under the guise of helping Effie unpack. Effie held up what looked to Tilly like a big plastic bag attached to a coat hanger and began to unzip it. A froth of sparkle-encrusted lemon sherbet frills and ruffles burst out of the bag. It was the most beautiful dress Tilly had ever seen.

"It's for the competition," said Effie, fluffing and primping the yards of twinkling net and chiffon before hanging it up on the edge of the wardrobe. "Do you like it?"

Tilly wasn't often lost for words, but she just couldn't think of any that were good enough. It was like trying to explain how far away the moon was. She nodded. As Effie lined up lipsticks, powders, perfumes, and various little pots and bottles of creams, colors, and potions on the dressing table, Tilly was wondering how she could ask Effie to help Cecily. As she stroked the head of a glass perfume bottle in the shape of a parakeet, she decided to go the long way round for a change, and turned to Bert.

"What makes a boy want to kiss a girl?"

Bert laughed out loud.

"What a question! Well, let's see ... A nice smile, sparkling eyes—preferably a matching pair—long, shiny hair, legs like a racehorse, and a father who owns a pub."

Tilly gave a heavy sigh. She didn't know anything about Cecily's father, but Cecily was more donkey than racehorse.

"So, who's the lucky chap?"

Tilly was horrified.

"It's not me! It's Cecily."

"That's a funny name for a boy."

Effie clipped him playfully round the ear.

"Stop teasing her, Bert. Now, Tilly, let's get this straight and start from the beginning."

"Cecily loves Sidney and wants him to kiss her, but he's not interested and she's a donkey. I thought you might be able to help."

Bert's laughter was swiftly diverted into a cough by a stern look from Effie.

"Who's Cecily?"

"She works for Queenie doing cleaning and things, and she's really nice and funny, but a bit messy like a scarecrow, not very pretty, and she can't smoke."

Touched by Tilly's concern for her friend and more than a little intrigued by the challenge, Effie agreed to give Cecily a few tips, but only if she wanted them. Tilly bounced off to tell Cecily the good news, and found her up to her elbows in washing-up. Cecily was thrilled, but told Tilly that she wouldn't be doing it for Sidney, but for herself. Tilly thought that somebody should tell Cecily about Bermondsey. She was just off to find Reg when a thought struck her.

"Cecily, what does your dad do?"

"He's a dustman."

31

Tilda

Theirs was a joyless god if his house was anything to go by. Dreadstone Hill Baptist Church, where my mother's parents wearied their knees in prayer, is the color of dried blood and squats sullenly at the top of the hill, encircled by cruelly spiked railings. Its windows are small and high and plain. With no beauty of their own, their construction thwarts any glimmer of it sneaking in from the world outside. This was the church where my grandparents learned to judge and fear and now they are buried in its shadow and I have come to look at their grave. Eli is sitting on the other side of the railings. He refuses to come in.

I came across their home address inside the walnut box. Now that the little blue diary has disappeared I have been looking through some of the other notebooks, and in one of them was an old letter that my mother had written to her parents but never posted. She must have come close, for it was sealed in an envelope and bore a first-class stamp. The letter told them that she was pregnant, that they were to be grandparents. Dreadstone Hill Baptist Church is the closest church to the street where they lived so it seemed like a good place to start. A single phone call to the rather surly church secretary revealed that they had been devoted members of its congregation in life and had remained so in death, choosing to be buried inside the iron bars of its graveyard. I wonder if my mother came to their funerals? They died within six months of each other, while she was living at Queenie's and I was away at boarding school. Did she take the bus from the other side of town in her best coat and sidle into the back of the church, or did she wait until they were buried and bring flowers to lay on the freshly heaped mound of earth? I wouldn't blame her if she did neither. But then I'll never know. They are buried in the same grave and for a moment, for the sake of my mother, I am tempted to stomp on it. Their headstone is a plain, granite rectangle the color of coal.

Reuben and Hannah Burns
Freed from sin by God's eternal mercy

A mercy they chose not to extend to their daughter.
"Did you know them?"
The woman standing at my side is tall and thin with a dark red birthmark just above her left eye. It looks like a thumbprint.
"I'm their granddaughter."
The woman smiles and waits. Her silence has purpose. It is bait to catch more conversation.
"I never met them. I don't even know if they knew about me. They disowned my mother before I was born."
The woman sighs and reaches over to place her hand

on the headstone, leaning heavily, as though it is the only thing keeping her up.

"It is hard to understand why a mother would abandon her child."

It is indeed. Like mother, like daughter.

"But sometimes it feels as though there is no other choice."

I shake my head in disbelief. What the hell would she know about it?

"Perhaps it was something they lived to regret."

She's trying to be kind, I know, but I'm surprised by how incensed I am by her polite platitudes about these people whom I never met, but who caused so much pain. I'm glad I didn't bring any flowers. I need to get away from her.

"Do you think it will be all right if I go inside?" I ask, pointing toward the church, which seems to glower down at me from its hill. I don't know why I need to look inside, but I do.

"I'm sure it will be fine. It's never locked."

I'm surprised. I thought most churches were these days, for fear of burglary and vandalism. As I turn to walk away, the woman holds me in her gaze.

"Your grandparents' lives were surely poorer for not having you in them," she says, and then she walks away.

Inside, the church is dark and cold and unwelcoming. I'm not surprised that even the vandals and the burglars stay away. St. Patrick's was full of magic, but this place is just an empty box of bricks and wood. The only adornment is a large, brass crucifix on the altar. It looks like a weapon. I could not pray in here if my life depended on it.

Outside, the sun puts in a welcome appearance and as I turn away from the church and walk back down the hill it warms my back and lifts my spirits. I have seen what I came to see and for now I can leave it behind. Eli is waiting at the gate.

"Come on, you. Let's go and see Daniel."

32

Tilly

R eg held the keys to the kingdom of heaven on
earth—or rather water, as they were now on the
pier. He unlocked the heavy double doors and flung
them open with a flourish. Tilly gasped in astonishment at the magical sight that greeted her. The ballroom was exactly how she imagined God's front room
to be. She had sometimes thought about what God
might do after his tea, at the end of a long day listening
to people's prayers, doing miracles, and sorting out
Bermondsey. She couldn't imagine him watching *The
Sweeney* or *Coronation Street* on the telly, or going to the
pub, but she could imagine him sitting in a front room
like this, being entertained by his angels, and anyone
else who had managed to get into heaven and had a
really good party piece. Sometimes, when they used to
go to Auntie Wendy's at Christmas or for one of the
grown-up's birthdays, everyone would do a party piece.
It would always be after tea, and the men would start
drinking beer and laughing, and the ladies would drink
Bambi Sham from glasses shaped like ice-cream-sundae
dishes, with pictures of Bambi on them. Kevin would

scrape out a painful version of "Greensleeves" on his violin while standing in the hall, and Uncle Bill always made the same joke about "should've used a hanky." Kevin played in the hall because he was too embarrassed to play in front of everyone, and Tilly could understand why when he was so rubbish at it. Karen always danced about a lot and sang a song from *The Sound of Music* about raindrops and kettles and warm, woolen kittens getting stung by a bee. Tilly liked the dancing but thought that the song was a bit soppy. Auntie Wendy would sing along to a Shirley Bassey song played on the record player, which made Tilly laugh because of the funny faces she pulled. Her daddy used to do his "Albert and the Lion," and Uncle Bill played the spoons on his hands and knees. Tilly would do impersonations of Mrs. Dawson at the Co-op, and Mr. Frittlecock, who came door to door once a week collecting a bob for the insurance. Her mother was reluctant to perform, but sometimes, after much persuasion and more Bambi Sham, she would say a poem about gold and silver cloths by someone called Yeats. Tilly didn't understand a word of it, but it didn't matter. The way her mother said it made it beautiful, almost like saying a prayer.

The ballroom was even bigger than the school hall where they had morning assembly. It was almost as big as the train station. Dangling from the scarlet-painted ceiling were three enormous chandeliers dripping with diamonds, which flashed and twinkled even in the gloom, before they were switched on. The walls were ruffled with boxes and balconies edged with gold, and richly decorated with flowers, leaves, and fat babies with little wings, like icing on a fancy cake. At one end of the room there was a shallow flight of gold stairs leading up to a very grand-looking stage, which was framed by deep purple velvet curtains that wouldn't have looked out of place in The Paradise Hotel, and crowned by an enormous gilded carving of unicorns, flowers, dogs, and mermaids. The wooden dance floor gleamed like golden syrup. Tilly thought that it must have been polished by thousands of pairs of dancing feet, but Reg laughed when she told him and said it was more likely the hours he put in with the electric floor buffer. Tilly stood wide-eyed and openmouthed like a baby bird, drinking in the spectacle and splendor. Reg, who had seen it all before, every day for many years, jingled the huge set of keys in his hand.

"Come on, sweetheart. Chop-chop! Miss Cynthia will be here any minute now, and I need to sort out her music or she'll have my guts for garters."

"Miss Cynthia has already arrived!" announced a self-assured BBC voice from the other end of the room, as an elegant figure swathed in pearls and lavender silk swept through the door in a cloud of L'Air du Temps. Miss Cynthia looked to Tilly like a woman made out of a broomstick. She was tall, thin, and very, very straight. She taught ballet, tap, and modern dance to classes of little girls who adored and feared her in equal measure, which made her the perfect teacher.

"'Chop-chop!' indeed, Reg." She wafted Reg away with slender hands whose long fingers were tipped with violet-polished nails. Reg scurried off, pretending to be suitably put in his place, but his grin and her wink reassured Tilly that it was only a game between friends.

Miss Cynthia placed her bag down on a chair, and turned her attention to Tilly.

"Good afternoon, young lady. I am Miss Cynthia. And you are . . . ?"

"Miss Tilly."

"I'm delighted to meet you, Miss Tilly. Are you here to join one of my dance classes?"

"Miss Tilly is my assistant," replied Reg, returning with a pile of records balanced on top of a record player and held in place with his chin, which he set down at the side of the stage.

"*Quel dommage!* She looks like a dancer to me. Well, never mind. She has no ballet or tap shoes, but perhaps if she could be spared from her duties for half an hour at the end of the afternoon, Miss Tilly might like to join my modern dance class for today."

Tilly wasn't aware that she had any duties, but she was desperate to join Miss Cynthia's modern dance class for today and hoped that her pleading expression was conveying this to Reg. Reg looked at Tilly thoughtfully, but apparently he wasn't getting the message.

"Tilly, sweetheart, do you need to spend a penny?"

Tilly's blushes were spared by the splendid Miss Cynthia.

"Mr. Reginald! Young ladies who avail themselves of cloakroom facilities do so in order to powder their noses," she exclaimed, "and gentlemen who speak about such matters so indelicately are not fit to be called gentlemen at all."

The tap lesson was first, and soon little girls dressed in black leotards and pleated white skirts began filing through the door like a stream of baby penguins. Their mummies and daddies left them at the door. Miss Cynthia didn't want any of her girls distracted by proud parents cooing and fussing. Discipline, concentration, and a little bit of magic are the qualities that make a great dancer, Miss Cynthia told all her pupils. She would provide the first two and the rest was up to God or the devil. Not all the parents were entirely comfortable with Miss Cynthia's alleged second assistant, but none was brave enough to question her, and there was no denying that she got results. Miss Cynthia soon had the girls arranged in three straight lines tapping and clapping as fast as their little hands and feet could manage. When their earnest concentration was mirrored on their faces, and tips of tongues crept out or crinkled frowns appeared, Miss Cynthia's voice would ring out above the music.

"Smile, girls! Smile! It's dancing, not darning socks!"

It became apparent that Tilly's duties as Reg's assistant consisted mainly of watching Miss Cynthia and her girls.

"You stay here, sweetheart, while I sort out a couple of things backstage. And keep an eye on Miss Cynthia; make sure she behaves herself."

Tilly was more than happy to watch the dancing, but she had no intention whatsoever of challenging Miss Cynthia, even if she were to set fire to the curtains and swing from one of the chandeliers. Tilly liked to think that she was pretty daring when it came to most things, but keeping Miss Cynthia in check, if she chose to misbehave, was definitely a job for a grown-up. As the baby penguins waddled out, the cygnets glided in. Miss Cynthia's ballet class was clearly a different species altogether from the tap dancers. Their hair was neatly coiled into buns and they wore pale pink leotards, soft, frilly skirts, and pink ballet shoes tied with broad satin ribbons. They all walked prettily and lightly, with their backs straight and their heads held high. Tilly immediately thought of Cecily. Perhaps her next stop after Effie should be Miss Cynthia. The last little girl to come into the class seemed vaguely familiar to Tilly from her seat on the steps of the stage. She took her place on the front row and waved happily at Tilly. She danced beautifully, as though she were completely alone in her own world of music. By the end of the ballet class Tilly was fizzing with nerves and excitement. She had no idea what "modern dance' was. What if she was as bad at it as Kevin was at playing the violin? As the cygnets floated out, a rather jumbled collection of creatures trotted, sidled, and lolloped in. This was a garden mixture of misfits, some bright and chirpy as robins, some plain and twittery like sparrows, and a big, fat pigeon of a girl whose podgy fingers were clutching a doughnut, which Miss Cynthia confiscated as soon as she saw it. The truth was that Miss Cynthia had started her modern dance class as a kindness to those who had a burning enthusiasm for dance, but were sadly hampered by a complete lack of natural ability and very little capacity to acquire any by instruction. The pigeon had no desire to dance, but her parents were determined that she should, if only for the exercise. Miss Cynthia stood in front of her motley clutch of fledglings and clapped for attention.

"Now, girls, this afternoon we are going to create a dance about love and longing."

There was some twittering in the back row from two

little sparrows that was quickly silenced by a raised eyebrow from Miss Cynthia.

"Imagine that you really love someone, passionately, devotedly, and with a flaming ardor, but that you cannot be with them, and then show me what that feels like in your dance."

Miss Cynthia's wistful expression was met with a row of vacant stares, except for Tilly, whose face lit up with recognition. She knew exactly what Miss Cynthia meant. She just didn't know if she could dance it. The fat pigeon scowled. The only thing she was missing was her doughnut.

"I don't know what you want me to do, miss," Drucilla moaned.

Miss Cynthia sighed heavily.

"Just do your best, Drucilla. Just do your best."

Miss Cynthia lifted the needle onto the record and the music began: "Je te veux' by Erik Satie. Miss Cynthia said it meant "I Want You' in French. Tilly soon forgot her nerves and was twirling round the room to the music, reaching up with her arms and then hugging them into her chest, skipping, leaping, and generally having a lovely time. She just listened to the music and it told her what to do. She got so carried away that she forgot she was supposed to be sad and missing someone, but Miss Cynthia didn't seem to mind, which was hardly surprising considering the efforts of the rest of her pupils. The two sparrows held hands and hopped from one end of the room to the other. A very tall, thin girl, who looked like a washed-out flamingo, crouched on the floor and then pretended to grow, like a beanstalk, swaying gently and very distinctly out of time to the music. The other pupils seemed to be copying one another in a lot of aimless wandering about and listless arm-waving, punctuated by the occasional jump or pause (although one of these was to pull up a pair of flagging socks and so couldn't really be counted as part of the dance). The pigeon shuffled round in a very small circle, weakly flapping her hands by her sides, but quickly exhausted by the effort sat down on the floor and roosted until the music had finished. Miss Cynthia began by shouting words of advice and encouragement over the music, but after a while even she became a little disheartened, sat down, and took a cigarette from her bag.

"I don't know how you put up with them." Reg offered her a light and shook his head in bewilderment. "I've seen zombies with more get-up-and-go!"

Miss Cynthia laughed and drew on her cigarette.

"I sometimes wonder myself. Look at the poor things. They haven't exactly been blessed with many God-given advantages, but every now and again, one of them actually seems to enjoy it. Look at Tilly; she's having a wonderful time. And the child can actually dance. She'd be welcome to join any of my classes."

She took a final draw on her cigarette, stubbed it out with her violet-tipped fingers, and stood up to rejoin the fray.

"Besides which," she said to Reg with a wry smile, "it pays my bills."

Miss Cynthia woke the somnambulant dancers with a burst of Rossini's "The Thieving Magpie," and she soon had them all flying round the room squealing with laughter and excitement. All except the pigeon, who refused to leave her perch.

After the dance classes had finished and Tilly had thanked Miss Cynthia, she waited for Reg to lock up so that they could go home for their tea before the ballroom had to be opened up again for the evening dance competitions. As Tilly waited backstage she inspected the pictures that were temporarily propped up against the wall while the foyer was being repainted. They were photographs of all the people who had performed in the ballroom, and in one of them she saw a face she recognized very well. It was Queenie.

"Oh yes, Queenie was on the stage," said Reg when Tilly pointed to the picture. "She was quite an act. But one day she just packed it all in. Said she'd had enough. That's when she bought The Paradise Hotel."

"But why?" Tilly couldn't understand why anyone would want to give up the magic of the ballroom, even for The Paradise Hotel.

"You'll have to ask Queenie. I'm sure she had a good reason. I just don't know what it was."

As Reg began switching out the lights, another photograph caught Tilly's eye. It was one of the older ones, a little faded, but still clear enough for Tilly to recognize the man in the hat and the overcoat, the one with the mustache she'd been seeing since her first day on the pier. The title on the photograph was "*Valentine Gray—The Great Mercurio—Thaumaturge Extraordinaire.*" Tilly didn't understand what it meant. She turned to ask Reg, but he was already walking away, jingling his keys impatiently.

"Come on, sweetheart. Home! We'll be late for tea and I'll tell Lily Lilo that it's all your fault," he threatened jokingly as he ushered Tilly through the front doors. Outside, the little ballerina who had been last to join the class was still waiting to be collected. She bounced up to Tilly and curtsied.

"I'm Bunny. What's your name?"

"Tilly. You're really good at dancing. How long have you been coming to lessons?"

Bunny grinned proudly.

"About ten years," she answered, "or maybe longer."

Tilly was doubtful. Bunny looked about six years old and was obviously as good with numbers as Tilly was with boiled eggs.

"Can you teach me to dance like you?"

The little girl twirled three pirouettes in a row and deliberately wobbled off the last one to land on her bottom in a fit of giggles.

"Of course I can."

Having locked the front doors, Reg was ready to go and whistled to Tilly, who was trying to copy Bunny's pirouettes.

"Come on, sweetheart. I'm dying for my tea."

Tilly said good-bye to her new friend and skipped off after Reg, who was already on the way home.

After tea, Tilly was sent to visit Gina in her room, while Queenie and her mother put their feet up and had a gin and tonic and what Queenie called "a girls' gossip." Tilly didn't mind. She was fascinated by all the things in Gina's room, and was now trusted enough to play with some of them. Her favorite things were the music boxes. She picked up the Eiffel Tower and carefully wound the key on its base. She set it back down on the dressing table, and did a little twirl in front of the mirror to the tune of "La Vie en Rose."

"I had a dance lesson today with Miss Cynthia and I made a new friend called Bunny."

"I used to be a wonderful dancer in my day."

"Yes, I know. You already told me before. But today's not your day, it's my day, and I want to tell you about me."

Gina laughed. It was strange, but Tilly felt more at ease with Gina than with any of the other grown-ups in the house. Strange, because in many ways she was the most difficult. You could never tell what kind of mood she was going to be in. She was bossy, fussy, and sometimes just plain rude. And sometimes she wouldn't talk to you at all. But somehow Tilly felt that they were equals. She could ask her anything, things she couldn't even ask Queenie, and she always got an answer. She wasn't always sure if the answer was true, but she always got one. And Gina never treated Tilly as though she were just a child.

"Come on then. Thrill me with your theatricals. Tell me all about your dance lesson."

Tilly wound up the key on the brass box with roses on it, and to the appropriate sound track of the "Waltz of the Flowers' described Miss Cynthia and her pupils in florid detail.

"The first dance I did was to a piece of music by Sarky called 'Shuh, Tuh, Vuh,' which doesn't spell anything in English, but spells 'I Want You' in French. Miss Cynthia said we had to dance as though we had a flaming Aga."

Gina smiled. She pointed to a heart-shaped wooden box painted with doves and flowers.

"Wind it up."

Tilly recognized the music instantly.

"Now you can show me."

Gina's room was considerably smaller than the ballroom, but Tilly did her best to re-create the original performance. Eli took cover under the dressing table. She ended with a dramatic flourish and collapsed on the bed to a round of applause from Gina. They lay in silence for a moment and Tilly could feel her heart beating in her chest.

"How can you tell if someone's dead and not just sleeping?"

Gina sat up and reached for her glass of gin and tonic.

"Bite them." She swigged her gin with enthusiasm. "What other music did you dance to?"

"*The Thieving Magpie* by Mussolini."

33

Tilly

Eli was watching Tilly struggling to get her feet into the proper position to begin a demi-plié. Her tongue was pressed hard onto her top lip and her forehead was crumpled into a frown of fierce concentration as she did her best to keep her back straight and her bottom tucked in, to avoid what Bunny called "looking like a duck doing a poo." She was giggling merrily at Tilly's rather ungainly efforts in between giving instructions in her version of Miss Cynthia's voice, pursing her lips into a prim little bow and pointing imperiously.

"Happy feet! Don't forget those happy feet!" she commanded, pointing her own toes to show Tilly exactly what she meant and then dissolving into giggles once more. Her laughter was contagious and it wasn't long before Tilly caught it and both girls were rolling around on the grass and clutching their tummies in helpless laughter. Eli watched them serenely from his own little patch of sunshine. They were playing among the gently whirring windmills in the back garden of The Paradise Hotel. A whole year had passed since Tilly's first dance class with Miss Cynthia and her windmills had long since spilled out of the flower bed that Queenie had given her when she had first arrived. She and Bunny had become firm friends and although Bunny didn't go to Tilly's school, they played together at the weekends and in the school holidays, and of course they saw each other at Miss Cynthia's classes. But it wasn't just dancing that made their friendship special. It was their daddies too—or rather lack of them. Bunny's daddy had gone away, and she didn't know where, and nobody would tell her. Sometimes it made her so sad that she forgot what it was like to be happy. Tilly could still remember what that felt like, but at Queenie's, happiness had gently trickled back into her life like melting butter through the holes in a hot crumpet.

"Where do you think my daddy is?"

Their laughter had worn itself out and Bunny sat hugging her knees, her big blue eyes staring solemnly at Tilly from beneath her blond bangs. Tilly shrugged her shoulders.

"Maybe he's gone away to work."

"Well, I'm still waiting for him to come back. I've been waiting and waiting for ages. I think he must have got lost," Bunny said sadly.

Tilly picked a daisy and twirled its stalk between her finger and thumb.

The girls sat in silence for a while, listening to the bees buzzing greedily around the honeysuckle and the clatter of pots and pans coming through the open kitchen window. Lil was cooking dinner for the guests and wafts of boiling potatoes mingled with the sweet, warm scent of roses and honeysuckle. Tilly wanted to help Bunny, but she wasn't sure how she could. She still thought about her own daddy; missed him; even cried sometimes, alone in the dark when a picture-thought of him would drift through her head staying only long enough to make her hurt. The thought that her daddy might still be stuck in Bermondsey worried Tilly like an impending visit to the dentist. What could he have done that had made God so cross with him? Maybe God had made a mistake and muddled him up with someone else. Tilly couldn't decide which was worse: her daddy being in such deep trouble with God, or God making a mistake. She knew that wherever he was, she couldn't find her daddy now, but maybe she could help Bunny find hers. She didn't have a clue where they might look, but at least they could try.

After Bunny had gone Tilly decided to go and see Queenie's mother. The old lady had been quite poorly for the last few days and hadn't left her room much. She had taken to having Cecily or Tilly serve her gin and tonic on a silver tray while she stayed in bed and listened to music. Perhaps she would know where they could look for Bunny's daddy. Tilly unfolded her crossed legs and stood up, rubbing her calves where the blades of grass had imprinted a pattern like raffia matting.

She went into the back dining room to fetch the gin and tonic and found her mother sitting at the table, drinking tea before the rush of the evening meal. Her mother had looked very different since they'd moved in to Queenie's. Her face seemed smoother and she smiled every day. She reminded Tilly of the statue of Mary in St. Patrick's Church, who had the most beautiful face that she had ever seen but always seemed just a little bit sad. She went over to her mother and stood a little awkwardly by her side, playing with the button on her cardigan.

"Do you miss my daddy sometimes?" she asked.

Her mother put down her cup and saucer and smoothed down Tilly's hair, holding her face tenderly in both hands.

"I miss him every day, Tilly. Every day."

Just a quarter of an hour later the evening meal service was in full swing and the dining room was packed. Tilly marched in looking for her mother. She found her with a plate of grilled pork chops, vegetables, and gravy in each hand, about to serve them to an elderly couple.

"Sofa Loren's dead," she announced.

Her mother nearly tipped a pork chop in gravy down the front of the old lady's spotless white blouse, but steadied her waitressing wobble just in time. Aware that Tilly's news had aroused a mild degree of curiosity among the diners, her mother forced a nervous laugh and replied, "Oh, I'm sure she's fine. I expect she's just asleep."

Tilly was indignant. She knew a dead person when she saw one.

"No—she definitely isn't. I took her a gin and tonic and when I got there she was dead. I need to find Queenie and tell her."

The occupants of the dining room sat with mouths open and cutlery suspended in midair. Tilly's mother set her plates down and attempted to usher the conversation with her daughter out of the room.

"Now, Tilly, you know how tired she's been lately. She's probably just in a very deep sleep."

Tilly wasn't budging. She folded her arms and fixed her mother with her most serious stare.

"She's not. I promise you she's dead. Cross my heart and hope to die."

Her mother looked away from her in exasperation and saw to her horror that Queenie had come in and was serving faggots and onions to a family of four in the corner. Determined to put a stop to Tilly's nonsense once and for all, she placed her hands on her daughter's shoulders and looked her straight in the eyes.

"How could you possibly tell whether she was dead or just asleep?"

"I bit her."

As Queenie set down the steaming plates in front of her guests, one of them clutched at her wrist.

"Excuse me, dear. I hope you don't mind me asking, but who is Sofa Loren?"

Queenie didn't miss a beat.

"Oh, don't worry, Mrs. Martin. She's the cat."

Queenie had been very calm and organized. She asked Gracie to finish serving dinner while she rang for the doctor. Afterward, she sat alone with her mother for a while. Tilly stood outside the door, which was left slightly ajar, listening to Queenie talking to her mother while she brushed her hair and straightened the bedclothes. When Tilly had found her, she knew the show was over and the entire cast had already left the stage. Ginger, Sofa, Grace, Marlene, Anita, and all the others who had made weekend guest appearances were gone. All that was left was an empty set. After the doctor and Queenie, they had all been in to see her and say good-bye, except for Cecily, who was too scared. When

Tilly bent over to kiss her cold, powdery cheek, she could smell gin, cigarettes, and Shalimar.

Later, they all sat together in the back dining room. The grown-ups were drinking gin and brandy and Tilly and Cecily were drinking cherry pop. Cecily was crying and hiccupping and sniffing, despite Lil's best efforts to console her. Gracie looked pale and shocked and even Reg looked a little shaken. Only Queenie looked normal. Just a little bit sad round the edges. And Sofa Loren, who was standing behind her waving a glass of gin in one hand and a cigarette in the other, looked positively jolly. It was just a shame that nobody could see her except for Tilly and Eli. What had used to be Sofa's body was still in the bedroom, laid out on the bed in a silk negligée, with her hair fluffed out on the pillow like an old man's beard. As Reg topped up their drinks, Queenie stood up and raised her glass.

"I should like to propose a toast to my darling mother, who was wonderful, adorable, fabulous, and absolutely barking mad. Thank you, we love you, and good night!"

As Tilly drained her glass and covered her mouth with her hand to muffle the inevitable burp, Queenie looked across the table at her and asked, "Are you sure you're all right, Tilly love?"

Ever since Tilly had been proved right about Queenie's mother, the grown-ups had been fussing around her as if finding a dead person was a terrible thing. Tilly still thought that finding a dead baby chicken inside a boiled egg would be much worse.

She found the first few days after Queenie's mother died a bit tricky. Everyone was sad, and her mother was very jumpy, as though she was in the bit of a horror

film where all the lights are broken and the scary man
is hiding and waiting to jump out and kill you. But Tilly
wasn't scared of horror films and she was finding it
hard to be sad. She wasn't sad, because the whole reason
why people were sad when someone died was because
they missed them, and you couldn't miss them if they
hadn't gone. And Queenie's mother hadn't gone
anywhere yet. Tilly was always bumping into her in the
corridors, in the garden, and in the back dining room.
She had even taken to wandering about in the guests'
dining room while they were eating. She hadn't caused
any trouble yet, but Tilly thought that it would only be
a matter of time. She had already made Tilly laugh at a
fat man slurping his soup by standing right behind him
and pulling silly faces. Tilly had had to pretend that she
was coughing, but the man still looked a bit cross. The
only place Queenie's mother seemed to be avoiding
was her own room. But Queenie was often in there, and
when she was, Eli would be with her. One day Tilly
heard her crying, and went in and sat on the bed next
to her and held her hand. Tilly wondered if she should
tell Queenie that her mother was still there in the
house, but she didn't know if it would help, especially
as Queenie obviously couldn't see her. In the end,
Queenie solved the problem for her. She was sitting at
her mother's dressing table trying out her perfumes,
just as Tilly had done so many times. She sprayed
Shalimar onto her wrist and said softly, almost to
herself, "I sometimes feel as though she's still here."

Tilly pulled a "what took you so long?" face.

"That's because she is."

34

Tilda

It's first thing in the morning, and there are two dirty mugs in the sink and an almost empty pot of still-warm tea on the table. Such simple things, but momentous too, evidence. It has been a very long time since anyone brought me tea in bed. Daniel has set off for the café, leaving me to bask in the domestic detritus that proves "we" are real. Daniel and Tilda, together. A couple of weeks have passed since *Breakfast at Tiffany's* but it feels much longer and Daniel's questions about my relationship with my mother are nagging at me like an unsolved crossword puzzle clue. He has shaken my complacency (or was it fear?) and made me curious. There are already three black, twisted matchsticks in front of me as I strike a fourth and stare into the flame, trying to understand what actually happened. I can't believe that for all those years I didn't try harder to find out why she sent me away. Of course, I have asked Queenie, but she couldn't help.

"I begged her not to send you away," she said, "and you pleaded with me to get her to change her mind, but she was absolutely determined. The best I could do was get you home for the holidays. Gracie said that she had no choice, but she couldn't tell me why. The strange thing was that she seemed utterly heartbroken about you going, but afraid to let you stay. In the end, I had to let it go. I was worried that if I pushed too hard she would leave and I would lose you both for good."

I wash and get dressed and creep reluctantly into my mother's bedroom. I sit down on the edge of the bed. The bed where I nursed her in her last few days. The bed where she died in her sleep and I found her the next morning. She had died as neatly as she had lived, with hardly a hair out of place. But I brushed it gently anyway, the way she had sometimes let me when I was a little girl. I still can't say whether it was relief or guilt I felt that day. Maybe both. The grief came later, but even now I can't be sure that I wasn't grieving because she had never been the mother that I had longed for, and now she never could be.

"My mother and I were never close"—my words echo in my ears, so familiar. But "never'? Is that really true? Convenient, yes; but now I have begun to doubt myself. Perhaps the truth is less tidy and more difficult to explain away. Perhaps I have been selective about the past, chosen the pieces that fit with the version it suits me to tell and jettisoned those that were incompatible. The fact remains that she did send me away from the place where I was the happiest I have ever been in my life. So far. I begged her not to, but she did it anyway. It was a deeply painful rejection for a little girl and, even now, a deeply embarrassing admission for a grown woman to make. My mother didn't want me. Except now it doesn't fit. Queenie said that my mother had been heartbroken and afraid when she sent me away;

Penelope said that I had been the most important thing in her life—perhaps too important. So, could it be something even worse? Could I have done something so terrible that she had to send me away? I have to know. I have to find that bloody diary!

I go back to the walnut box. I know that it's not in there, but maybe one of the other notebooks can shed some light on what really happened. Flicking through them, it seems that most are diaries for the years that I was away at school and afterward, but there is one that looks different from the rest. Thin and a bit tatty round the edges, it has a red cover and lined pages like a school exercise book. On the cover, in faintly scratched letters, it says "Diary of a Madwoman." Inside, the writing is in pencil.

They have put me in the asylum. Stevie and that bloody doctor. I'm not myself, apparently. Well, I pity the poor sod that I am. I'm so tired. I'm too tired to be anyone, let alone myself. I don't think I'm mad, just bad. Mum and Dad were right. I married a sinner and now I shall be sinned against. Punished. And serves me right. But why should my baby be punished too? Who will look after her? They want me to write down my thoughts. It's supposed to help. Ha ha ha! It's my homework. Except I'm not at home, am I? They're my loony bin lessons. They won't give me a pen. It's too dangerous. I might hurt myself, they say. Or someone else. The pencil is nice and safe. Blunt. They won't give me a sharpener in case I eat it or sharpen my pencil into a weapon, or use it to escape or die. Maybe if I just lie down and stop breathing I could die. Maybe I don't need a pen or a

pencil sharpener. Maybe I could outwit all their stupid
rules and just die by giving up. In the meantime I shall
write down my thoughts like a good girl:

Tilly Tilly Tilly Tilly Tilly Tilly Tilly Tilly Tilly Tilly
Tilly Tilly Tilly Tilly Tilly Tilly Tilly Tilly Tilly Tilly Tilly
Tilly Tilly Tilly Tilly Tilly Tilly Tilly Tilly Tilly Tilly Tilly
Tilly Tilly Tilly Tilly Tilly Tilly Tilly Tilly Tilly Tilly Tilly
Tilly Tilly Tilly Tilly . . .

Day after day, page after page, she has written just
one word. *Tilly*. I was her only thought.

Until eventually, a few pages from the back of the
book . . .

I have made a friend. And he has done me more good
than all their pills and electric shocks and bloody basket
weaving. Evelyn has helped me to believe that I'm just
as good as anyone else, as good as Stevie and the doctors
with all their clipboards and questions. He says that
being normal is overrated. He has only been here a few
weeks, but already he has found his answer. He says that
his life feels like one big practical joke, so he's decided
to laugh in its face. He makes me laugh too. And I can't
remember the last time I laughed before I met Evelyn.
Once a week, we have dance in the gymnasium. They
make us stand up and move around while the music
plays. But that's not dancing. You can't make someone
dance. They have to want to. I always dance with
Evelyn. He will be leaving soon, and I'm not staying
here without him. So now, I'll have to get better.

Who the hell was Evelyn?

Daniel and I are very close. Julietta, our dance teacher, has instructed the ten couples in front of her to stand sufficiently close to each other for it to feel "almost indecent in public." Daniel and I are happy to comply. We are learning to rumba. It was Daniel's idea. When he found out how much I loved dancing with Miss Cynthia, he surprised me. Of course, the ballroom and Miss Cynthia are long gone, and we are in a sparkling rectangular box of wooden floors and mirrored walls called The Rhythm Studio.

"It'll be much easier for you. You've done all this before," he declared. "So you'll have to be patient with me."

He was a natural from the start. But a dreadful pupil. He spends most of our lesson dancing beautifully, trying to make me giggle and usually succeeding, which plays havoc with my posture. Miss Cynthia would most certainly not have been amused.

Tonight, after the class, we walk back to the flat hand in hand, and almost as soon as we are through the door we behave utterly indecently in private. Rumba is clearly a euphemism for foreplay. I hope Eli isn't listening.

Later, as we lie in comfortable and exhausted silence on the disheveled duvet, my thoughts turn, rather annoyingly, to my mother. I try to distract myself by running my fingers through the fuzz of hair that covers Daniel's soft, slightly rounded belly. It has been a long time since I traced by touch the topography of a man's naked body. Daniel convulses at my tickling.

"Hey! Get off my fat bits!" he laughs, moving my hand higher onto his muscled chest.

But now my mother has entered the room, albeit only notionally, she is refusing to leave and I can't settle. I get up to use the bathroom and return via the kitchen with an open bottle of wine and two glasses. Daniel throws back the duvet to let me back into the bed.

"What's up?"

How does he do that? I'm beginning to think that he can see inside my head. I smile at the thought.

"What do you mean?"

He wags his finger at me and laughs.

"Come on! I can hear the cogs whirring and clicking from here. And you've got your deep-thinking face on."

"What's my 'deep-thinking' face?"

"The one that'll stick if the wind changes and then you'll be sorry. So, stop thinking and tell me."

I pour wine into each of the glasses.

"It's that whole thing with my mother. After all these years, why can't I just leave it alone? Why won't it leave *me* alone?"

Daniel flings his arm around me and hugs me close.

"My darling girl, I have no idea. Maybe just because it's time—time for you to know. And maybe it will be a whole Pandora's box of worms," he says, mixing his metaphors shamelessly, "but I'll be here."

He kisses the top of my head.

"I'll even pick the worms out of your hair."

35

Tilly

The funeral was on a Thursday, so Tilly assumed that they would be burying Marlene. After much pleading on Tilly's part, and persuasion on Queenie's, her mother had agreed that Tilly would be allowed to go. She had never been to a funeral before and was very curious to see what would happen. They all gathered in the hallway waiting for the cars to arrive. Lil was carrying an enormous handbag that was full of tissues, judging by the endless stream she kept producing to mop up Cecily, who had already dissolved into tears. Reg was looking very smart in a black suit and Tilly's mother looked pale and nervous. Queenie was beautiful in a plain tight black dress, several long pearl necklaces and a large-brimmed hat with a veil of black-spotted net. Marlene's coffin arrived in a big black shiny car and was covered in white lilies and red roses. Tilly had hoped that they would be getting in the car with the coffin, but the flowers took up so much room that the undertakers had had to send another car for them to ride in. They set off so slowly that Tilly thought the men driving the cars must be beginners. She noticed that people on the streets were watching them as they passed by and the men were taking off their hats. Tilly felt a bit like the queen. She waved at a couple of the people through the car window until her mother took her hand and placed it firmly in her lap. But Queenie smiled.

Tilly was expecting a church, but the building they drew up outside looked like no church she had ever seen. It looked like a village hall with its pebble-dashed walls and shallow pitched roof clad in corrugated iron. The building was in a garden surrounded by chicken-wire fencing attached to concrete posts, and fixed to one of them was a colorfully painted wooden sign that said "*Welcome to the Church of Cheerful and Blessed Souls in Jesus.*" Tilly was hugely relieved. It was a church after all. It was bad enough worrying about her daddy in Bermondsey, without Marlene having a funeral in a village hall and then ending up God only knows where. But if St. Patrick's was God's house, this looked more like his holiday chalet at Hunstanton.

Waiting for them at the door was the biggest man Tilly had ever seen, at least as big as a polar bear, but the color of Marmite. Marlene was lifted out of the car and, when everyone was ready, the man led their procession into the church. Inside, the place was as cheerful as its name implied. There were lots of wooden chairs facing a long table at one end of the room, which was covered in a brightly colored embroidered cloth. The window ledges were filled with china vases of flowers, some fresh and some plastic, and lots of different china statues. There were Jesus, Mary, and a few angels, but more unusually, a couple of horses, several swans, Laurel and Hardy, and a St. Bernard. Colored fairy lights were woven through the statues and the vases on the ledges, and strung above the big table that Tilly supposed was the altar. In the middle of the table was a big statue of Jesus on the cross surrounded by more vases of flowers, candles, and all sorts of other sparkly bits and pieces, including a snow globe with an angel inside, a unicorn with a glittery horn, and a doll dressed up as a bride. Tilly wondered if they were going to have a church bazaar after the funeral, and if she had enough pocket money left to buy the snow globe.

The wooden seats were all occupied by the most fascinating people that Tilly had ever seen all in one room in her short life. The ladies looked very glamorous, dressed in black, but with lots of jewelry and makeup and some spectacular hats. They were all different, but for some reason they all reminded her of Queenie. The men were smartly dressed in dark suits but with bright ties or scarves, and some had flowers in their buttonholes. Tilly wondered if the flowery ones were supposed to be at a wedding and had gotten the wrong church. She hoped not. One of them was wearing red lipstick and a red rose behind his ear. She knew that he was in the right place. As she gawped in delight and amazement at the dazzling congregation, more than one face seemed familiar. It wasn't just that the ladies reminded her of Queenie. She knew some of these people. She just didn't know how. It was like a tune that you could hum all the way through but couldn't remember the name of. Her ponderings were interrupted by a real tune being bashed out enthusiastically by a lively little leprechaun of a man on an electric organ. He was accompanied by a pair of wizened old ladies with false-teeth smiles, in pink frocks and wrinkled stockings, who were banging and clattering tambourines; and by a plump young woman with pink cheeks and National Health glasses parping away on a trombone. Marlene's coffin was placed center stage in front of the big table, and once everyone had settled back down in their seats, the big man spoke. He stood next to Marlene and placed his hand on her coffin, just about where her left knee would be, Tilly thought.

"Good afternoon, ladies and gentlemen," he began, in a voice deep and loud enough to rattle the windows.

"My name is Pastor John-Winston Benjamin, and I should like to welcome you all to the funeral of our dear sister Ruby. Together we shall celebrate her life—a life that brought so much love, joy, and excitement to so many. We shall thank our Lord for her light and laughter, which touched all our lives; and we shall say our final farewells before we send her off into the loving arms of Jesus."

Tilly was horrified. Either they were at the wrong funeral, someone had put the wrong person in the coffin, or Pastor John-Winston Benjamin didn't know what he was talking about. She turned to Reg, who was standing beside her. He squeezed her hand and whispered, "It's all right, love. Ruby was her real name."

A warm wave of relief flooded through her. But she still wasn't convinced that Pastor John-Winston Benjamin could really be Marlene's brother. They didn't look anything like each other. Still, he said some lovely things about Marlene, and how proud she had been of Queenie, and they said enough prayers to make Tilly's knees itch from kneeling on the prickly red cushions that were provided for the purpose. They sang two hymns, accompanied by the musicians: "Abide with Me," which she knew, and "The Old Rubber Cross," which she didn't. Tilly was amazed at how beautifully the congregation sang. In her experience, singing in church was usually a bit all over the place with the tune and the timing, unless it was the proper choir. But this lot sounded good enough to be singing on the stage at the end of the pier. After the second hymn the man with the red lipstick came to the front to say a poem. He said that some of the happiest days of all their lives had been when Marlene was the owner of The Banana Blush and that the poem the name was taken from was one of her favorites. She had asked for it to be read at her funeral, but that it should be taken in the spirit in which she had intended it. Tilly had no idea what he was talking about, but thought that the spirit must be gin. She would ask Queenie about The Banana Blush later. The man didn't need a piece of paper. He knew the words off by heart. The poem was called "Sun and Fun' by a man called John Betterman and was about squashed tomato sandwiches and spiders.

After the poem, Pastor John-Winston Benjamin walked over to Queenie, took her by the hand and led her to the front of the church. He raised both his arms up, taking Queenie's with him.

"Dear Heavenly Father, and all your angels, bless us today and wrap your loving arms around us. Dry our tears and fill our hearts with peace as we say good-bye to our beloved sisters Ruby, Marlene, Anita, Ginger, Grace, and Sophia. Welcome them into your heaven, and cherish her soul as one of your precious rainbow of treasures for evermore. Amen. And now Queenie will sing our final song."

Pastor John-Winston Benjamin gave Queenie a hug and then stood to one side. Queenie leaned over her mother's coffin and rested her cheek against the cool, dark wood between the red and white flowers. She turned her face, and with a final kiss stood up and took a deep breath. Her eyes were wet with unshed tears but her back was straight and her head held proudly. She started singing on her own in a soft, husky voice, but, much to Tilly's relief, the musicians soon caught up. The song, called "Cabaret," was about a lady called Elsie, and knitting. By the end, Queenie was belting it out better than Shirley Bassey, and the congregation was on its feet whistling, cheering, and clapping. The old ladies were waving their tambourines in the air, the trombonist's cheeks were the color of cherry brandy, and Pastor John-Winston Benjamin was dancing in the aisle with the man with red lipstick. There were lots of tears too, but all the faces were smiling. Even Cecily had stopped sobbing, but from the look on her face it might have been through shock. Tilly was in heaven. If all funerals were this good she couldn't understand why people didn't want to go to them.

"I wish Daddy could have had a funeral like this," she said to her mother on the way back to Queenie's in the car. Her mother squeezed her hand and said nothing, but, for a moment, Tilly thought she looked almost afraid.

Back at The Paradise Hotel there was a party, which Tilly thought was a lovely idea. All the people from the church came, including Pastor John-Winston Benjamin. She even spotted the two old ladies in pink frocks eating sausage rolls and drinking sherry in the guests' sitting room. Most of the others gathered in the guests' dining room to eat the buffet that Lil and Cecily had spent the morning preparing, and drink funny-colored drinks that Queenie said were "cocktails." She let Tilly taste the one that she was drinking. It was the color of boogers and smelled of fruit.

"It's called a Banana Blush," Queenie told her as she took a tentative gulp, answering her question before she had a chance to ask it. It tasted lovely, like a banana and ice pop with a hint of medicine. But Tilly couldn't see how it would have kept Marlene happy for days. It wouldn't have lasted five minutes. She sat down next to Queenie.

"Why did you stop going on the stage?"

Queenie shrugged her shoulders and then smiled.

"It didn't make me happy anymore. It was just pretend. I needed a different kind of life."

"And why do daddies go away?"

Queenie took another sip of her drink before answering.

"I wish I could tell you. People often do things that other people can't understand. But sometimes they have a very good reason, even if you don't know what it is."

She gave Tilly another sip of her drink.

"And if someone loves you like your daddy did, the love never goes away, even if the person does."

"You won't go away, will you?"

"No, Tilly love, I'll never go away. I promise."

Tilly got up and wandered round the room staring at all the people as though they were animals at the zoo. They were such exotic creatures that Tilly was spellbound, unlike Cecily, who was hiding in the kitchen. All at once, she realized how she knew them. She saw them every day. These were the glamorous show people in the photos with Queenie that hung on the wall. And now they were actually here. In her house. Tilly thought that she might actually explode with pride and excitement. The piano had been moved into the dining room and once the guests had eaten enough of the buffet and drunk enough cocktails, the music started. The man with the red lipstick (that had been refreshed after the buffet) took a seat at the piano and began to play. He was good. Tilly thought that he was even better than Liberace, who had been Mrs. O'Flaherty's favorite. The guests took it in turns to sing, some by themselves, others in groups. Even Queenie sang again. And people started dancing. Her mother went over to Queenie and took her hand.

"Dance with me," she said. "It'll be like old times."

Tilly was surprised and a little jealous to see Lil dancing with Pastor John-Winston Benjamin. Her mother and Reg danced very close together, and her mother's head was on his shoulder. Tilly thought it looked more like a walking cuddle than dancing. She danced with Queenie and several of the other ladies before Pastor John-Winston, to her great delight, swept her up into his arms and whirled her round the room until she was giddy and helpless with giggles. Once she had gotten her breath back and taken a few sneaky sips from all the drinks that looked like the one Queenie had let her try,

Tilly danced on her own, weaving between the couples on the floor and making every move Miss Cynthia had taught her, as well as a good many of her own. She had never felt so fizzy and sparkly and twirly and fluffy. Eventually the dancers, even Tilly, grew tired, the music slowed and the party began to fade away like a sunset slipping into the sea. Queenie stood, a little unsteadily, by the piano and raised her half-full glass.

"To all of you; my friends—no, my family. Thank you for coming. Thank you for loving her almost as much as I did, and for loving me as much as I love you. She would have adored this."

Tilly looked at Marlene lolling happily on top of the piano, with a cigarette in one hand and a Banana Blush in the other.

"She did," said Tilly to Eli, who was sitting next to her on the floor. And then she was sick on the carpet.

Part 3

*The truth, the whole truth,
and nothing but the truth*

36

Tilda

November 19
Tilly will never forgive me.

W hen I got back to the flat this morning, Queenie
was there and the little blue diary was open and
perfectly placed in the middle of the kitchen table. She
smiled at me and said she thought that now I was ready
to read on. And then she left.

It's Boxing Day and Daniel has gone to visit his family. He asked me to go with him, but I'm not ready to
meet them just yet. I'm a bit awkward with the whole
family thing and Daniel's is a big family. I need a while
longer to work up to it. We spent Christmas Day at the
café: me, Eli, Daniel, Joseph Geronimo, and Miss
Dane—Penelope. Daniel cooked, I waitressed, Joseph
Geronimo entertained, and Penelope sat back and
thoroughly enjoyed herself. Penelope has taken quite
a shine to Joseph Geronimo and was relieved to avoid
spending Christmas with her niece, the inappropriate
food shopper. Daniel thought she might like a Snow-
ball to drink, but Penelope turned out to be more of a
whisky and ginger kind of girl. We had crackers, wore

paper hats, read out loud the dreadful jokes, and listened to Christmas music on the jukebox. It was one of the best Christmas Days I can remember since I was a child. After tea, which was really just a continuation of lunch, Joseph Geronimo took Penelope home before heading out on a date with a new lady friend called Fatima-Jane. Daniel and I spent the evening in his chaotic but cozy living quarters above the café, doing all the proper things that make Christmas happy. We played Scrabble, making rude words and cheating. We watched some awful television, ate satsumas and roast chestnuts that were burned on one side and raw on the other and fell asleep in front of the fire halfway through the *Poirot* Christmas special. It was like the second movement of Beethoven's *Emperor*: quietly magnificent.

But now this. November the nineteenth is my birthday. What is it that I shall never forgive my mother for?

Once more I find myself alone on the pier, staring out to sea. The cold, gray waves are rising and roaring, flecked with rabid foam, and the bitter wind is shunting gunmetal clouds across a low sky that is full of menace. The noise of the sea and the wind is already deafening and the threatened rain soon joins the crescendo, beating furiously onto the wooden boards of the pier and drumming gunshot percussion on the metal roofs of the shelters and kiosks. But I am perfectly still in the eye of the storm. I can only stare out to sea, seeing nothing. Perhaps now she has finally killed something in me too.

I don't know how long I stay like this before something makes me look up. I don't know what it is, but when I do I catch just a glimpse of a passing figure. Not even as substantial as that; a mere shadow, a ghost. But I know who it is. It has been a lifetime since I saw him, but I know. Shock fires adrenaline through my leaden limbs and I set off down the pier to find him. There, again; the back of his dark coat and his hat held on with one hand as he dodges between the shelters and kiosks. I'm running now, freezing rain slashing against my face. I reach the fairground and I see him ahead at the galloping horses, but he's getting away from me.

"Valentine!"

I scream it so loudly that I can feel it searing my throat. He turns for just a moment and looks straight at me through the veil of driving rain. And then he's off, running toward the end of the pier, and I have lost him again. When I get there, of course, he is gone. I grip the metal railings with icy hands. My knuckles are blue; the color of fresh bruises. A giant warm hand covers one of mine and Eli appears on my other side. Joseph Geronimo nods toward the bleak wilderness of water.

"Let him go."

He waits patiently for my silence to be long enough for me. The comfort of his warm hand on mine eventually pulls me back.

"Did you know him?" I ask.

"I know who he is." Joseph Geronimo hands me a cigarette and puts another between his lips. He lights them both and takes a deep draw.

"I also know that he's long dead and doesn't belong here anymore."

"I knew him when I was a little girl."

It seems to me that I'm bound for Bedlam no matter what, so if I can't avoid the madness, I should at least give myself the satisfaction of trying to explain it. Joseph Geronimo says nothing and waits for me to continue.

"My mother met him when he was alive; years ago, before I was born."

I tell him that she met Valentine as his daughter lay broken and bloody in the middle of the road, and that she held the child's hand and watched Valentine sobbing as his little girl died. I tell him about the entries in my mother's diary for the date of my seventh birthday, and the days after. He shakes his head in disbelief and gives me a wry smile.

"Jesus, Tilda, you're much more trouble than you look, aren't you?"

He flings an arm round my shoulder and squeezes me hard.

"Come on. Let's go and talk to Penelope."

Half an hour later we are all in Penelope's sitting room, drinking tea jollied up with whisky and eating mince pies. I feel like I'm having an out-of-body experience. This morning I learned something that has erased an entire volume of my life story and left only blank pages, and hours later I'm sitting calmly drinking tea and comparing mince pie recipes. Eli is asleep in front of the fire. I think even he's had enough for today. I have decided that Joseph Geronimo and Penelope are to be my interpreters. The past described in my mother's diary has become L. P. Hartley's foreign country, and I need some help trying to understand what happened there. I hand the little blue book to Penelope, open at the page where I want her to start reading. Aloud. Penelope nudges her spectacles a little farther up her nose and clears her throat as though she is about to make an announcement.

November 19
Tilly will never forgive me.
   She must never find out what I've done. I did it for her, but she must never know.

November 21
God forgive me, I killed him. I never meant to. I didn't plan it. It just happened.

Penelope looks up, her face stretched with horror and bewilderment. I meet her eyes with a steady gaze. "Go on."

The night before Tilly's birthday I got drunk. I'm not supposed to drink at all with my pills but I always do. I couldn't face what I knew was coming. I knew that she thought he would be there; her perfect daddy, home for her birthday. But I knew that instead he was going to break her heart. So I washed it all away with the drink. Because I'm a coward. Poor Tilly, what chance does she have? Her father's a selfish, ungodly bastard and her mother's a pathetic, drunken coward. A mental case.
   I didn't even hear her get up. She made her own breakfast and took herself off to school without a single "happy birthday' from anyone. I was so ashamed when I eventually managed to drag myself out of bed. I was sick; whether it was from the drink or the shame I don't

know. On my knees in front of the toilet, stinking of vomit, my face wet with snot and tears, I hated myself for being me. But I tried. I cleaned myself up, and then the house. I invited Wendy and Karen and Mrs. O'Flaherty to tea. I rushed round making sandwiches and a cake with Smarties—Tilly's favorite, even though I knew it would count for nothing. He was still everything. But I had to try. I just wanted my little girl to have a happy birthday. When she came home from school her disappointment was like a slap in the face. Bless her heart, she played the game. She opened her presents and ate her tea. And I stood there, the fake mother between the genuine articles, Wendy and Mrs. O'Flaherty. They seem to find it so easy; kids, husband, housework. To them, it comes as naturally as breathing. I just feel like I'm suffocating. Tilly hated the doll I got her. I don't understand why she asked for it—she never plays with dolls. But still she went along with it, pretending to be pleased. But then Karen had to mention him: Stevie, the specter at the feast. It wasn't her fault, but that was the end of the "happy birthday' game. The others went home and left us alone again. Tilly sat and looked at her presents. I could see that she was desperately holding herself together, like a sandcastle being lapped by the waves. And we both knew that the tide was coming in. I think she was doing it for me, protecting me from her hurt. She acts like she's the mother and I'm the child. So what did I do? I drowned my sorrows. Again. Pathetic, despicable, worthless bitch that I am, I drank myself to sleep. Again.

I don't know what woke me but I knew straight away that something was wrong. I couldn't breathe. I knew it was Tilly. The sight of her in the garden will haunt me every moment until I die. I didn't know how completely, unconditionally, and desperately I loved her until I saw her against the flames and smoke, howling in misery. All she wanted was him. So I gave her the next best thing—a cast-iron alibi for her daddy. It was the only thing that could keep him from her on her birthday if he loved her best in the world. He was her hero; nothing could stop him except this. My twisted gift to Tilly was to keep her dream daddy alive. To keep him perfect, I had to kill him. I panicked and I lied. And now I must find a way to live with the lie and make it true. I have to find a way to keep him dead.

"Jesus, Tilda, and I thought the doll was bad enough." Joseph Geronimo does the rounds with the whisky bottle, while Penelope pauses to take in what she has just read.

"I buried that bloody doll in the garden. Just like my mother buried her secret in her diary." I giggle. It's not funny, but it's the whisky. I can never drink whisky. Penelope "huh-hmms," ready to continue.

November 24

The questions have begun. At first Tilly was too upset to ask. She clung to me as if she were afraid that I might disappear as well. She cried until she was sick. And I have had to watch and listen to her misery, knowing that I have caused it. But I only did it to save her from knowing that her daddy doesn't care anymore. And surely that would have hurt her more. But now she wants to know things, details. I have to be so careful. I have to tell her enough to satisfy her but not too much in case I get muddled. Stevie sent her a birthday card. I told her that he must have posted it just before he died. I told her that he drowned on the way back to the pub one night. I didn't say he was drunk, but maybe I implied it. Slipped and fell into the sea and that lots of people saw it happen, but it was dark and rough and no one could rescue him. I said that I couldn't tell her straight away, because I didn't want to spoil her birthday; that I was going to tell her a few days later. But she's so sharp. I try to keep my story straight but I can see that she doesn't trust me. I would willingly die for her but she doesn't even trust her own mother.

Jesus Christ, he's gone. Why can't she just accept that he's never coming back? But she couldn't and so there were more questions, more salt in the wounds. She pushed me too far and I lost it. What little control I had left after a cocktail of pills and a bottle of whisky as a chaser. God only knows what I did and said. I don't remember and I don't want to, because it frightened her to death. My beloved baby girl is terrified of me and now she is all I have left. I've lost Stevie for good. If he ever finds out what I've done, he'll hate me forever and take her away. And then I'll have nobody. Nothing. I may as well be the one who's dead. In a moment of madness I've sacrificed my husband for our child and I've got no idea what to do next.

Penelope is quiet for a moment. She and Joseph Geronimo both look at me, perhaps to check how I am coping. The whisky is washing my wounds and dulling the pain. But I'm glad she didn't remember what she did and write it down. I don't think, even now, I could bear to hear it spoken out loud; that I was so afraid of my own mother that I wet myself.

November 25

I must make a new life for Tilly and me, and I have to do it soon. Stevie's job will finish in the new year and he's talking about coming home in January. I write to him and send him Tilly's letters, but I always burn his replies. After I've read them. We have to disappear before he comes back. It kills me to think that I will never see him again. Never hold him again. But I had to make a choice, and I chose Tilly. I need to show her that I can be a good mother. After Christmas I'll think of something. I just have to try to keep this mess from Wendy and the others until I do. Though God knows how. The drink doesn't help. It loosens my tongue and I say things I shouldn't, especially to Tilly. But without it I couldn't carry on. It softens and sweetens and muffles and blurs. It cushions me in case I fall. I'll give it up soon, but I need a little help for a bit longer. And then I'll stop.

"Me too." It comes out a little bit louder than I intended. "Soon," as I wave my empty teacup at Joseph Geronimo. He obligingly refreshes it. Penelope puts the diary down and takes a sip from her cup. And then another. She looks across at me, seemingly nervous.

"Ta-dah!" Again, it's a bit too loud. The whisky is playing havoc with my volume control. "What do you think of that, then?" I inquire of each of them in turn with my hands and eyebrows raised. "It's no wonder she took to spending so much time in church!"

The discussion that follows is made both easier and more difficult for me by the whisky. Easier because the people and events we're talking about feel once removed, more distant, like a cousin. More difficult, because I'm finding it increasingly hard to concentrate and not laugh. Penelope struggles at first. She knew my mother well, but the diary is that of a complete stranger to her. After a lot of brow furrowing and a bit more whisky, she speaks.

"I know without doubt, Tilda, that she loved you more than her own life and nothing I have read here casts any doubt on that. But she was obviously ill and desperate and terrified of losing you. It doesn't justify what she did, but perhaps it helps to explain it. Sometimes good people do terrible things because they truly believe it's the only thing they can do." She looks at me, trying to read my face. She won't find anything sensible there.

"Bloody awful for you, though," she mutters, almost to herself. She sips more whisky from her cup.

"Oh, for pity's sake, there's no tea in this anymore. Where are the bloody glasses?"

She gets up and fetches some cut-glass whisky tumblers from the sideboard. I am fighting the urge to giggle at Penelope's "language," as my mother would have called it. Hearing Penelope swear is like hearing a nun fart. This was supposed to be a serious discussion, but I'm really struggling now.

"She didn't have to tell you any of this." Joseph Geronimo takes out a cigarette, but remembering where he is, doesn't light it. "It takes a shit load of guts to admit to something like this, especially to the person you were trying to protect in the first place. And she didn't bury her secrets forever. She knew you'd find the diaries. She meant for you to find them."

"Yes, but she knew she'd be dead before I did. It's easy to be brave when you're a corpse."

Penelope goes to say something at this point, but decides to have another sip of whisky instead.

"Even so, she could have taken her secret with her forever, so why didn't she?" Joseph Geronimo puts his cigarette between his lips and takes it out again.

"Oh, for heaven's sake, man, light it. And can I have one please?" Penelope passes him an ashtray and he offers her his packet. She grins like a naughty schoolgirl. Her cheeks are looking very rosy as she draws tentatively on her cigarette.

"I haven't had one of these for years."

I am trying to muster up some proper anger toward my mother but somehow I can't find the will to do it properly.

"She bloody well knew she wouldn't have to answer to me for any of this. I can hardly go and stomp on her grave."

Joseph Geronimo smiles. "Well, you could, but I don't expect it would help you much. For what it's worth, I think she was trying to put something right."

Penelope is getting back into the swing of her smoking now.

"Perhaps your mother spent the rest of her life answering to herself, and God, for what she did. I'm sure it never left her a moment's real peace."

"I don't know who I am anymore." It's not a wail. I

sound more like someone who's cross because they've lost a glove.

Joseph Geronimo smiles at me tolerantly, as though addressing an overtired child, but his tone is serious.

"Of course you do. You're still Tilda. You can't change any of the stuff that happened before and none of it changes who you are now. But now, at least, you know the truth. What you do with it is up to you. But the worst bit's over. You've faced it and nobody died."

"No. Not even my dad, apparently."

My inappropriate explosion of laughter must be blamed on shock and an excess of strong drink, but Joseph Geronimo has only half my excuse. The pair of us are soon helpless with laughter. Penelope kindly ignores our childish behavior.

"Well, my dear, it's too soon to decide anything yet. The water's far too muddy."

A bit like my head. I wish I'd eaten something more substantial than a mince pie before I decided that I quite like whisky after all.

"Now, I suggest we all have something to eat."

Penelope must have read my mind.

By the time Daniel arrives (by process of elimination—he'd been to the café and my flat already) we are sitting among the ruins of a Fortnum & Mason hamper, still drinking whisky and singing "Danny Boy," which, when Daniel appears, I find absolutely hilarious, along with just about everything else by this point. It's late, and we leave Penelope tottering off to bed having tucked up Joseph Geronimo in a blanket on the sofa, much to his delight and amusement. Reluctantly, Eli leaves his warm spot by the fire to follow us back upstairs. Daniel has failed to extract a sensible explanation out of any of us, but at the door he remembers a question he has for Joseph Geronimo.

"How did it go with Fatima-Jane?"

Joseph Geronimo raises himself onto one elbow and shakes his head.

"I was hoping for belly, but she was more into Morris."

Daniel clearly has no idea what he's talking about.

Joseph Geronimo winks broadly. "Dancing, Danny boy, dancing!"

37

Tilda

Never, ever again. Never again shall whisky pass my lips. I make my solemn vow from the cold, hard floor of the bathroom where I am engaged in a desperate embrace with the lavatory. I have been horribly sick and I can feel an encore approaching. If I move my head even slightly, all the little goblins inside it start using my brain as a bouncy castle and the wicked fairy of hangover stabs my temples with her hatpin. My stomach feels like a washing machine full of compost on a slow spin cycle. I think I might be dying. Daniel knocks on the bathroom door far too cheerfully and much too loudly.

"I've made you some breakfast."

The washing machine immediately clicks onto fast spin and begins to empty. Daniel beats a hasty retreat. Ten minutes later he tries again.

"Come on, Tilda. Out you come. I've made you some toast. You have to eat something with your acetaminophen."

He's got a point. Gingerly I loosen my grip on the white porcelain and drag myself up from the floor. I break the journey to vertical by sitting on the edge of the bath for a bit before finally standing up. The goblins are now performing *Riverdance*. The woman in the mirror staring back at me has skin the color and texture of putty and the eyes of a bloodhound. It's not my best look. As I leave the safety of the bathroom Daniel greets my appearance with gentle laughter.

"Holy Mary Mother of God! I've seen corpses with more life in them."

He gives me a tentative hug while sensibly turning his head to one side and leads me to a chair at the kitchen table. There is a glass containing a rather suspect-looking liquid in front of me.

"Now drink that up and I'll get you some nice dry toast."

"What is it?"

"Best not to ask. But I promise it will make you feel better. And don't sip it. Drink it all at once, and then hold your mouth shut until it goes down."

It's like standing shivering at the edge of a very cold sea in your bathing suit. You know the best thing is to dive straight in but you have to steel yourself. I pick up the glass, but halfway to my lips my courage fails me and I put it back down. On my third attempt I finally take the plunge. The liquid is cold, a little slimy, and has a hot, spicy aftertaste with a hint of banana. I spend a full five minutes with my hand clamped over my mouth, sitting bolt upright assisting gravity to keep the liquid where I've put it. After several escape attempts it settles down and I can risk speaking.

"God, Daniel, I'm so sorry. And I'm so embarrassed."

"Well, don't be. It seemed like quite a party you were having. I'm sorry I missed it."

He places a plate of toast in front of me. It has a thin scraping of butter and is cut into rounded abstract shapes like clouds.

"I thought I'd save you the bother of all that fiddling about and cutting it into tiny squares."

It takes me a while to brave the toast but when I do, he's right. I do feel better. Not great, but definitely better. Daniel sits opposite me, occasionally looking up from his monumental fry-up, smiling and shaking his head with amusement. After my second cup of tea I get up and fetch the diary. I open it at the page where Penelope began reading aloud. I hand it to Daniel and ruffle his hair.

"Thank you for my horrid drink and my toast clouds. I'm going to have a bath and try and turn myself back into a living person. If you read this, you'll understand what last night was all about."

I stay in the bath until my skin is wrinkled, like a forgotten apple lurking in the depths of the fruit bowl. I wallow in a cloud of steam and bubbles, hoping that my hangover will seep out through my pores and disappear down the drain along with the bath water when I finally emerge. By the time I'm dried and dressed, with a bit of makeup on and out of direct sunlight, I look reasonable and feel more like myself. I'm very grateful that the hangover fairy seems to have left the building, taking all her little goblins with her. Daniel is still sitting at the table drinking tea. The diary is open in front of him but he has stopped reading.

"Well, I reckon it's a bestseller."

He speaks gently, allowing his tone to offer the sympathy that he knows I couldn't cope with in words.

"What did your drinking companions say?"

I try to remember.

"Penelope said that good people sometimes do terrible things and Joseph Geronimo said that by leaving the diaries for me, my mother was trying to put something right." I sit down opposite him and steal a sip of his tea. "And what do you think?"

Daniel looks at me and shrugs his shoulders.

"I think it's all about love."

I stare blankly back at him. He may as well have said "sneakers." Perhaps my hangover is finding its second wind. Daniel stands up. He needs more room to air his explanation. Even Eli is sitting up now and giving Daniel his full attention.

"Think about it, Tilda," he says, throwing his arms in the air. "All that stuff, that madness, that heartbreak. It's all about love. It makes you crazy and you can end up acting like an idiot. Oh yes, love might be 'a many splendored thing,' but it's also a right royal pain in the ass!"

I'm stunned, and Eli has tipped his head to one side in apparent confusion, but Daniel is warming to his subject now and adds striding about to his arm waving.

"Look—Gracie loved you and she loved Stevie. But she loved too hard, and it drove her crazy because she didn't love herself and so she didn't think that anyone else could. She gave up everything for love but didn't feel loved in return. And yes, she was ill and thought God had disowned her, which probably didn't help, but in the end it was all about love."

Even in my slightly befuddled state Daniel's words strike home. Sometimes a simple truth is like a hammer blow. Daniel sits down again and checks his mug for tea. It's empty.

"And at this point, I'd also like to take issue with Lennon and McCartney for propagating the ridiculous notion that all we need is love. I can think of at least five more things just off the top of my head, and given more time for proper consideration I'd probably come up with a few more." He looks sorrowfully into his empty mug. "And one of them is definitely tea."

I get up and put the kettle on.

Later, as we are walking hand in hand along the promenade to open the café for any teatime trade, Daniel starts swinging my arm backward and forward. It's something he does when he wants to say something and doesn't quite know how to say it.

"All that stuff about love being a right royal pain in the ass . . . I don't mean with you. It's not like that with you."

He carries on swinging my arm.

"The madness, and the making you crazy, sure enough. But not the pain in the ass."

At the café, we switch on the lights and turn the jukebox on. I set the tables while Daniel fires up the coffee machine. It's still only early afternoon but already it's almost dark. As I watch the strings of colored lights flicker into life along the pier, I finally voice the thought that has been chasing round and round inside my head.

"Jesus, Daniel. What if he's still alive?"

38

Tilda

Looking back, I always thought that my mother had killed him. And I never once doubted that he was dead. I thought she had driven him away and that if he had stayed at home with us he wouldn't have died. I always blamed her and I was right. She murdered him for me. I wasted years mourning, praying and lighting candles for a man who wasn't actually dead. And now, after all this time, I have to consider the possibility, however remote, that he might not actually be dead.

These days I remember my childhood like an old movie shot in soft focus mellowed by distance and nostalgia, that jumps and jerks from one frame to another. Some of the characters are just shadows in the background, some have starring roles, and others are out of the frame altogether. Bits of the film are missing or blurred and it is shot entirely from one perspective. With the content of my mother's diaries it will be completely remastered and restored in high definition and glorious color. But what if I prefer my original screenplay?

I have finished reading the first diary now, rushing through it, searching for clues about what really happened to my dad. I remember that first Christmas without him. My mother tried so hard to make it happy for me. I remember the red sweater with reindeers that made me itch, and going to church with Mrs. O'Flaherty on Christmas Eve. I prayed so hard for my dad in case he was stuck in Purgatory. I loved St. Patrick's. It was such a beautiful place and full of magic. And dead people. The dead people didn't bother me then. People were just people and I either liked them or I didn't. Whether they were dead or alive made no difference to my opinion of them. It was only later that they became a problem, and that was my mother's lesson. She lived in fear and made it my inheritance. But it made me fear the living, not the dead. That year Father Christmas brought me a heart-shaped locket engraved with a "T," which, according to the diary, was sent by my dad. She never told me the truth about where it came from but at least she gave it to me. In the diary she also tells the truth about the letters. So many lies undone; the fragile fabric of her fabrications unraveled at last by the truth. She told me when I wrote them that the letters were taken to my dad by a special angel. She didn't tell me that the angel was an employee of Royal Mail.

The next diary will take me and my mother to Queenie's. And that is where I am going today. Of course, it's not Queenie's anymore. When Queenie retired, my mother and Reg ran it very successfully together for another ten years. When Reg died of a stroke my mother sold The Paradise Hotel and moved into her flat. It is now, according to its website, a luxury boutique hotel run by Aubrey and Austin, whose aim is to make each of their guests feel cherished and pampered.

I can't wait to meet them but I am uneasy about revisiting my sacred childhood sanctuary and finding it wrecked beyond recognition. I have rung ahead and asked if could visit. I said that I lived there as a child, but nothing more. I'm not sure if it was Austin or Aubrey I spoke to, but he was both delighted and delightful.

It takes me only ten minutes to walk from the flat to what will always be "Queenie's" to me. A new rococo, black and gold wrought-iron sign proclaims The Paradise Hotel's status as a "bijou and boutique hotel." The profusion of plastic potted petunias and marigolds from my childhood has been replaced by miniature bay trees topiaried into pom-poms, but the Union Jack remains. Either side of the front door are two black artificial Christmas trees, scattered with tiny white fairy lights and topped with silver replicas of Michelangelo's David, wearing black net tutus to preserve their modesty. I ring the doorbell to be greeted by a full orchestral rendition of Carl Orff's *Carmina Burana*, and two men who appear simultaneously to answer the door.

"You must be Tilda. We're so excited to meet you. Come in, come in."

The speaker is a slim, well-groomed man in his early forties, with very short fair hair and an engaging smile.

"I'm Austin, after Healey—I was conceived in one, according to my mother—and this is Aubrey, after Beardsley. His father was a fan."

Aubrey is a little shorter and heavier than Austin, with dark hair thinning on top and heavy, black-framed glasses. His violet shirt is immaculately pressed and his square silver cuff links blink and wink under the hall lights as he shakes my hand.

"Delighted to meet you, Tilda. Do come through and have a drink."

The hallway, staircase, and corridor through to what used to be the guests' sitting room are wallpapered in a striking pattern of enormous black and white roses punctuated with Venetian glass mirrors. There is not an aspidistra in sight. I suddenly realize that in coming here I am desperate to find a trace of my old life, but after so many years, incredibly foolish to believe that I shall. I am wrong. The old wooden reception desk has been replaced with a gleaming black marble monster with lascivious curves and curlicues. Sitting on top of it, in majestic splendor and protected by a huge glass dome, is Queenie's stuffed corgi.

"It looks like you've found an old friend."

Austin is watching me as I gasp with astonishment and then clasp my hands with delight.

"Well, finally, we may have found someone who can settle this once and for all."

Aubrey is affectionately patting the top of the glass dome and looking at me expectantly.

"What the devil is this chap's name?"

"Queenie always called him Prince Phillip."

There is a brief but significant silence shattered by an explosion of squeals, shrieks, OMGs, and hand clapping. I always thought that it was quite funny, but not that good.

Finally, Aubrey composes himself sufficiently to take both of my hands in his, and in an almost reverential tone, barely louder than a whisper, asks, "Did you actually know Queenie?"

Austin and Aubrey are Queenie's biggest fans. They

have an enormous collection of programs from Queenie's brief but apparently illustrious career, a couple of albums she recorded, signed photographs and ticket stubs, and a feather boa she once wore on stage. They even have some footage of her shows. They have spent a great deal of time and money lovingly gathering memorabilia of a person they have never met and are much too young to have seen perform live, and yet they seem to love her almost as if they knew her. They certainly know far more about her time as a performer than I do. Queenie will always be a star to me, but I had no idea that she was actually quite famous. I learn all of this while drinking prosecco in their private lounge that was, in Queenie's day, the guests' sitting room. Except for the carpet and curtains it is exactly how I remember it and exactly what I need, a happy childhood memory still intact and—most important—still true.

"When Queenie died we cried for days and we were desperate to get hold of this place when it came on the market. The woman who sold it to us had inherited it from Queenie herself. It came with most of its contents included in the price. We thought we'd died and gone to heaven."

Aubrey wanders round the room proudly surveying Queenie's treasures. The china dogs still sit on top of the piano, the clock on the mantel is still ticking, and the man in the boots and hat still has his eye on the young lady's oranges. Even the plastic flowers have survived.

"Of course, we would have left the whole place pretty much as it was when we bought it, but it's not what people want now, is it? They watch too many property shows on TV, telling them what they should and shouldn't like. So now it's all minimalist chic and statement piece this and en suite that. I ask you—what sort of person wants a lavatory in their bedroom? But at least we still have all this."

"What was she like, the woman you bought the place from?"

I have to ask.

"We never met her, did we, Aubrey? It was all done through solicitors and estate agents. But she left us a bottle of champagne and a note to welcome us, saying she hoped we'd be as happy here as she had been, so she must have been nice. It was a lovely thing to do."

I keep quiet. That confession can wait until another day. And I'm sure that there will be another day with Austin and Aubrey. After two bottles of fizz and endless questions about Queenie and The Paradise Hotel, they allow me to leave. Daniel is at the café, getting ready for his New Year's Eve party tomorrow, and I promised that after my visit I would go and help. Before I leave, I invite Austin and Aubrey to come. They see me to the door and stand together in the porch light between the Christmas trees to wave me off. As I turn to leave, Aubrey places a hand on my arm and says, with a sincerity that tugs at my heart and fills me with pride, "It's a privilege to meet someone who really knew her. In her time, you know, she was the best. No other drag queen even came close."

39

Tilda

The heart-shaped wooden box was at the back of the bottom drawer of the tallboy in my mother's bedroom. The drawer is full of paperwork that I haven't got round to sorting out yet. When I first went through my mother's things I dealt with the easy stuff first: clothes, linen, surplus household stuff, and furniture I didn't want to keep. A quick glance in the drawer was enough for me to dismiss its contents as a job for later, and I missed the box. But now my mother's papers have taken on a new significance in the search for Stevie, so I have returned to the drawer. The box had been Queenie's mother's. As I lift the lid the music that I danced to at my first class with Miss Cynthia sparkles out of the box and into the air: "Je te veux." Inside nestles a ragbag of treasures. The silver "Mother' brooch is still bright and shiny as the day I gave it to her. There is a lock of baby hair tied with a scrap of pink ribbon and pinned to a knitted baby bootie, and three milk teeth wrapped up tight in a child's handkerchief. My silver christening bracelet is there too, and a program from Miss Cynthia's Christmas Concert when I danced a solo to "The Glow-Worm." It is as pristine as the day

it was printed, and inside my name is carefully under-
lined and the note in the margin in my mother's handwriting reads "She was beautiful." There is a gold locket
engraved with a "G." I remember my mother wearing
it. Inside it is a picture of my parents on their wedding
day. I unscrew the lid of a half-empty bottle of after-
shave and sniff gingerly. It smells of my dad. Queenie's
watch is in there too, a small, round face on a gold-
colored expandable link bracelet. And lastly there is a
photograph of a man and woman in their late forties;
respectable-looking. God-fearing. The woman has a
birthmark just above her left eye. It looks like a thumbprint. She is the woman I met in the graveyard. "Mum
and Dad," it says on the back of the photograph; my
grandparents. It seems these were my mother's most
precious possessions and she made this box her reli-
quary. I think Daniel must be right. It was all about
love. If only I'd known.

I shouldn't have started this now. I haven't got time.
I still have Queenie's watch in my hand. I no more expect it to work than I did the Christmas tree lights all
those years ago, but several tentative turns of the winder
are rewarded by a gentle, rhythmic ticking. I slip the
bracelet over my wrist. I need to get ready for the party
and collect Penelope, who has, once again, managed to
evade the niece and her New Year's Eve Thai turkey
curry extravaganza with wines recommended by *Good
Housekeeping* and mince-pie ice cream *à la* Delia. Penelope is coming to our party instead. Daniel is already at
the café with Joseph Geronimo, no doubt sampling the
food and drink and generally getting into the party
spirit. Last night I told him all about my visit to The

Paradise Hotel, and Aubrey and Austin, but he was more interested in Queenie.

"You never told me Queenie was a man," he said.

It was hard to explain. You had to have been there. And then.

"I was a little girl. Queenie was just Queenie to me. I suppose I knew almost from the start. I mean, I don't remember it ever being a shock or a surprise. But you had to know her to really understand. She was so much more than just a man, or a woman for that matter. She was a fairy godmother crossed with a fire-eater and we all loved her. But to me she was perfect, the soap powder mummy that I had always longed for. It really was as simple as that."

"And what about straight-laced Gracie? From what you've told me, I can't imagine that she would have approved, let alone lived and worked with her. It doesn't make sense."

But of course it did. It made perfect sense. I hadn't really thought about it before. As a child I had simply accepted the situation for what it was. I was happy and secure and I didn't need to know any more. But as soon as Daniel had asked the question, I knew the answer.

"She was a mother to Gracie as well; and Gracie knew that Queenie, unlike her real mother, would never abandon her no matter what. Queenie made her feel safe, needed and loved. She understood what it was like to be different and she accepted Gracie for who she was, just like her own mother had accepted Queenie. In fact, at The Paradise Hotel, my mother fit in very nicely. Everyone there had been cracked in the kiln in one way or another. Lil was afflicted with terrible mood swings and rages, Marlene and her friends were the barking side of eccentric, and nowadays Cecily would be labeled as having 'learning difficulties.' Even Reg had a glass eye."

"And what about you?"

"Well, apart from dissecting my food with geometric precision, a phobia of boiled eggs, growing windmills in the back garden, and believing that God sent sinners to Bermondsey, I was completely normal."

We both laughed and I thought how right Queenie had been about Daniel. She was the best mother I had ever known, despite being a man with no children of her own.

"And what about seeing ghosts? Is that normal?"

Bang. The sixty-four-thousand-dollar question, out of the blue. No one was laughing now. This was my big moment. The one where others have cut and run. Or I have. Daniel had thrown me a hand grenade and my answer would be the pin: out or in?

"It is for me."

I watched his face and waited. There was no shock or horror. He looked like he was trying to decide what to choose from a menu.

"Have you seen Queenie since she died?"

"All the time. She promised me years ago that she would never go away, and she never has."

Daniel gripped his chair in mock fear.

"Is she here now?"

I'm weak with relief. "So you don't think I'm mad?"

His whole face broke into a smile. "Of course I do. It's part of your endless charm. To be honest with you, I find the cutting up the food thing much more annoying than the dead people. God, it takes you a whole day to eat a slice of toast. Longer if it has beans on it. A man could starve to death while you're still on your starter. But that's okay because we have that in hand now, don't we?"

There was a slight pause before a wicked grin broke across his face.

"I have to ask. Queenie—she's not around when we . . . you know?" He winked at me and I thumped his arm, laughing.

"Of course not!"

"So . . . when did you last see her?"

"Yesterday, at The Paradise Hotel, she was in the guests' old sitting room."

"What was she doing?"

I smiled at the thought.

"Checking for dust."

"Did you tell Austin and whatshisname?"

"Aubrey. No."

"Why not?"

I don't know why. I'm sure they'd be thrilled to know that she still pops in. In fact they'd probably be chasing her round the house with a Ouija board.

"Maybe because I'm so used to hiding it. It's normal for me to see what I see, but it's also normal for me to pretend that I don't. It scares people."

"Jesus, Tilda, you must have been hanging around with a right bunch of wimps until now."

I didn't tell him that, until now, I haven't really hung around with anyone unless they're dead.

"What about your mother? Have you seen her?"

I laughed out loud.

"Now there's one thing that's never going to happen.

It's more likely that Jesus wants Saddam Hussein for a sunbeam."

Daniel raised his eyebrows theatrically.

"Because . . . ?"

"Because she was the one who told me it was wrong, the work of the devil. She said that it was a one-way ticket to Bedlam and basket-weaving for basket cases. And if you're really lucky, they'll plug you in and light you up like a Christmas tree."

"Perhaps not, then. What about your dad, have you seen him?"

He took it all very well. It was almost as though we were talking about a hobby I have, like the piano. Could I play "Chopsticks' or "Für Elise'?

"Daniel, I'm not like he was, I never learned how to control it. I can't pick and choose. I'm not a medium and I don't know how it works; I can only see them if they want me to. I can't make them come, and I can't make them go away. I just have to live with them."

Daniel was quiet for a moment, but he still wanted to know.

"Yes, but have you seen him?"

"No. Not once."

"Then that must mean he's still alive. If he was dead, he surely would have found a way."

I denied it.

"It's not that simple, Daniel. I told you. I've no idea how it all works."

But I have to admit, the same thought had crossed my mind.

Now, Queenie's watch tells me that it is already seven o'clock and I'm running late. After lighting a single match and taking a quick shower I get ready and call for Penelope. The cab is already on its way. The unseasonably miserable woman who took my call warned that "We don't take no drunks, stags, hens, or dogs." I tell Eli, but when the cab arrives he gets in anyway. By the time we arrive the party is rocking and rolling, and the café is almost full. Eli seeks refuge behind the counter. I introduce Penelope to Austin and Aubrey and leave them to bond over champagne cocktails and sausages on sticks. Daniel is busy serving drinks and as he blows me a kiss I can tell by the twinkle in his eye and the tilt of his smile that he has already served a fair few to himself. Joseph Geronimo is at the jukebox with Queenie. I join them and, kissing him on the cheek, steal Joseph Geronimo's choice.

"I love this song. Dad used to sing it to me."

He looks up and grins.

"I haven't been able to stomach it for years. I used to drink in a pub where the landlord played it over and over. It drove me crazy. But it's been a while. I think I can take it now. Just for you."

For me, it's like an old friend.

> *Her eyes they shone like the diamonds,*
> *You'd think she was queen of the land,*
> *And her hair hung over her shoulders*
> *Tied up with a black velvet band.*

40

Tilda

January brings a welcome "new broom" freshness; a bucket of clean water to wash away the dust and dregs of the weary old year. My head feels clear and my heart strong as I start, once again, with the diaries. I settle down in a chair by the French windows with a mug of steaming tea and allow myself a few idle moments of gazing out at the glittering, marbled sea before beginning to read.

January 2

We have to run away. Tilly has let the cat out of the bag to Wendy. It was only ever going to be a matter of time but Wendy has forced my hand and so we must leave as soon as we can. She went mad. Said that what I'd done was the wickedest thing she'd ever heard and that she would find Stevie and tell him or report me to social services. It breaks my heart to lose Wendy. She's been such a good friend and it's hard to know that she thinks badly of me, especially when she's always taken my side. But she doesn't understand. If I lost Tilly it would destroy me. Stevie's still in Ireland, or so he says, but according to his last letter he'll be back in a couple of weeks. If we don't leave now it will be too late. It kills me what I'm doing to Stevie. But I'd rather do this than have him find out that I killed *him*. So, I'm going to Queenie's. I haven't seen her since we were both in that God-forsaken hospital. Without Queenie I wouldn't have gotten through it. We wove footstools, laughed, cried, and even danced together, in that stark, echoing gymnasium with tinny music blaring from an ancient gramophone. The weekly Patient Socialization Dance, it was called, but we called it The Psychos' Shuffle. Of course, he was Evelyn then, but desperate to be Queenie, which is why he ended up there in the first place. But he was strong enough to stop pretending and be the person he really was. When he left he made a new life as Queenie. When I left I just made my old life worse, and I still have no idea who I really am. We stayed in touch; just a few cards and letters, but Queenie always said that if I ever needed a friend I only had to ask. Well, now I've asked, she said "yes," and we're going. Tilly thinks that we're just going to the seaside for a holiday. I'll cross that bridge when I come to it.

The winter wind is howling outside, whipping the waves into froth and foam and sweeping stinging swirls of sand along the beach. But I remember that day the sun was bright, the frost sparkled on the lawn, and the sky was a faraway, perfect blue. I remember the angry shouting and the tipping, squeezing fear I felt when I heard it, and Auntie Wendy's face as she stormed out of the back door. I thought she was going to say something to me, but in the end she left without a word. I never saw her again. Two days later we turned up on Queenie's doorstep. Queenie, who used to be Evelyn.

January 10

Queenie is a blessing and a miracle. She welcomed us with open arms and has offered me a job that comes with accommodation, here in the hotel. Tilly loves The Paradise and Brighton, and she loves Queenie. I don't think I'll have any trouble persuading her to stay. I think we have found the perfect hiding place.

January 20

For the first time in a very long time, I don't feel mad. I feel like I've stopped holding my breath and listening for the bogeyman to knock on the door. Maybe this is what it feels like to be happy. It's been so long, I can't remember. Or maybe I've just stopped being alone. Nobody here thinks we're strange and nobody asks any awkward questions or whispers behind our backs. Instead of standing out like we normally do, tagged and tainted by our differences, here we blend in. Here, at Queenie's, with one abracadabra, we can disappear and be free.

I wonder what she told Queenie about Stevie, or if she told her anything at all? Queenie was never one to pry. She was a good listener and loved a good gossip, and she was happy to give advice when asked. But she would never force a confidence and she's never mentioned anything about it to me since. The diary entries for February and March are less frequent. My mother was probably too busy helping Queenie to write much. But maybe she didn't need to. She had real people to talk to now, who were a kind of family. Perhaps they were enough. She did mention that she never sent the postcards I wrote to Auntie Wendy or Mrs. O'Flaherty.

I can't risk Wendy finding out where we are but I am sorry about Mrs. O'Flaherty. She will worry about Tilly and wonder what's happened. She was very good to her, without making me feel like a bad mother. Maybe one day we'll be able to see her again and thank her.

She describes how Queenie arranged for Reg to take her in a van to pick up all our things from our old house.

I was terrified one of the neighbors would see us and tell Wendy, and sure enough, she turned up soon after we got there. But Reg told me to stay in the house and keep out of sight while he dealt with her. He told her what I had asked him to. It was the first thing that came into my head; a distraction to make her look in the wrong direction, if only for a little while. When she turned awkward he sent her away with a flea in her ear. Queenie wouldn't even let me pay for the van, but at least Reg let me buy him a drink.

She talks about Lil, Cecily, Queenie's mother, and Reg, describing their antics and eccentricities with surprising tolerance and obvious affection. But it is clear from her diary that Queenie was the star.

Queenie has saved me again—from myself and the private hell I was hiding in. She has given me back a life worth living and provided me and Tilly with a happy home and a new family. But that doesn't mean I will ever stop loving Stevie; I can't forget him and what I've done. And if I could find a way of giving Tilly her daddy back, I would. But how can I do that now?

But maybe now she has. At least her diaries have given me the chance to look for him.

And so to me. What does her diary say about me? Outside, the wind has dropped, and a pale silver specter of the winter sun backlights the somber clouds. She says that I am better than I was. Much better. Happy. Very happy. I have made new friends. Everyone at Queenie's loves me, and I love all of them. I'm doing well at school. I'm having dance lessons.

But.

Tilly will always have our bad blood in her; an unstable mother and an ungodly father. She still sees ghosts. I wish I could make it stop.

She never did. And now, at last, I realize that I am glad. Eli is staring out of the front window into the street. I join him just in time to see Penelope being dropped outside by her niece. She sees me and waves. She is looking tired, and the walk to the front door seems long and laborious. She told me yesterday that she thinks her candle may be burning down. I told her not to talk rubbish, but I think she may be right. I make a mental note to go down in a little while and make her a cup of tea. And I make another one to start my search for Stevie before his candle burns out altogether.

41

Tilda

The sun is hot on my face and Eli is sleeping at my feet. I close my eyes and breathe in the warm, sweet scent. I love the smell of lilac. It is a beautiful spring day and I am wearing the new dress that Daniel bought me. It has been four months since I started looking for Stevie but he is still lost. It seems that he has disappeared as successfully as we did all those years ago, and all the wizardry of new technology has yet to pull this particular rabbit out of the hat where he is hidden. There have been false hopes and false alarms and many trails that have just grown cold. I tried finding Auntie Wendy and found her obituary instead. She died ten years ago of a heart attack, just a year after Uncle Bill, and Karen emigrated to Australia soon afterward with her husband and two little boys. Her brother, Kevin, still lives a few streets away from Wendy's old house, and he told me what he could. He remembers only bits and pieces: the day Reg collected the things from our old house; Wendy's fury at whatever it was that Reg had told her; Stevie sitting at their kitchen table on the day he came home looking for us with his head in his hands, sobbing. It meant precious little to Kevin at the time, but now, to me, every scrap of information is precious. The O'Flahertys had grown up and moved away, Teresa taking her mother to live with her after Mr. O'Flaherty gently died while happy and drunk in the pub one afternoon. She comes back every now and then to visit old friends and Kevin promised to give her my number and ask her to call me when he saw her next. I didn't hold my breath. "Oh ye of little faith," Daniel had said. And he was right. Yesterday I went to see Mrs. O'Flaherty.

Mrs. O'Flaherty had her own bedroom, sitting room, and bathroom in an annex to Teresa's smart new four-bedroom, mock-Tudor detached. At nearly ninety she was a physical miniature of the woman I remembered, but her warmth and spirit were undiminished.

"May God in heaven preserve us! It's Miss Tilly," she cried, as I stood hesitating in the doorway. "She's come back home to Blighty!"

She patted the seat of the chair facing her, and as I sat down, she took both my hands in hers.

"Let me look at you." She examined my face with her watery eyes. Once they had been the color of a summer sky, but now they resembled the winter sea.

"You look well, Miss Tilly. And happy. There must be a man." She raised her eyebrows and smiled. But Mrs. O'Flaherty knew I wasn't here to talk about now. I was more interested in then. But first, I had to ask, "What do you mean, 'back home to Blighty?'"

"From Van Diemen's Land?" She chuckled at my uncomprehending "shipping forecast" face. "Like the song?"

She sang her explanation in a cracked but still tuneful voice:

"Far away from my friends and companions,
Betrayed by the black velvet band."

The song meant so much to me, but I had no idea what Mrs. O'Flaherty meant by singing it to me now. She saw the confusion in my face and started again at the beginning. She hadn't known at the time what my mother had done, but she had suspected that something wasn't quite right.

"I thought at the time they had simply parted. It must have been hard. Your mother loved you both but it didn't seem to bring her any joy. You could see the hurt in her eyes. And as for your daddy, I'm sure he loved Gracie and he worshipped you, but he was a handful sometimes—like another child for your mother to mind. And he certainly had an eye for the ladies, but I don't think he ever strayed. I didn't know what to make of it. Then when he lost his job there were rumors of course; that he'd gone back to Ireland; that he was working in a pub and giving readings; even that he'd gotten another woman. And there were cruel things said about your mother by ignorant people with small lives who knew no better. But that's all they were: rumors, tittle-tattle and nasty gossip."

"But he didn't lose his job, he was sacked, wasn't he?" I remember the entry in my mother's diary and the furious rows just before he went away.

"Apparently so. He was supposed to have gotten into a fight with one of the other men. He accused Stevie of being a fraud and taking advantage of grieving folks with his readings. Punches were thrown and the other fella came off worse. But that's only what I heard. It was so long ago, and I don't expect we'll ever know the truth now. I'm not sure it even matters anymore."

It does to me.

After we disappeared, Wendy told Mrs. O'Flaherty about my mother's first lie, which I knew about, and a second about emigrating, which I didn't.

"Wendy was so angry with her, but I felt sad for all of you. Your mother was a broken woman, looking for something to fix her, but she'd a good heart. She tried so hard on that birthday of yours. I remember she looked like a ghost but she was the one who was haunted.

"And then you put the tin lid on it by setting the shed on fire."

She shook her head and chuckled softly to herself, but even after all these years I can still taste the tears and the smoke.

* * *

High up in one of the lilac trees a blackbird is singing and, despite the constant hum of traffic, I can just hear the sound of the waves. This place is a little heaven of fresh green, foaming mauve, sunshine and birdsong. I sit with Eli and wait. I have no idea what we are waiting for but I have a feeling that something or someone is coming.

* * *

I sat and drank tea with Mrs. O'Flaherty from blue-and-white willow-pattern cups and saucers.

"When that man came to fetch your things from the house, Wendy was sure she saw your mother inside and she was furious. But even more so when she heard from the chap that your mother was taking you and emigrating to Australia. 'Joining the Ten Pound Poms,' he said."

I tried to swallow the tea past the lump lodged in my throat. Among the photographs on the windowsill there was one that I recognized from the old house. It was the white-haired lady I used to see at St. Patrick's sitting behind Mrs. O'Flaherty. She followed my gaze, and then my train of thought.

"We missed you at St. Patrick's. But I used to light a candle for you."

"All those candles I used to light for my dad . . ."

She took hold of my hands in hers again and squeezed them tightly.

"A candle lit in God's house is never wasted, Miss Tilly." Then she continued, gently, "I know what you want from me, child, but I don't know where he is. I wish I did, but I don't."

She hadn't even seen Stevie when he'd been back to Wendy's.

"The only thing I know for sure is that he did come looking for you, but Wendy told him what the man had said and he went away with his heart broken. They all believed you'd gone. And so did I. Until now."

She shook her head in disbelief and then fixed me with her steady gaze.

"Don't you give up, Miss Tilly. You can still find him. And I hope and pray with all my heart that you do."

Before I left I promised I would visit her again, with Daniel, and that if I did find out anything about Stevie, I'd let her know. But where the hell was I going to look now?

Bermondsey?

*   *   *

301

Here in the public gardens, heavy plumes of tiny star-burst blossoms bow the branches of the lilac trees, and the blackbird sings on under sunshine and a bright blue sky. It was here my mother sat with blood on her new dress. It was here to her hometown that she brought me, the safest place, the perfect double bluff. Who would search for an arachnophobe in a spider's web? Here, where she was cruelly cut off by her parents and abandoned by her god. Here, where my mother's illness began, and where, just pregnant with her first child, she watched another die. She hid us in the last place in the world where anyone who knew her, especially Stevie, would look. It probably never occurred to her that the Australian story would actually work. Even though Queenie was here to support her, it was still the birthplace of all her terrors. But even so, she came back. Because of me. Her love was absolute.

I press my back into the hard wooden slats of the bench and stretch my arms behind me. The sun and scent of lilac are seducing me to sleep. Footsteps break the charm. Eli is sitting up and staring intently across the gardens. The elderly lady might easily have been one of Queenie's friends from the look of her. She walks with a stick but her frail frame is still proud and straight. She has the posture of a dancer and the look of a show-girl. Her gray hair is spun into a candyfloss chignon fixed with two pearl hairpins, and her lips are a slash of red Chanel. Her female companion is about my age and looks as though she has stepped straight out of a Pre-Raphaelite painting. She is carrying a red balloon. They make a striking pair but it is the older woman who unsettles me most. She is somehow familiar. I don't recognize her face. I don't know her at all. But somewhere there's a connection from her to me, like a ley line. It makes me nervous and I look away. I pass the time with fifteen Hail Marys, two Our Fathers, and five The Flight from Bootle's. The poem and the prayers are my worry beads. When I look round again, the women are gone, but the red balloon is tied to the wooden bench where they were sitting. I feel sick, but nonetheless I am compelled to look. The bench is in the sunniest spot of the gardens, and a brass plaque glints against the blistered varnish of the dark wood.

In loving memory of a precious daughter, "Bunny' Joy,
who was tragically killed, aged 6 years,
and her devoted father, Valentine,
who couldn't live without her.
Forever loved.

42

Tilly

Today they were going to look for Bunny's daddy. Tilly had promised. The Paradise Hotel was packed with guests and her mother and Queenie were rushed off their feet, so Tilly felt sure that she would be able to slip away unnoticed for a bit. She just had to wait for the right moment. Lil was banging and crashing round the kitchen trying to prepare twenty-two breakfasts while Cecily stood, with a dopey smile on her face, gazing at the photo she was holding.

"Isn't he gorgeous?" she asked, thrusting the snapshot at Tilly, who inspected it carefully.

"It's Sidney," she replied.

"Yes, I know it's Sidney. Isn't he lovely?"

"No. He's Sidney."

Lil hurled a frying pan into the sink and turned to face Cecily, her hands on her hips and her face the color of the tomatoes burning under the grill.

"I don't care if it's Frank Si-bloody-natra! If you don't sodding well shake your skinny-boned useless bloody ass over here and help me with these buggering bloody sodding bacon and sausages, I'll swing you round the garden by one scrawny buggering leg until your guts and gizzards fly out of your bollocking bloody bumhole ass fuck."

Lil's temper was always worse when she was really busy, and Tilly had learned an impressive number of new swear-word combinations from her. In fact, if the Brownies had a badge for swearing, Tilly thought she'd be able to get it without even practicing. If she'd been a Brownie. Even Cecily had grown used to Lil's outbursts, and whereas once she would have collapsed in tears, now she tucked the precious photo into her pocket and began turning the sausages in the pan, poking her tongue out at Lil while her back was turned. Over the months, Effie had worked her magic on Cecily, and with some makeup lessons and hand-me-down dresses had transformed her from an ugly duckling into a perfectly passable mallard.

Several dates with Sidney had followed and Cecily's confidence had finally blossomed. Or as Lil put it, "That girl's more daft in the head than ever now!"

"Tilly, love, could you pop this through to Mr. Johnson on table nine? He's very particular about his sauce and someone forgot to put it on his table."

Lil handed Tilly a bottle of brown sauce and she skipped off down the corridor to the guests' dining room. Mr. Johnson had already started on his sausages and was reading a magazine that was propped up on his teacup.

"What's it about?" Tilly asked, as she plonked the bottle of sauce down in front of him.

"Stamp collecting."

"Oh, so you're a pervert then?" she replied in her best "be nice to the guests' manner.

Mr. Johnson nearly choked on his sausage.

"I beg your pardon, young lady?"

"She said, 'You're a convert.'" Queenie swept over like a guardian angel. "To brown sauce," she continued smoothly. "Most people prefer red, but Tilly likes brown best too, don't you, love?"

Tilly nodded. She had absolutely no idea what Queenie was talking about, but had the distinct feeling that she had just been rescued and swiftly made her escape. Bunny was waiting for her in the back garden and the pair of them slipped out of the gate unnoticed and headed off toward the pier.

May 29

She looks so pale and still and small. They have washed her and brushed her hair, and the white sheet that covers her is neatly folded back, but already, to me, she looks like a ghost.

Tilly and Bunny skipped along the promenade hand in hand. Tilly waved to Ena and Ralph and then Conrad in passing, and when they reached the pier they sat down on a wooden bench to catch their breath and decide where to look. Tilly tried to remember what a policeman would do on the television if he was trying to find someone who was lost. Of course, if they had Lassie it would be easy. One word and she'd be off in a flash, and back before tea with the missing person in tow. But they only had Eli, who seemed on edge, and was sticking very closely to Tilly, watching her carefully with troubled eyes. Tilly thought it must be because she had gone out without telling anyone. Anyway, he clearly wasn't going anywhere without her. She chewed thoughtfully on a loose thread from the sleeve of her cardigan. Suddenly it came to her. Of course! A policeman would ask questions. Usually by knocking on doors and asking women in their curlers, or men wearing sleeveless undershirts and smoking cigarettes. But Tilly thought that failing that, the best place to start would be with Bunny. She just wished she had a pencil to lick and a notebook to write in. She put on her best "Dixon of Dock Green' face and began her interrogation.

"What does your daddy do?"

"Magic."

Tilly sighed and with exaggerated patience replied, "No, I meant what does he do for a job?"

"Magic. He does tricks."

"Does he have any hobbies?"

With a pang, she thought about her own daddy, his garden, and the smell of creosote and matches inside his shed.

"Yes. I already told you: magic."

This wasn't going well. Tilly gave it one more, slightly wild shot.

"What's his favorite color?"

"Pink."

"Are you sure?"

"No. But it's mine. It used to be red. But now it's pink."

Tilly sighed again. They didn't seem to be getting anywhere, and she couldn't stay out for too long or she would be missed and she didn't want her mother to worry. She stood up and offered Bunny her hand.

"Come on. Let's just go and look in as many places as we can think of."

The nurse says to speak to her and hold her hand because she will know that I am here. So I hold her hand, which is still warm. But I can't think of anything to say, so instead I write this.

They trotted down the pier, searching through the constant ebb and flow of faces. But Tilly didn't even know who she was looking for. Bunny's description had simply been "He looks like Daddy." When they reached the ballroom the doors were open and people were lining up to buy tickets for that afternoon's tea dance. Tilly and Bunny worked their way along the line and into the foyer with its plush scarlet carpet and newly painted walls covered in photos and posters. Tilly was about to suggest that they should head back home when Bunny squealed with delight.

"There he is! That's my daddy!"

She was pointing at one of the photographs. *Valentine Gray—The Great Mercurio*. It was Tilly's man. The man she had been seeing ever since she came to Queenie's. Even from her first day. Who needed Lassie now? She grabbed Bunny's hand and marched her out of the doors. She half ran to the galloping horses, pulling Bunny along with her.

"What's the matter?" the little girl asked in a worried voice.

"Nothing," gasped Tilly, not even bothering to stop and look at her. "I know him, and I think I might know some places where we might find him."

They were at the galloping horses now and Tilly was eagerly scanning the faces in the crowd of people gathered around the ride. Bunny kicked her hard on the ankle. Surprisingly, it really hurt. She finally looked at Bunny, whose face was rumpled into a furious scowl.

"Why didn't you tell me you knew him? We could have found him ages ago!"

"Because I didn't know I knew him until you showed me his picture. Now, come on!"

She dragged Bunny round all the places on the pier where she had seen Valentine, her heart pumping with excitement. But the magician was nowhere to be seen. Tilly had one more place up her sleeve.

I didn't even notice that she'd gone. If Queenie hadn't asked me to go to the bank, I wouldn't have known anything about it until the police came knocking on the door.

Just before they reached the public gardens, Tilly spotted him walking ahead of them, his black hat bobbing along in the sea of heads. He was holding a red balloon and walking so fast that Tilly had to run to keep up, holding on tightly to Bunny's hand. Weaving in and out of the slowly moving crowd and terrified that she would lose sight of him, she wanted to scream out loud at everyone to get out of her way.

It was the bone-chilling sound that made me turn around and look. Like the howl of a dog in unspeakable pain.

Opposite the gardens, Valentine turned to cross the road. Bunny yanked her hand free from Tilly and ran after him, straight into the path of the busy midmorning traffic, and without a thought Tilly followed. The last thing she saw before the blackness hit her was Bunny lifted high in her daddy's arms.

I turned and saw Tilly run straight across the road as though she were chasing after someone. I couldn't see who it was but I saw the car that Tilly didn't. She rolled across its bonnet and landed head first on the cold, hard stone of the curb. And now she is almost gone. The harder I cling to her, the further she slips away. She has been here for almost three weeks and each day she grows weaker. The doctor says I should prepare myself for the worst. Stupid, stupid man. How should I prepare myself? Buy a black dress and choose a coffin? Queenie keeps telling me to go home and rest, but how can I do that either? She comes and sits with us, smiling and laughing and holding Tilly's hand and telling her about anything and everything. She even sings to her. Where do people learn to do that? I am almost frozen with fear and useless. I can only watch and write.

Tilly dreamed that she was riding on a bus through beautiful countryside on a sunshine-bright day. With her were Granddad Rory and Grandma Rose, Mr. and Mrs. Bow and the lady with the white bun from St. Patrick's, Marlene and Conrad with their eternal cigarettes, and Bunny and her daddy, Valentine Gray. Mr. and Mrs. Bow were chatting to her grandma and granddad, and Mrs. O'Flaherty's mammy was busy knitting, but Tilly couldn't quite make out what it was she was making. Bunny was holding her red balloon and jiggling up and down on her seat with excitement. Tilly watched out of the window and wondered where they were going. She hoped it was to the seaside.

June 4

Dear God, please help me. I know you probably gave up on me a long time ago, but finally now I understand. I disobeyed you and I shamed Mum and Dad, and I still do, because I still love Stevie. I am wicked and selfish and this is my punishment. I married an ungodly man and mixed bad blood with bad blood to have a child. Her father taught her to sin against you and make friends with the dead, play with ghosts. I was too weak to stop him and I deserve to be punished. But Tilly doesn't. She believes in you. She loves you and she goes to church. She's just a little girl. I know you had to choose the punishment that would hurt me most, and you chose well. But there is another way. I will do anything to save her. I swear that if you let Tilly live, I will give her up. I'll send her away so that she can't be near me and catch the wickedness that taints me, and then she'll stop seeing things she shouldn't and forget. She's not like me. She's good and kind and funny and people love her. Give her the chance to grow into the woman I never found the courage to be. My daughter deserves a wonderful life. And if I let her go, I'll still be punished—perhaps even more than if she dies.

They traveled on and on, but Tilly didn't recognize any of the places they passed through: the little villages with duck ponds and greens for playing cricket; the patchwork fields and the tunnels of towering pine woods. She was growing tired but she was desperate to stay awake until the bus reached its destination. But Tilly wasn't staying on the bus. Bunny wouldn't let her.

"You have to get off here," she said, leading Tilly to the door as the bus slowed to a halt in a street that looked safe and vaguely familiar.

"This is your stop."

When Tilly got off, Queenie was waiting for her.

When Tilly woke up, she knew she wasn't dead because she wasn't on the bus. She was in her hospital bed and Queenie was there, smiling and holding her hand.

43

Tilda

The trail of clues that has led me to Stevie was as fragile as a daisy chain but, against the odds, the links were made and held long enough for me to find him. This week I shall visit both of my parents and neither of them will know anything about it.

It's the first time I have visited my mother's grave since her funeral. The bright summer sunshine is reduced to a confetti of scattered light through the dense leaves of silver birches. The cemetery is cool and green and shady and the trees, tall and spindly like ships' masts, sway and clack in the gathering breeze. Crows and magpies swagger through the grass like avian pirates and hop on and off gravestones, charting their territory. My mother's grave is just off the path in a row as yet incomplete. I have brought her red roses. A marble headstone in the form of a cross has been installed and in accordance with her final wishes has been inscribed with the words:

My God, I have put my trust in thee

She made a deal with him, and kept her promise to the bitter end. She was so desperate for me to live that she gave me up and I spent the rest of her life punishing her for it. The note she left asked me to forgive her. I wonder if she ever forgave me.

The Sea View Care Home is a large Edwardian villa with sweeping lawns carefully mown into broad stripes. In the distance where the stripes converge there is an iron fence that reminds me of a toy farm set I used to have when I was a little girl. Beyond the fence the fields drop gently away toward the glittering sea. When I first arrived I was shown into the residents' lounge to wait for Mrs. Parsons, the manager. It was lunchtime and the chairs were all empty except for one that was occupied by an elderly man staring straight ahead, apparently enraptured by the pattern of the wallpaper. He looked up at me when I entered the room and although his green eyes still sparkled, the expression on his weary, sunken face was a screensaver, registering neither emotion nor understanding. He ignored my greeting and returned to his study of the wallpaper. His name is Seamus and, according to the young woman who brought me in here, he arrived on the same day as Stevie and the pair of them became good friends. But he has no idea who I am and clearly no desire to find out. I leave him in peace and return to the corridor where the sound of cutlery on crockery and the smell of nonspecific savory food pervade the warm air. It reminds me of all the awful dinners I endured at the boarding school I hated so much. I need to be outside. I tell the woman at the reception desk that I'll be in the garden. Eli is by my side and once we reach the lawns he lifts his head and sniffs the breeze, his black nose twitching. I can't, or perhaps don't want to, imagine Stevie sitting inside that stuffy lounge with its floral wallpaper and orthopedic armchairs, but here in the garden, where the flowers are real and the views boundless, I feel closer to him than I have since I was that little girl who held his hand and hung on his every word. Eli suddenly takes off in the direction of the iron fence and, sensing his urgency, I follow. Stevie is here. But will he know that I am, or is it too late?

We were moving Joseph Geronimo's things into the flat above the café. Daniel lives with me now; no, we live together in my mother's old flat—me, Daniel, and Eli. Joseph Geronimo and Daniel were downstairs unloading the van. I was upstairs surrounded by boxes. Eli had been restless all morning, pacing up and down and endlessly fretting. He sniffed each box frantically when it was brought upstairs and finally found what he was searching for. He grabbed a cardboard corner and shook his box of choice violently. I heard breaking noises. He stopped and looked at me to see if I had gotten the message. Apparently not. The barking began, urgent, insistent, and demanding. Even Daniel heard it. I opened the box and the barking stopped. As I knelt down, his black face appeared a whisker away from my cheek. I picked the shards of glass from the front of a photograph in the top of the box and a ghost stared back at me. Joseph Geronimo and a few friends stood in front of a bar with glasses raised, but the man serving the drinks was Stevie, the landlord who drove his customers crazy playing "Black Velvet Band." Eli barked one more time. I had found what he wanted me to. All that time, without knowing it, Joseph Geronimo held the key.

It didn't take much to track down the man himself after that. The pub was still there and so was the juke-box. The dark interior was hushed by heavy curtains and a burgundy carpet patterned to hide the spills that the stale, beery odor betrayed. The old men drinking in the back bar were pleased to have someone new to talk to. Cradling half-pints of Guinness in purple hands knotted and gnarled by old age and arthritis, some of them even still alive, they told me all about my dad. He had been the landlord here until he had retired, and some of them were his friends. They visited him when they could. They told me that he talked about me, that he had never forgotten me. Their pale eyes watered and their cold bony fingers clutched at my arm as they smiled and said how pleased he would be that I had come back. They even told me where he was, right down to the postcode and the telephone number— ridiculously easy after all these years.

"It's Tilda, isn't it? I'm Mrs. Parsons, but everyone calls me Pat." The woman striding across the lawn is younger than I expected. She offers her hand and her condolences. "I see you've found him then?" My hand is still resting on the simple brass plaque attached to one of the fence posts, which marks the place where my dad's ashes were buried just six weeks ago. "Your father loved this view," she says, shielding her eyes from the bright sunlight with one hand and gazing at the band of water that shimmers on the horizon. She goes on to tell me how popular Stevie was with the other residents—a bright spark, full of life right until the end. I know that she is trying to be kind, but her words are like pebbles falling down a deep, dark well. I am too late. Sensing that silence is what I really need, Pat turns back toward the house. Her perfume is overpowering and seems to trail in her wake as she follows the stripes across the grass. The scent remains, growing stronger if anything, and my mistake becomes clear. Chanel No. 5. Perhaps my mother has made her peace with Stevie now, as well as me.

The soft clut of the letterbox is shortly followed by Daniel dropping a small package into my lap on his way to the kitchen to make me toast clouds for breakfast. I can see by the postmark that it is from the Sea View Care Home. It's a letter from Pat Parsons with some forms for me to check and sign in order to be able to collect what remains of Stevie's belongings. Apparently he had asked her to keep them safe. Just in case. I don't want to think about it now. Those precious scraps are all that remains of him, but I would trade every last one of them just to be certain that he knew, even at the moment of his death, how much I loved him. That I have eked out every memory of our six short years together to keep our bond secure throughout the rest of my life without him. That he has always been and will always be my dad.

I shove the forms back into the padded envelope, but the wad of papers resists. There is something at the bottom that I have missed. A small red and white Woolworths paper bag, grubby and tattered, with its top folded over and stuck down with a scrap of tape turned brittle and yellow with age. I check Pat's letter again and it's there in the final paragraph.

This may seem a little strange, but when your father was dying he insisted that you would, one day, come back to find him. His belief in this was unshakeable. He told me that I should make sure, above all else, that you receive the enclosed package as soon as possible. I meant to give it to you on the day you came to visit, but you left before I had the chance. He was so insistent about the urgent nature of his request that I felt I had to send it to you straight away. His exact words were, "A promise is a promise and she's waited long enough."

Inside the bag is a black velvet band.

Acknowledgments

Wow! Book three—who'd have thought it?

My first acknowledgment this time is not of a person, but a place. I'd like to thank Brighton. Thank you for your splendid pavilion, your fabulous pier, and your magical carousel of galloping horses. Thank you for your madness, tolerance, and sheer exuberance. You are my happy place and invaluable inspiration for my writing. Brighton—I love you!

Thank you to my brilliant agent and friend, Laura Macdougall, for always having my back, telling it like it is, for being an all-round excellent human being and an absolute privilege to work with. Thanks also to the whole team at United Agents for all their hard work.

Thank you to the wonderful Lisa Highton for her gentle but firm editing hand, her patience and humor, and for shepherding me safely through airports and the perils of public transport. Thanks also to all the team at Two Roads, particularly Alice Herbert, Jess Kim, Emma Petfield, Kat Burdon, Sarah Clay, and Megan Schaffer. Thank you to Amber Burlinson for doing a damn fine job of the copyediting (again!), and to Diana Beltran Herrera and Sarah Christie for producing yet another truly exquisite cover.

Thank you to my readers all over the world for buying my books and for all your wonderful messages of support and encouragement. And, of course, for all the photos of your dogs—you know the way to my heart!

Heartfelt thanks to all the booksellers and book bloggers who help my readers to find my books, and particularly Nina Pottell and Dave Wilde for their unstinting support and early quotes.

Thank you to my parents for telling everyone about "Their daughter, the author' (although, to be honest, they're getting a bit blasé about it now), for their joy and pride each time I have something published or get mentioned on the radio, and thanks, Dad, for press-ganging everyone you meet to attend my local book events.

Thank you to all my friends (you know who you are) who share my highs and lows and also keep my feet on the ground and stop me from getting too big for my (admittedly rather fabulous) boots.

Peter at The Eagle Bookshop still hasn't finished one of his own books but continues to be my writing buddy and offer invaluable support and advice. And tea. Thank you.

A big shout-out to Ajda Vucicevic. Finally, Tilly and Queenie will be unleashed into the world. You never lost faith—and you were right. Bless you.

Lastly, I should like to thank my husband, Paul, and my beloved dogs Squadron Leader Timothy Bear and Zachariah Popov. (Zach—you scared the bejesus out of me, but you were absolutely worth it) You guys are home.

P.S. Tilda and Joseph Geronimo both smoke cigarettes on the pier. It's not big and it's not clever—it's fiction. Smoking on The Palace Pier is strictly forbidden.

Insights,
Interviews
& More...

Meet Ruth Hogan

Harpur Studio

RUTH HOGAN was brought up in a house full of books and grew up with a passion for reading and writing. She loved dogs and ponies, seaside piers, snow globes and cemeteries. As a child she considered becoming a vet, show jumper, Eskimo, gravedigger and once, very briefly, a nun.

She studied English and Drama at Goldsmiths College, University of London where she hennaed her hair, wore dungarees, and aspired to be the fourth member of Bananarama. After graduating, she foolishly got a proper job and for ten years had a successful if uninspiring career in local government before a car accident left her unable to work full-time and was the kick up the butt she needed to start writing seriously.

It was all going well, but then in 2012 she got cancer, which was bloody inconvenient but precipitated an exciting hair journey from bald to a peroxide blond Annie Lennox crop. When chemo kept her up all night, she passed the time writing and the eventual result was her debut novel *The Keeper of Lost Things*.

She lives in a chaotic Victorian house with an assortment of rescue dogs and her long-suffering husband. She describes herself as a magpie; always collecting treasures (or "junk" depending on your point of view) and a huge John Betjeman fan. She still loves seaside piers, particularly the Palace Pier at Brighton, and would very much like a full-size galloping horses carousel in her back garden. ❧

Ruth Hogan on Mothers and Daughters

Mothers and daughters . . . their story can be complicated . . . but it can also turn out to have a happy ending.

This tag line from *Queenie Malone's Paradise Hotel* could also be a comment on my relationship with my own mum. She was a product of her generation and class. While her brother was encouraged to further his education and make a career for himself, Mum was expected to content herself with marriage and children. She was bright and beautiful, and a talented artist who dreamed of art school. Instead, she got a job in a local manufacturing company, married, and had two daughters.

The injustice of an education cut short and a talent never nurtured haunted her adult life. She was determined that her daughters would not suffer the same fate. My sister rebeled; she hated school and got married at nineteen, and so I became the sole channel for Mum's aspirations. Her standards were exacting. The results of every math and spelling test mattered. I passed my 11 plus with flying colors and a scholarship to the local girls' school followed. Mum was thrilled.

But our relationship was complicated. The joy of picnics in the park and holidays by the seaside were tempered by a constant fear of letting her down. I was the first person in our family to go to university, but when I was awarded a lower second her only comment was that I could have done better if I'd worked harder. It took me many years to realize that the eggshells I trod on fearfully as a child became the rock-solid foundations of my future. My education gave me the choices and opportunities that she never had, and everything she had put me through she did because she loved me. ⌒

Reading Group Guide

1. *Queenie Malone* explores the theme of mother-daughter relationships, both conventional and unconventional. Of the many pairings, whose relationship do you think is the most successful?

2. Brighton is a character in itself in the book—how do you think this manifests itself? Would the novel have been as successful in a more anonymous setting?

3. All families have some secrets, and the secrets in *Queenie Malone* are well-intentioned, but very damaging. What other choices might the characters have made? Is there ever any justification for withholding the truth?

4. The story is told through the twin points of view of Tilly the child, and Tilda her older self. How much of Tilly the child can you see in Tilda the adult, and how does that change as the novel progresses?

5. What is true and not true is constantly brought into question throughout the book. This is a challenge not only for the characters but for the reader—how much did this add to your enjoyment?

6. Ruth Hogan describes her most interesting characters as those who've been "cracked in the kiln." The Paradise Hotel is full of eccentric and memorable people, who fit together and support each other, without judgment. What role do they play in supporting both Tilly and then Tilda?

7. One of the common themes running throughout Ruth Hogan's novels is that of redemption. Whatever tough times people have gone through, and however lost they may be at various stages of their life, it's never too late to make peace with the past and move forward. Would you agree? ∾

A Bonus Short Story From Ruth Hogan: *The Man From Howard House*

I never saw his face, but I fell in love with him nonetheless. His broad shoulders and dignified stance captivated me from that first glimpse through the glass panels of the front door. Howard House was a confident cube of classical architecture on a pristine plot with manicured lawns framed by ornamental box hedges, in a street where estate agents added a "poshness" premium to prices purely on the strength of the postcode. Granchester Gardens was a parade of highly desirable residences built in rows either side of a green planted with pine trees. It was barely a ten-minute walk from the Victorian semi that I shared with my dog, Wilfred, and my husband, but another world entirely. The houses here boasted chandeliers and sweeping staircases. One had a grand piano in the sitting room, another a harp. Gleaming cars parked in the driveways purred prosperity while protected by electric gates. This was my favorite route to walk Wilfred in the late afternoon. While he sniffed the gateposts and snuffled through the grass, I snooped through the windows. I liked it best in the autumn and winter when the nights drew in and before the curtains were drawn. Cloaked in twilight I could gaze with impunity as the chandeliers lit up the treasures within. It was in November that I first saw him. There were hyacinths sprouting stiff, green shoots in glass jars on the shelf beside him that would be in full bloom in time for Christmas.

It was August now, and Wilfred's swagger had slowed to a waddle as he panted in the afternoon sun. Clarissa Clements was dead-heading her roses in the garden of Vermont Villa. She waved her secateurs at us and wandered over to the gate.

"What is it with men and their balls!" she exclaimed.

She gestured toward the privet hedge of the neighboring property which had been recently coiffured into cubes and pyramids, each topped with a perfect sphere.

"That buffoon next door is obsessed with them! He's got a season ticket for Arsenal, a tennis court in his back ▶

A Bonus Short Story From Ruth Hogan:
The Man From Howard House (continued)

garden, plays bowls every Thursday and now this! If he had to take up topiary, he might at least have come up with something more creative."

Clarissa and her neighbor, Gordon Grindstone, weren't on friendly terms. In fact, they barely spoke. When they did it was for him to accuse Clarissa's Siamese cats, Yum-Yum and Ko-Ko, of desecrating his flower beds and for Clarissa furiously to deny it. Wilfred and I liked Clarissa. She was the only person in Granchester Gardens who spoke to us.

"Have you seen your fancy man today?" she teased. I had confided in her about the man in Howard House, hoping that she might know who he was, but she didn't.

"You be careful your husband doesn't find out," she warned.

I smiled. "I've already told him. He's not the jealous type."

Summer ripened into autumn and our walks became littered with lengthening shadows and crisp, fallen leaves. The air was pungent with woodsmoke and turned our breath into steam. Gloves and scarves replaced sandals and sunglasses, and Wilfred regained his swagger. The second blooms of Clarissa's roses were fragile from the first frost while Gordon Grindstone's

topiary balls flourished. And in the
fine houses of Granchester Gardens
the chandeliers lit up once more. I saw
him most days and sometimes I would
loiter at the front gate, but occasionally
the house would be in darkness and
I would wander home disappointed.
The hyacinths returned in their glass
jars, and candle-lit vegetables appeared
on doorsteps. Trick or treat was a refined
affair in Granchester Gardens, with
clutches of well-behaved children
dressed as wizards and witches and the
occasional rogue fairy or Harry Potter
character, knocking only on doors
giving permission with a pumpkin.
But Halloween had a nasty shock in
store for me. Clarissa was decorating
her porch with flashing fairy lights and
fake cobwebs when she saw us and
hurried over to share the news.

"I'm afraid Howard House has been
sold. It looks like your man will be
moving."

I hadn't even known that it was on
the market. But then this wasn't the
type of street where it was necessary
to display "For Sale" signs. Properties
were sold quickly and quietly for eye-
watering sums of money. I resolved
to make the most of what little time
I might have left. I even considered
knocking on the door on some pretext, ▶

but then I was rather old for trick or treat and besides, neither Wilfred nor I were in costume. The following evening Clarissa was waiting impatiently for us while pretending to take down the decorations from her porch. Gordon's balls were strewn across his lawn.

"What on earth happened?" I asked her. Clarissa grinned broadly as she surveyed the ruined hedge with obvious satisfaction.

"I expect it was trick or treaters," she said slyly. "But it serves him right. He soaked my poor little Yum-Yum yesterday with his hose. He *said* she was scratching up the bulbs in his flower bed, but I don't believe a word of it."

Bonfire Night burned brightly. The hyacinths bloomed, and Christmas came and went, but the occupants of Howard House remained. I never did find the courage to knock on that door, and then one day in February they were gone. I stood on the pavement staring at the empty space where I had seen him last and a tear trickled down my cheek.

Clarissa was pruning her rosebushes.

"He's gone," I told her.

"I know. Come inside. I've got something for you."

Wilfred and I followed her through her front door, and there he stood, almost as tall as me, propped against the wall—the painting of a retreating soldier that I had fallen in love with from Howard House.

"I found him in a skip outside the house on the day that they moved out. He's yours now!" ❧